HER EVERY
SECRET

G.L. Redding

To Mike

For embracing my wild dreams, igniting courage, and standing by me through the uncharted territories. This book is a tribute to your unwavering support that helped shape my journey.

CONTENTS

Silence.

"Sir, what's the number you're calling from?"

Nothing. *Don't freak out.*

"Sir, can you tell me what's happened?"

My chest tightens, and I struggle to keep my breaths calm. *Please, please give me an answer.* I hate losing control of my emotions. This prank has gone on long enough.

A sigh from the caller sends a chill down my spine. The voice doesn't sound like a teenager. It's cold, cruel, and calculating.

"You know what? I've changed my mind. There is no emergency. I'm driving away from the young girl. I think I scared her; she's running back up the driveway."

The line goes dead. Nausea builds as I stare at my ten-year-old computer. Why I'm allowing a prank to get me worked up? That wasn't real. My fingers rest on the keyboard, and I breathe deeply and close my eyes. I try to convince myself this was a prank.

But he said my name. I *never* give my name. *Fuck.*

"Sally, I'm running to the bathroom—you have the calls covered?" I ask and push away from my desk.

There's a break in Sally's incessant humming as she waves me off. As the newest dispatcher, I have the worst spot and the shittiest desk. The muted shades of brown and beige in the hub of four cubes blend as I rush past, making it hard to focus on anything.

With force, I open the bathroom door, step in, and lock it. My hands grip the edges of the sink as I stare at myself in the mirror. Fear covers my face. I glance away. *Get it together. This was some idiot thinking he's funny. Let's just get out there and finish this shift.* My eyes close and I can't stop what's beginning to play in my mind.

CHAPTER 1

Zoey

"Nine-One-One. What is your emergency?"

"It's not my emergency, *Zoey*. It's *yours*."

"What's the address of your emergency?"

"I'm on a farm road."

My eyes roll. There are only farm roads here.

"Do you know which farm road, sir?" I take a deep breath and goose bumps spread down my arms. My eyes close as I wait for him to answer.

"The one with a little girl waiting for the bus at the end of a long driveway."

My eyes spring open and sweat builds on my palms. My teeth clench. Letting out a deep breath, I remind myself I can stay calm in any emergency in this middle-of-nowhere place. It's incredibly dull compared to the Chicago PR world. With a slow inhale and deep exhale, I release the building tension.

"Is the young girl in distress?"

"Not yet," he responds tersely.

The cool tone and the lack of panic in his voice are uncharacteristic of an actual emergency call. As I put the pieces together, the tightness in my shoulder's eases, knowing this is likely a prank. Regardless, I must act like it isn't.

"Sir, what's your address?"

I'm eleven years old. It's a wintry day for southern Missouri. It didn't stop me from donning the outfit I'd been working up the courage to wear to school for weeks. I'm wearing a skirt for the first time—which also ended up being the last time. I've got on deep teal tights and a miniskirt with a unique maroon, navy, and teal pattern. The oversized sweater is a matching teal, and my shoes are slip-on dress shoes—another first for me. I usually dress to beat the boys at tetherball.

As I started down the driveway, I buzzed with excitement. I'd only ridden the bus two or three times to school. We moved here recently, and my parents put a mobile home on the land for us to live in while our house is being built. Usually, my mom drove the few miles up the road to drop me off at school. But that morning, my parents met with the architect before my dad went to work. My only option to get to school was to take the bus.

The thrill of independence fueled me as I prepared for my half-mile walk down our driveway to catch the bus. It was something new, just like my outfit. I put on my neon pink winter coat with a neon yellow collar, loaded up my backpack, and grabbed my trumpet.

As I made my way down the driveway, I heard what I thought was the bus coming up the hill. I ran the last quarter of a mile to make it before the bus arrived. I didn't want anyone to see me running in this outfit. It was awkward with my trumpet, and my slides didn't help. The effort it took to keep them on my feet had me regretting my decision to dress up for the first time.

When I made it to the end of the driveway, out of breath, I looked up. It was not the bus. It was a green pickup truck with a red dinosaur on the side from one of those old gas stations. The driver had stopped right in front of me. As I caught my breath, I looked at him. He stared at me. And then panic hit.

I turned and started running back up my driveway. I was all alone. There were no houses anywhere. You couldn't see our trailer from the road. Crap. My shoes flew off, I dropped the trumpet. I made it almost a third of the way back up the driveway when I heard the truck move along the road. I looked back, and he was gone.

My heart was pumping hard. Was I more embarrassed or afraid? As I slowly caught my breath, I heard the rumble of a vehicle again. Was that the bus? I looked to the left but couldn't see anything because we were on the top of a hill, and the road dropped off. I looked to my right, at the long road and farm fields, and that's where I saw it. The truck was coming back. I turned and dropped everything and started sprinting and screaming. My shoes were gone, and I ran back up my gravel driveway as fast as possible, ignoring the rocks that pounded into my feet.

I turned back to see if I was being ridiculous, and he was pulling into the driveway. A scream escaped me again as I ran as fast as I could. I was halfway up. I cried out as loudly as possible. Only a little more to go and our trailer would be visible. I kept screaming. He was close, but I was fast. I made it to the place where the trailer was visible and saw my parents step out the door. I turned around, and he was backing up. He must have seen the house and my parents. By the time I made it there, he was gone.

My eyes open to see the old, dingy bathroom floor. I haven't thought about the specifics of that event in years, but it's always with me. Anytime I walked home from a college party, from a bar in Chicago, or went running in the neighborhood before sunrise, the fear would thrum underneath the surface. I shake my head and start counting my breaths. In one, out two, in three, out four, up to ten, and then restart. I repeat the process a few times and begin calming down. There's no link between this caller and my past. This is just triggering my fears. I'm overreacting. Thoroughly convincing myself I'm being dramatic, I stand up, wash my hands, and return to my desk.

For the first time since taking this job four months ago, I'm annoyed we haven't upgraded our systems so we can trace cell phones. Desperate to put my mind at ease, I take a deep breath. Okay, all I need to do is get through this shift. Then I can go home, forget about all this, and continue binging *The Walking Dead*.

Sally stops humming and asks me if I'm okay. I say, "Yeah. Just tired." The computer screen lights up. We have another 9-1-1 call. "I'll grab it," I say. Grateful for the distraction from the last call.

"Nine-One-One. What is your emergency?"

"I changed my mind, *Zoey*. There is an emergency. I'm heading back to the little girl waiting for the bus, and this time, I'm going to take her."

My hands shake uncontrollably, and my breaths are stuck in my chest. I'm panicking. *Shit.* I've never panicked in a crisis or on a call. The certificate of achievement for how I handled the call when Nick had that tractor accident steals my focus. It was a frantic scene, with Nelly too agitated to help control the bleeding. I stepped in to calm her down. The doctors say it saved his life, the way she contained the bleeding before the paramedics got there. I'd only been on the job for six weeks. With a deep breath, I channel my confidence and steady my nerves. I got this.

"You're quiet. Don't you need to ask for the address of the emergency?"

Shit. I need to get a hold of the police. *Jack.*

My eyes close and I focus on calming my voice. "Sir, what's the address of your emergency?"

"I've already told you, a farm road," the caller sighs.

Okay, my mind is clearing. I need to keep him on the phone and get in touch with Jack. "Can you describe the farm road? Are there any landmarks nearby?"

"Nice try. You really are a natural at handling crises. Stories of your career success in Chicago weren't exaggerated. Shame you're wasting your talent answering Nine-One-One calls in West Plains."

My hands tremble as I'm fumbling with my phone to text Jack. It's all I can do right now; I want to avoid any extra attention from Sally. It'll cause me to lose my focus.

"Can you give me the number you're calling from, sir?" I ask.

As I'm bringing up Jack's messages, I see his last one from three days ago that I haven't responded to. What can I say to him? My heart races, I don't have much time. What's going to get him here the quickest?

The caller isn't responding to me. His deep, heady breaths fill the silence on the other end of the call.

Help!!! Can you come to my desk ASAP? Weird call. Please.

A knot forms in my throat, and I swallow, hoping he comes. He's always there for me, even when he shouldn't be.

My attention shifts back to the caller. "Sir, I need you to describe the situation so I can dispatch the appropriate services."

I continue, keeping up the ruse in an attempt not to draw Sally's attention. She'll come over and stand too close to me, and I'll won't keep my composure. She's already started looking back at me. I wave her away, signaling I have this under control. It's not uncommon for us to repeat questions when some callers are more hysterical during incidents.

"That's enough. Don't you know this call isn't going to follow any of your crisis scripts?"

"Yes, sir. I can see that. Can you give me your name?"

"Ned."

"Okay, Ned. What is it you need help with?"

Out of the corner of my eye, I can see Sally staring at me. I refuse to look at her; I need Jack here. This call will be unmanageable with Sally's overbearing presence. He can run interference.

"Have you reached out to Jack yet? Do you think he'll come running to your side?" Ned's cruel laughter echoes through the line.

My hands go cold, and my stomach turns. How does he know these things about me? He knows about my job in Chicago. He knows about Jack. My eyes squeeze shut.

"Yes, I have. Is there a problem with that?" I ask with forced composure.

"Actually, that's perfect. He should be here for what comes next."

Just as Ned finishes, Jack steps in and comes my way. My stomach tightens at the sight of him in uniform. I'm not sure I'll ever get over how the fit enhances his muscular frame. He smiles at Sally and turns to me with a blank face, as if to say he's here because of his job, not me. Okay, I deserve that. Now that he's here, I can ask questions that will clue him in to the situation.

"Alright, Ned. Can you tell me about the girl? Is she still on the farm road?"

Jack's eyebrows raise toward me. I nod at him, trying to convey this is an actual situation. Not another game.

"No, she's with me," Ned says bitterly.

Shit. Fear rises to the surface while my stomach drops. A deep pain settles in my gut. My fingers are shaking. My breath is fast. I can't count my breaths right now; I don't have the time. Jack grabs my hand, looks me in the eye, and nods. I take a deep breath.

"Is the girl in any distress?"

"What do you think?" Ned responds flatly.

"I think she is probably highly distressed right now. A stranger has taken her from her bus stop. What can we do to help her in this situation?"

Jack nods at me with approval.

"I think you mean, what can *you* do to help the girl, *Zoey?*"

"Okay. What can I do to help the girl?"

CHAPTER 2

Zoey

Jack's eyes are laser-focused on me. I can see his concern. *Dammit.* I don't like it when he looks at me like this.

"Good girl. Now you're asking the right questions," Ned murmurs.

I nod slightly at Jack, signaling that I'm making progress. He's texting and I'm sure he's reaching out to his boss, Sergeant Graves.

"Let's start by you telling us more about Cassie," Ned says. Us? He means him and Jack and anyone who will end up hearing this recording. *Fuck.*

My chest is tightening, unable to take in a full breath. I try to count my breaths. In one, out two, in one, out two. It's all I can get up to. Jack is looking at me. Concern radiates off him. *Dammit.* No, not this. What does this man, Ned, want? What is his game?

"You're awfully quiet right now. No crisis script for your own life?" Ned sighs.

My hands are sweating, fingers trembling again. Jack puts his hand on top of mine, looking at me like he has all the confidence in the world that I can handle this. Doubt shivers down my back.

"Alright. It seems like I need to get through to you. To know more about your emergency and this little girl, you first must start talking about what happened with Cassie," Ned barks.

He's angry and wants nothing but the truth.

"Cassie, okay. Ned, what would you like to know?"

Jack looks at me, puzzled. He doesn't know this Cassie or any Cassie that I know of. We've only been seeing each other for a few months, and I've certainly not let him in below the surface, despite his efforts. I don't deserve his love, and when he finds out the things I've done, he won't want me anymore.

"Well, I'd like you to explain what happened with Cassie," Ned states.

Who the hell is this man? How does he know about what I did to Cassie? That was the lowest point of my life. What does he want from me? He wants me to be humiliated by telling this story publicly. But why?

"If I tell you about Cassie, will you give us information about the little girl and where you are?" I ask and my stomach churns, bile rising in my throat.

"I'll give you information, but *Zoey*, I need you to tell *all* the details about Cassie," Ned commands.

Shame is pressing down on my shoulders. I look at Jack and take a deep breath. My eyes close and I'm back at my desk in the top PR firm in Chicago. Packing up my stuff. Alone. No one looks at me, and no one talks to me. I've never felt so cold, and it's the middle of a hot Chicago summer day.

My eyes open again. And with one more glance at Jack; he looks at me with uncertainty. He wants to understand what I need. I know it. That's just what he's like. Loyal and supportive.

"We can take a break if you need one. I can call back later. When is your next shift? Oh that's right, Thursday, at 6:00 a.m.," Ned states.

"No, no. Don't hang up. I can tell you about Cassie." My shoulders straighten. "Cassie was my coworker at the Pellman Group. We were friends."

Out of the corner of my eye, I see Jack wave Sally away, glaring at her, and then turn back to me. He nods, then glances down at his phone and shows me the screen; Sergeant Graves is on his way in. Awesome, just what I need, a larger in-person audience for me to share one of the worst decisions of my life. One that turned my life in Chicago upside down and landed me back in West Plains, Missouri, as a 9-1-1 dispatcher.

"Now, *Zoey*. Let's not play games here. I think we both know this is not what I want you to share about Cassie," Ned sighs.

I'll do anything to help find this little girl. My eyes squeeze shut as my stomach churns.

And I'm back at The Pellman Group's legendary holiday party, on the ninety-fourth floor of the Hancock building. It's one of the biggest perks of working there. Clients, coworkers, spouses. Free food, free drinks, and a designer swag bag. I went all out that year, especially since I was without a plus one.

My hair and makeup were professionally done. I wore a black jumpsuit that clasped at my neck and opened down my back, showing off that I had nothing on underneath. My favorite red lipstick coated my lips, hiding how inferior I felt as I drank fabulous champagne and mingled with the Chicago elite.

That night started off great as I scoped the room for any single guys. The only thing that was on my mind was finding a good no-strings screw to take the edge off before I headed back home for Christmas. I knew that the moment I arrived home, the familiar weight of my mom's drama would drag me down.

With a sip of champagne, I swallowed down my impending dread and met the eyes of a man in a mismatched suit and scuffed shoes. He raised his glass to me. Nope. Just nope. As I turned away, I spotted Lucy and walked over to her for some idle chitchat, not wanting to leave myself open for any guy to approach me. I wanted to be in control. Single the guy out and then go in for the kill ... or fuck, in this case.

As I nodded at Lucy's story about a new houseplant, I saw a few promising guys. My eyes landed one with a reddish-brown beard, a nice sport coat, and the right shoes—that classic camel leather color. I loved those. I made a mental note to keep track of him. You never knew who could hold their liquor at these things, so I needed to keep my options open throughout the night. And then my gaze stopped on a man that was tall, dark, and athletic. Sharp dresser. I could have a lot of fun with that man. He moved to the top of my list.

Satisfied with my prospects, I glanced down at Lucy's picture of the new plant stand she was showing me. A tingling sensation hit me, and I scanned the room and made eye contact with a man who looked like he was ready to devour me. He was intense. He had nice hair and just the right amount of five-o'clock shadow. Good shoes. Satisfied that I had options, I downed the rest of my champagne. Now it was just a waiting game to see who could keep their wits about them throughout the night.

As I was telling Lucy I needed a refill, I heard a low voice behind me that whispered along my neck. "See any prospects?" His warm breath sent a tingle down my back.

I turned, and it was Joey, Cassie's husband. Cassie and I were club friends outside of work. At least one night a week, you could catch us at a bar or club. Joey knew my drill. He always teased me about how I hunt and conquer. They had finally given up trying to set me up.

The idea of settling down made my skin crawl. That would have required me to trust a man enough to let him in. The problem is, I didn't trust my instincts. So, it was easier keeping things casual.

"You know, I like to size them up from a distance. I'm taking my time tonight."

"You better not take too long to find your mark; or you'll be fighting them off tonight in that outfit. You look sensational." Joey smirked.

My spine tingled at the compliment as I smiled and studied his face. He was kind, and I understood why Cassie loved him. He knew how to make a woman feel seen. "Did you and Cassie save me a spot at your table?"

"Yep, made sure you weren't left to the vultures," Joey said with a laugh.

Cass was always there for me, no matter what. I asked him how his work was going. He was an attorney at some big law firm in Chicago. I found his work boring, but I feigned interest.

"Wow, Zoey. You've really gone all out tonight," Cassie exclaimed.

My eyebrows raised at her and I told her she looked fantastic, too. Cassie's slinky red dress made her curves pop. She took my arm. "Enough, Joey, about your blah blah blah legal work." She looked at me. "Let's go get some more champagne. Tell me who is on your shortlist," Cassie said, and then winked at Joey.

As we walked away, I looked over my shoulder at Joey; our eyes locked. I felt a charge of energy. Ignoring the sensation, I walked to the bar with her.

"So, tell me, have you noticed the guy in the green velvet sport coat? He looks like he'd be fun." Cass bumped me with her hip as we walked.

"Not yet. Where is he?" And before I could ask her to be discreet, she pointed right to the other side of the room at him. "Thanks, Cass." I raised my empty glass to him and gave him a coy smile.

"Anytime," Cass says with a smirk.

Once we got our champagne refills, Cassie left me to go check on the swag bags. She was on the committee that year and wanted to make sure the interns hadn't mucked anything up.

As I stepped up to an empty cocktail table, I let out a deep breath and enjoyed the silence for a minute. Before I knew it, Joey sidled up to me again. "Where did she head off to?" he murmured.

"Checking up on the interns." I smiled over at him and noticed he was drinking something brown, probably his usual bourbon.

"She doesn't have an off button," Joey sighed.

"Don't I know it. She keeps me on my toes at work; I have to put in extra effort so she doesn't show me up."

"That's not true. You're a genius in a crisis," he said as he bumped me with his arm.

I laughed. "You're right. I have a talent for turning messy situations into opportunities. I'm going to head to the bathroom before we sit down for dinner."

"I'll escort you; I need to make a stop, too," Joey said.

We walked in silence out of the ballroom and toward the bathroom. As soon as we turned the corner, I saw the long line for one of those unisex single-stall bathrooms I hated.

"Hey," he whispered, "there's a secret bathroom one floor down. I doubt it has a line."

I felt both relieved and mischievous at the same time. "Perfect. Lead the way."

We headed down a floor, and sure enough, he was right.

"Ladies first." He put his arm out, pointing the way.

As I entered the bathroom and glanced in the mirror, I stopped. I looked great tonight. The jumpsuit hugged me in all the right places. As I smoothed my hair, it hit me. I didn't think about how I would get out of it to pee throughout the night. Feeling stupid for overlooking that detail, I reached for the two clasps at the top closure but couldn't get them. Dammit. I kept trying as my embarrassment grew. Joey's going to think I've dropped a load in here. I opened the door and peeked out at him.

"Hey, this is embarrassing, but I can't get the clasp on this thing undone," I said sheepishly.

"I was wondering what was taking so long. Here, let me in, and I'll help," he laughed.

As he entered, I turned around, and then Joey moved my hair over my shoulder and out of the way. I felt his hand move to the clasps, and his fingers came around and brushed my collarbone. He paused and took a deep breath that sucked the air out of the room. His hand held my shoulder as he slowly brought his other hand up to the clasps.

After he unhooked one clasp, he paused again. My heart started beating faster. I'd felt nothing toward Joey in the past. We were friends. We both loved Cassie. But something was happening in that bathroom.

He let out another breath, and it caressed my neck. Had he stepped closer? As he unhooked the second clasp, my top came undone. That was all the help I needed, but he didn't move. I took a ragged breath, and his breath followed. We were frozen. Then gravity took hold. My top fell forward, and my breasts were exposed. And then he moved.

His hand came from behind, sliding down to my front and cupping my breast as his head leaned forward and he kissed my neck. My breath left me. "Joey."

He gave a slight moan and squeezed my breast with a slight pinch at my nipple. I gasped as his teeth slid up my neck. What was happening? Not him. Not kind, lovable, handsome Joey.

He reached his other hand around me and then up to my other breast. I moaned as he pushed his hardness against my backside. I wanted to step away, but I couldn't. His touch, his desire, reached that unlovable part of me I had locked up.

I turned, and our eyes met. Heat filled his gaze. And before I knew it, his lips were on mine, and he was kissing me like I was his lifeline. He parted my lips, and his tongue was on mine, exploring and tickling my mouth. It was unexpected and wonderful, and I couldn't focus. What was happening? I couldn't stop kissing him. It was like I was standing on the edge of self-loathing and just wanted to fall.

"Joey?"

"Yes," he mumbled.

And then his hand slipped down my front, grazing just below my belly button. My breaths quickened, and my mind numbed. His finger slipped lower, and he rubbed my bundle of nerves. I ran my hands through his hair and moaned. He moaned in return. Everything intensified. He was hungry with desire, and I couldn't get out of the freefall of pleasure with him. I pushed him against the wall, and his hardness pressed against me.

"Zoey," he said, pleading.

A gasp escaped me and then I kissed him harder, rubbing my hips up against his circling fingers. I pulled back and looked at him. I saw his eyes—the regret and lust all in one look. How could they hold both at the same time? He glanced down at my breasts, reached for one, and gently floated his hands over them.

I don't know if it was the look of longing and regret or the tenderness of the exchange, but it confirmed how terrible I was. The bitterness of shame filled my mouth as I reached for his belt and undid it. He gasped and held his breath for a moment. I slowly lowered his zipper, just like he did with my clasps. He moved his arms around my back and pulled me in for another disarmingly gentle yet passionate kiss.

My hand plunged into his underwear. He was hard and smooth. I slid my hand down his length, and he raised on his toes, dropped his head back, and moaned. My grip was firm around him, and he snapped his head back to me and made eye contact. And then I brought my hand out to the side of his pants and slowly lowered them as he lifted his arms over my shoulders.

Then I looked down and glanced back at him. His stare was piercing; I lowered myself to my knees, placed my hand around him, and slid it down to the base. He yelped, and then I took him entirely into my mouth. He grasped my hair as I reached around him with my other hand, grabbed his ass, and pushed him forward so that he thrust into my mouth with his hips.

I was on my knees, with my top around my waist, and with each thrust, my breasts bounced in rhythm with the words "I'm broken" in mind.

"Zoey," he whispered. "Zoey, oh God."

I was in it then; I was letting him fuck my mouth. My eyes watered as I gagged. It hurt, but I welcomed the pain of what I was doing to Cassie. He sped up and pumped my head along with his hips; he moaned and then shuddered as he sprayed into my mouth. I sucked once, twice, and then pulled away, wiping my mouth.

Our eyes met as I looked up at him and so many unspoken words were in that one moment. Regret, care, loathing, kindness, emptiness. I stood up and turned away from him.

"Zoey," he whispered.

"I need to pee. Can you wait outside so you can help me with my top?"

"Yeah, sure," he said.

My stomach churned with disgust after he left. I counted my breaths a few times and then opened the door for him to help me get my top back on.

That night added another brick to my wall of shame. I wore my mask and laughed at Cassie's quips about the interns. Showed genuine excitement for the swag bag she curated for the party and then went home alone. There was no one that I could take home that would help me forget the night's events.

"Zoey, did you change your mind about the break? Want me to call back on Thursday?" Ned asks.

My eyes snap open and I whisper, "No." I take a deep breath and let it out. "I gave Cassie's husband a blow job in the bathroom at the company holiday party."

Jack flinches so quickly I almost miss it. A tear rolls down my cheek as a layer of my wall crumbles with the confession.

"Excellent. But I'm not sure that's all, is it?" Ned asks.

My eyes shift over to Jack. He's calm; he looks at me like I didn't just say what I said. My stomach is queasy knowing that he won't ever look at me the same after today.

"That's all that happened between Cassie's husband and me. She found out this summer, and I got blackballed from my job and friends, so I left Chicago. I did what you asked. Now, what will you tell me about the little girl?"

My shoulders straighten as I force the shame away so I can focus on finding this little girl. My teeth grind in anger that Ned just forced me to reveal that I'm a slut.

"You're right; a deal is a deal. I found the little girl on Farm Road One-Thirty-Nine. She's scared but unharmed *for now*," Ned states.

"Is she still on Farm Road One-Thirty-Nine?" I ask.

"Tsk, tsk, *Zoey*. We have more to go over."

I look at Jack, shake my head, and see his boss, Sergeant Graves, walk into the room. He follows my gaze, turns around, and gets up to brief the sergeant, giving him the rundown. As they walk back over, I hear Jack tell him I have things under control.

How could he say that? Desperation to find this girl is crushing me. I feel anything but in control right now. Jack looks at me and motions his hands in a circle, signaling to keep Ned talking and then writes something down. It's the name of the little girl that lives on Farm Road 139, Madison Pike.

Madison. My heart sinks. My worst fear is now her reality. She is living through what I've always feared—being taken. I force myself to release a breath and continue playing Ned's game.

"What else would you like to go over?"

"We have more to discuss. However, this morning has been quite eventful, don't you think? Let's take a break for a couple of hours, and I'll call back soon." Ned hangs up.

Panic explodes out of me, and I lose all control. "Ned? Ned? He hung up! What do I do? How do we get him back? How do we find Madison?" I scream out to everyone and no one.

Realization settles in me, and I sink back into my chair. Someone has kidnapped a little girl waiting for the bus. My hands are shaking and my heart races with fear. My chest is tight, and I can't catch my breath.

"Zoey, Zoey, look at me. Zoey, *look at me*. Good." Jack is sitting in a chair next to me, leaning toward me with his elbows on his knees. He reaches out to grab my hands.

"Take a deep breath. Good. Another one. You did great; we have her name and the location of the kidnapping. Did he say he was going to call back?" I nod, uncertainty consuming me. "He'll call back." He assures me.

Jack pulls me in for a hug, wrapping his arms around me tight. I count my breaths. In one, out two, in three, out four, on and on to ten, and then starting over again. A little girl was just kidnapped, and it's my fault. In one, out two, in three, out four.

After about my fourth round, I return to my body. Jack's still clutching me in a hug that says, "I've got you." How? I just shared one of the most shameful acts of my life. How is he touching me? And now everyone in town will know. I count my breaths one more time and my breath evens out. I slip my crisis mask back on.

This is what I'm good at. Crisis, figuring it out, seeing the opportunity. I can do this. We can find Madison. I pull back and meet his eyes. "What's next?"

CHAPTER 3

Jack

Zoey is trembling in my arms. I need these few moments to assess this situation. A caller has stated they kidnapped a girl, Madison Pike, on Farm Road 139, and Zoey is supposed to help her. Then she was talking about a friend in Chicago, her friend's husband, and a blow job. My mind catalogs the details as I put the pieces together. I draw her in closer and wrap my arms around her in a tight embrace.

She shudders in my arms. What has happened to her over the last decade that made her value herself so little that she would give a married guy a blow job in a public bathroom? Sadness and guilt overwhelm me.

The look of despair on her face is heartbreaking, her shoulders slump in anguish. Why taunt Zoey with her past mistakes? And Madison, she's just an innocent necessity to make her confess. What's his motivation to force her to reveal what happened at the holiday party? He wants her humiliated. I clench my jaw. How did we become strangers?

Zoey charmed me instantly when we met our freshman year. And I became a lovesick teenager that took on whatever role she would give me in her life just so I could stay close to her. A friend, a study partner, a ride to the party, a boyfriend's buddy, or last-minute prom date. During the first couple of years of college, I kept in touch and made sure we hung out every break.

As time passed, she became the standard I compared to every girl I dated. I even got drunk one night during our senior year of college and called her and confessed my love to her. Zoey laughed and said, "I love you too, Jack. You've always been one of my best friends and always will be." Solidifying I would forever be in her friend zone.

As time went on, we continued to grow apart. Zoey started bringing home a boyfriend for the holidays, and it just wasn't the same when we got together to catch up. Eventually, we stopped staying in contact altogether. We graduated from college, and neither of us moved home. I landed my dream job in Nashville. A big city cop.

Zoey goes still in my arms. It snaps me back to the situation at hand, and I go into cop mode. I'm just a patrol officer now, but I'm the most experienced on the team because of my time on the force in Nashville. She pulls back from me, and I'm startled to see a mask lower over her face. She becomes calm and determined, and asks, "What's next?"

Another first for me with her, putting on a front. It was always easy to know precisely what she was thinking. She wore it on her face. Her lack of a poker face was one of our first inside jokes. I pause, look at her deeper, and she doesn't waiver. I can't dwell on her shift; we have a little girl to find.

"Sergeant confirmed Madison did not make it to school today, and we issued an Amber Alert. It's not a lot to go off of because we don't have details about the vehicle, but we have all available officers on the road looking for suspicious cars."

She nods. "Okay, good. What about tracing the call? Oh shit, we can't do that, dammit. Our technology is old and doesn't trace cell phones." Her shoulders drop in defeat.

"We'll work with what we have," I say, reassuring her.

Sergeant walks over. "You're correct, Moore." He looks down at Zoey. "You're the only lead we have."

She stiffens her shoulders and lifts her chin, conveying a confidence that takes me back. For a moment, I study her. The front she's putting on stuns me. Before

I can get to my next question, Sergeant continues. "Do you know who this Ned is?"

Zoey looks down quickly. If I wasn't studying her to understand how the girl I knew so well turned into this woman, I would've missed it. Sergeant didn't see it. My eyes meet his and give him an incredulous glare, and he holds firm.

"There is a missing little girl out there. We don't have time to waste," Sergeant barks.

"I know this, Sergeant Graves. I know this deep in my bones, and we'll find her," Zoey responds boldly.

Before this exchange turns into a battle of wills, I turn to Sergeant. "Have you listened to the recording of the calls?"

"No, I'll get on that; in the meantime, get some answers from her."

Holding in a grimace, I nod at him and turn back to Zoey. "Hey, hey." I try to get her to focus on me and not staring daggers into the back of Sergeant's head. She turns to me and makes eye contact. A flash of pain and distress crosses her face, and then it quickly vanishes.

"No, I do not know who Ned is. No, I do not know Madison. I don't know anything that isn't on those calls."

Sergeant makes a few clicks on the computer, turns around, glances at Zoey, and then picks up the headphones on the desk and starts listening to the calls.

"I don't believe you have anything to do with this kidnapping. You couldn't fake how shaken up you are. I believe you, and we'll find this girl."

She nods at me and closes her eyes, taking a deep breath, sealing the crack that I saw appear a moment ago in her mask. I knew something went down in Chicago to bring her back here, but every time I tried to learn more about her time there, she brushed me off, saying it was just too much. Too much noise, too many people, too much traffic.

I let it go because I've been so grateful to have her back in my life and even more scared to do anything that might push her away. Living out my teenage dreams has been a surreal experience that I never thought would happen. Our chemistry is undeniable. Sex with Zoey is passionate and free. But it turns out friends with benefits isn't right for me.

As time has gone on, our interactions have become empty, lacking any genuine connection. I want something more meaningful. I've been balancing on a tightrope, trying to keep her in my life by keeping her in my bed.

As I return to the present, she opens her eyes and looks at me with determination. I let out a breath and refocus on finding Madison. "Can you tell me about the calls?"

"I answer the call, and it's immediately strange. A man tells me a little girl is at the end of a driveway all by herself." My eyes widen, and she nods in confirmation.

At that moment, Sergeant walks over and interrupts. "It was more than just that. He seemed to know a whole hell of a lot about you, like he was targeting you." I clench my jaw. He needs to change his tone. This isn't on Zoey.

"What do you mean, Sarge?" I ask.

"Well, he tells Zoey it's *her* emergency, and he knows about you, Jack, and her past job and life in Chicago. It's almost like he's baiting her with Madison's kidnapping," he accuses.

"It's because when I was in fifth grade, someone tried to kidnap me from the bus stop," she deadpans at Sergeant, chin held high.

"Did you file a police report?" Sergeant demands.

"I don't know. I was a kid and terrified. I told my parents, and maybe they did, but I never asked about it again. I went to school late and tried to forget the entire event."

But I know she never did. Sergeant's rubbing his temple. He's grasping at straws. Our small-ass town only deals with unruly teenagers, escaped livestock, and occasional domestic disputes from the town drunks. During the pause in his questions, I step in. "Do you think this Ned knew about this incident in your past?"

"I don't know; it's not like it's a secret. I've told the story a few times to people throughout my life." She looks contemplative.

The first time I heard it, I remember it clearly. I finally got up the nerve to ask her on an actual date, and she'd agreed. About an hour before I was supposed to pick her up, Zoey called me.

"Jack, someone's at my house," Zoey whispered.

"What do you mean?"

"I came upstairs to borrow my mom's curlers and saw headlights from the upstairs hallway," she squeaked out.

"Are your parents home?"

"No, they're at an event; they're not supposed to be home until eight."

"Do you want to call the police?"

"No, what if it's someone just turning around? I don't want to waste anyone's time." She sighed. "Can you just talk to me while I get ready?"

"How can I get to your house on time if I'm talking to you?" I heard her fear through her shallow breaths. This wasn't like her: the most carefree, loving, kind, and fun girl I knew. I'd never seen her be afraid or back down from any challenge. Like when she was the only girl that jumped from the cliff into the lake, when one boy claimed girls were too afraid to do it.

"Here, why don't you talk with my dad, and I'll head over early. That way, if anything happens, he'll know, and I'll wait while you finish getting ready." She agreed, and I rushed to take the quickest shower of my life and head over.

Once I got there, she answered the door, a little disheveled but cute in an almost too-short T-shirt and the phone to her ear. I pointed to it. "My dad?" She nodded. I reached my hand out for it. "I'm here; we're good. Nope, no one else is here. Okay, will do, Dad."

"Thank you!" she burst out as she jumped into my arms for a hug.

I laughed. "Are you ready to go?"

She laughed and slapped my shoulder. "I need to change, Moore."

All my friends called me by my last name. I smiled at how affectionate it sounded from her. I waited for her to get dressed, and when she came back downstairs, my teenage heart raced. As we approached my car, I opened the door for her. When I reached the driver's side, I looked over, and she was back to her bubbly self, tapping her feet.

"Hey, can I ask you why you were so scared?" I glanced over, and she looked at me and told me the story about when she was in fifth grade waiting for the bus. She thought she was going to get kidnapped. Telling the story, she was as confident and carefree as if she were recalling her last family vacation.

I was stunned and in awe of how she could be so casual about a terrifying event. How could she have been so scared an hour ago and so carefree with me now? Like nothing phased her, she just kept moving forward, knowing life is an adventure she was determined to make the most of. I smiled at her. "You're amazing." She grinned and just shrugged. "What movie are we going to see?"

We laughed at dinner, cuddled in the movies, and made our way back to her house. I pulled off into a farm field nearby, not wanting the night to end. I steadied myself for our first kiss, a moment I'd spent way too long imagining.

Then I leaned over the center console. Our tongues swiped at lips, trying to find a rhythm. It was awkward and sloppy. She pulled away too soon and told me she needed to be home before curfew. She thanked me again for the night and for always being there for her as I walked her to her door.

When I reached my car, I suppressed a fist pump. I couldn't believe I finally got my date with Zoey and kissed her.

That was the beginning and end of our romantic relationship until four months ago, when she returned home out of nowhere.

"It seems like this would be quite the coincidence if this isn't related to you," Sergeant says accusingly. Judgment and disdain ooze from him after hearing what she confessed to the caller.

Sergeant needs to get out of this room before I do something I regret, like punch him in the face. His attitude toward Zoey is triggering my protective side.

CHAPTER 4

Zoey

"**H**ey, Sarge, I agree this seems more than a coincidence." I snap my head to Jack, steeling myself for his matching tone of disgust that Sergeant Graves clearly has.

"What's best is if I work with Zoey to uncover what we can about this caller before he calls back." He's trying to smooth out some of the tension in the air.

"*If* he calls back," Sergeant Graves barks.

Jack takes a deep breath and stands, taking a step toward Sergeant Graves. "I am going to believe that he will call back, and I'll work with her to get some clues. Can you work with the officers on their search efforts and keep things running smoothly?"

Sergeant Graves' face reddens. It's clear he's not a fan of his. It's also clear Jack is much more suited to be a sergeant. I'm grateful for his presence, even though I've been trying to keep him at a distance. Sergeant Graves glares at me. I keep my chin high and my composure strong. I will not let his judgment affect me.

"Spreading our resources out is what's best here. I'll run command of the officers in the field. I'll also take the lead with the Pike family; I've known them for years. You can take the lead with her," he says as he looks down at me and huffs.

Sergeant Graves turns and takes long strides out of the room on his short, stubby legs. The door closes, and I let out a deep breath. Jack turns to me, sits back down, leans forward, and grabs my hands.

"It's going to be okay. We'll find Madison, and we'll figure out who this son of a bitch is, and he'll regret ever messing with you."

I study him for a moment, to make sense of his kindness toward me. He's heard about what a treacherous cheater and horrible friend I am, on top of everything he's already put up with from me in the last four months. And yet, he still looks at me like I'm the only one in the room who matters. I can't bear it. I turn away toward the dingy brown wall.

He has always been too good for me. Always listening, always supportive, even after our last conversation. As much as I want to lean on Jack, I can't. It's how I got into this mess in the first place—expecting a guy to help me feel better about myself.

Yet here we are. One text, and he is by my side. I'm not worth his concern. We need to be focused on finding Madison.

"Tell me about Madison. What grade is she in?" I ask him.

"She's in fifth grade. Small for her age, but bubbly and friendly to everyone." I flinch, thinking of this happy, carefree girl with a stranger.

"Can you recall anyone that may know you and Madison?" he asks. I shake my head. "No, I don't know Madison or the Pike family. I don't know if there is a connection."

My eyes squeeze shut, and I rub my temples, trying to make sense of what's happening. Searching for any connection, but only coming up with reasons that this is all my fault.

Sally's humming interrupts my self-loathing and I begin grinding my teeth. How can she be humming with what's going on? I glare at her; she's trying to bring the attention to her, so she's a part of the action. It takes everything out of me not to roll my eyes. Jack must sense my annoyance and turns to Sally.

"Sally, I'm so grateful you're here today. You're our best dispatcher," he tells her. Ha. She *was*, but I'm the best now.

"Can you man the calls while we figure this out? We need Zoey to focus on what she knows about this caller and be prepared for when he calls next," he says, giving her a charming smile that would melt ice. I've never seen this side of Jack. Charming a woman and bending her to his will.

"I think you're our only dispatcher who could maintain her composure while everyone else here is losing control," he coos.

Seriously. I'm holding every ounce of self-control to not react to his words' effect on her. Why am I shocked? This thirty-year-old police officer version of Jack is merely an acquaintance. Since we reconnected, I've kept a safe emotional distance between us. I close my eyes as he continues to charm Sally into staying out of our conversation.

He was the last person I expected to run into when I went to Littles that first week I moved back. I'd spent the better half of the week hiding and feeling sorry for myself. My mother's neediness finally drove me to the edge. I had to get out of the house, find a job and a place to live in this small-ass town I never wanted to live in again.

A stop at Littles, the worst dive bar on this side of the Mississippi, was a safe place to venture out. Only cheap drunks, guys that worked at the railway manufacturer, would be there. And underage teens looking for some booze, if it was anything like when I was a kid.

I walked in, and it was like a time machine. It hadn't changed. Particle board ceilings and walls, not a TV in sight. The same dingy pool tables were tucked in the back, but a shuffleboard table had been added. That could have been fun if I wasn't trying to hide out and not to speak to anyone that night. I was right. Already a few old men at the bar, and in the back, some kids who were a little young to be drinking were giggling.

I slid onto the oversized pleather bar stool and waited for the bartender to turn around. I recognized him and immediately regretted my bar choice. Andy. What the hell was he doing as a bartender here?

I shouldn't have been surprised; he was always the good-time guy, avoiding responsibility like it was a full-time job. I always envied his lack of ambition and complete contentment with taking each day as it came, never plotting to get out of this town. He made eye contact with me, paused, and then his eyes lit up.

"No fucking way! Zoey! What the hell are you doing in town, and at Littles?!" he yelled way too loud.

I looked around. Everyone must have been used to his volume, because no one looked my way. "I'm looking for a drink, *Andy*. Got any vodka?" I asked, dripping with sarcasm.

He laughed. "Just the shitty stuff!"

"Great, I'll take it with some club soda." He gave me a wry smirk. "Or anything to take the edge off the shit part."

"Sprite and vodka coming right up! And don't ask for lime; we don't have any of that fancy stuff you're used to in Chicago!"

I held back a cringe. My life there was the last thing I wanted to think about. As I waited for my drink, someone entered the bar and he looked at the door.

"Hey, hey! Man! It's your lucky night!" he screamed.

Geez, he's loud. I didn't even bother looking over. There wasn't anyone that could enter this hellhole that I'd care about seeing.

Andy walked over with my drink, and his eyes were big and mischievous. I rolled my eyes; he hadn't changed at all. I sensed someone sit next to me; he looked next to me at the person with knowing eyes and then back to me so quickly that I couldn't help but look at who was now sitting next to me. Holy *shit*.

"Jack?"

"Zoey?! You're the absolute last person I expected to see here tonight," he quipped. Me too, Jack, me too. I gave him a genuine smile. I was so happy to see him, but my heart quickly sank. He's a variable I didn't factor into my plans.

"I thought you lived in Nashville."

"I thought you lived in Chicago," he responded.

"Well, now I'm here; you? Visiting or living?"

"Ha! Jack left the big city four years ago, and now he's a small-town cop!" Andy interrupted.

I looked at Jack quizzically, and he held my stare. It's then that I noticed his hazel eyes had changed; they had become greener. They used to be so young and naïve, but now they were strong and experienced. He was broader, too. His jawline had sharpened, and his hair was short on the sides and a little messy on the top. He was no longer that cute teenager who was one of my best friends. He had become a man. My stomach tightened. Jack was *hot*.

Andy slid a beer over to him as he turned on his barstool to face me. I turned to face him. Our knees bumped and his leg settled between mine, and mine fumbled between his. We sat close to each other; closer than I would have liked, but I couldn't pull away. His warmth comforted me. I looked at him again, and I was safe. It was always that way with him, but now there was also something different. A curiosity at what his touch might feel like.

He held my stare for a moment, contemplating where to start. "When did you get back?" he asked.

"On Monday. I've been hiding out at my parent's."

He nodded. "How long are you staying?"

The thought of doing this made my stomach churn with unease. I didn't want to answer the questions that hung in the air, asking why I'm here again. I just wanted to move forward.

I shifted in my seat as the warmth of his leg against mine spread through me. He didn't move to create space between us. His touch sent a tingle down my back. I studied his face, looking for a reaction.

"I'm looking for a job and a place to rent."

"Look at that! Hell has frozen over! Zoey is moving back home!" Andy yelled as he slapped his hand on the bar. I flinched at the noise. God, he is loud.

Jack cocked his head slightly. "Want to get out of here?"

"Yes, please."

He slapped a twenty on the table. "Sorry man, I'll catch up with you later."

Andy clutched his heart and barked out through his mock pain. "Protect yourself!"

He was still just as goofy as ever. I followed Jack out to the street. Not ready to go home yet, but I didn't want to go anywhere for fear of running into someone else from my past. I leaned up against the side of Littles and looked up.

"Thanks. Andy was a bit more than what I was looking for tonight. I just couldn't stay another night in at my parent's."

"Andy is always more," he laughed.

"Yeah, he doesn't seem to have changed much." I tilted my head forward to get a full look at him. "Unlike you."

His eyes locked on mine, and my heart picked up. His gaze deepened. And it was like he was trying to see the last ten years of my life written on me. He wasn't going to find it there. I had buried my past so deep it wouldn't come out. He broke the silence.

"My place is a few blocks down if you want to grab a drink that won't burn a hole in your stomach?"

Yes. *Shit*. No. *Dammit*. My hands were sweating. This was not part of my plan to build my life back. He watched me silently as the conflicting thoughts in my mind clashed.

"Come on, let's catch up; what has it been? Eight or nine years? You seem like you could use some good vodka after suffering through Andy's yelling."

As he turned, I stepped off the wall and walked up to him. "A decade."

"Yeah, it's been a long time," he confirmed.

We walked in silence as I thought about how much we'd changed. A West Plains cop. He had wanted to be a cop for as long as I had known him. At least some of his plans had worked out, unlike mine. We both had dreams of leaving West Plains for bigger cities, but here we were, back again.

As we walked to his apartment, questions swirled in my mind about how he ended up back here, but I couldn't ask him. I feared they'd lead to questions about me.

"Here we are," he pointed at a door between buildings. He lived in an apartment above an antique shop downtown. And as if I'd lost all rational thought, I followed him up the stairs and into his place.

"You want vodka and soda? Is that what you were suffering at Littles?"

"Do you have any wine?" I hadn't asked for it at Littles. I figured it would be an old box of wine that would've led to the worst hangover of my life.

"Yeah." He pulled out an already open bottle from his fridge and raised it. "Chardonnay?"

I nodded, and he grabbed a stemless wine glass from his open shelf. While his back was to me, I scanned his place. It was charming and masculine, with brick walls and an open kitchen. It was like a big city loft.

He took long, confident strides as he opened a beer and met me at his oversized, brown leather couch. I reminded myself that Jack used to be one of my best friends as I willed my racing heart to settle. My hand reached out to take my wine, and I sat down close to him. He grabbed the remote off his coffee table, which looked like an antique trunk, and clicked on the TV.

"You know, there is an open position for a Nine-One-One dispatcher down at the station. I'd be happy to make an introduction for you. It would be better than working at Walmart," he offered.

The idea of answering 9-1-1 calls tossed around in my mind. "You make a convincing argument." I say with a smirk. It would add a level of excitement to my life. Not like handling PR crises in Chicago, but as close as I could get in this tiny town. "I'd appreciate that." I shrug.

"Why are you moving back?" he asked.

My breath caught in my throat and I didn't answer. Where would I even start?

I sat my wine on his coffee table, let out my breath and slid on his lap, straddling him. He looked up at me with shock and curiosity in his eyes. Heat spread in my core. I rocked my hips, and he hardened underneath me.

His hands snapped to my waist, and his fingers slowly slid under my shirt along my waist, brushing my hip bone. I rocked again. His gaze steadied, and a sly grin appeared. I looked down at his mouth and back into his questioning eyes. I gave a tiny nod, and his lips were on mine.

It was unlike the sloppy kisses I remembered from my one and only date with him. His lips were soft, and his tongue teased mine. I parted them, and he gave my lower lip a little nip. I gasped, rocked my hips against him, increasing the friction, and then I was gone, lost to the unexpected pleasure of Jack's kiss.

"I'd like to go on the premise that this guy is after you and not Madison. Let's work off the assumption that Madison's kidnapping was an opportunity to get to you." Jack's attention is back on me.

He's worked some magic on Sally, as she isn't even humming anymore. He tries again. "This may be hard to internalize, but I think this Ned is after you."

Jack thinks I'm freaking out, but I'm not. I have my well-formed crisis mask on. I can think clearly in any situation. "Well, he isn't going to get very far," I say confidently.

That's the one thing I learned in PR: If you act confidently, people take you at your word. You can be very wrong, but if you're confident in your stance, people usually follow it.

"Let's start by reviewing your interactions since you've been back. There may be a clue in your activities these past four months."

My life isn't much here. I come to work, and I fuck him. That's all I do. "My routine here is simple. It involves this job and you." I stare at him knowingly. "There's nothing else I do. I haven't been back to a bar since that night at Littles. It's rare for me to make it out to my parent's."

He nods and looks at me with sympathy, and I can't stand it. I turn away, studying the speckled brown fabric of the cube wall.

"Then we should start talking about your past." Jack pauses, touches my chin, and guides my face back to his. "We need to identify who in your past knew what happened to you in fifth grade and what happened in Chicago."

A wave of nausea washes over me. Could Ned be Cassie's husband?

CHAPTER 5

Jack

I gently touch Zoey's chin and turn her face towards mine. I look at her deeply, conveying to her I'm here, she's safe, and can trust me with her past. Her gaze turns cold. She pulls back, releasing her chin from my touch, folds her arms, and holds my stare. *Shit.* This hard Zoey is foreign to me. My heart is quickening, and I break first, glancing at her computer.

I pick up a pad of paper from her desk. With a deep breath, I try a different approach. "Can we start with anyone from your life in Chicago you think may want to cause you harm?"

She glances down at the pad of paper now in my lap. I reach and put my hand on hers. "Zoey, I get this isn't something you want to discuss. I *know.*" I squeeze her hand. "But there's a little girl out there right now scared to death, and you are …"

"I *fucking* know I'm the only one that can help her, *Jack,*" she interrupts as she rips her hand away.

Every muscle in my body tenses as I force myself not to flinch. She retreats into herself and her walls rise. I don't even recognize the woman sitting in front of me. She closes her eyes and takes a deep breath. When she opens them, I see her mask slip into place.

"There's Cassie and her husband, but I really couldn't see them doing some-thing like this. She's a PR girl; she got her revenge the PR way by demolishing my reputation beyond repair in Chicago."

The bravado in her tone jolts through me. "Can we at least add Cassie's husband's name to the list to look into?"

She shrugs. "Joey Banks."

I write the name down. "How long did you live there?" I ask quietly.

I don't want to spook her, but I need her to trust me with her past. We haven't spoken in three days. We have solely spent our time together over the last four months having sex. Zoey hasn't once slept over or agreed to go on a proper date with me. Four nights ago, she showed up at my apartment and I was cooking her dinner, hoping she would sit down and have a meal with me.

Zoey knocked quickly and opened my door. As she walked into my apartment, she lifted her shirt above her head. She dropped it on the floor by the couch, and my eyes followed her every move. She strutted toward me wearing a sinful black lace bra. My shoulders tensed as I returned my focus to the pasta I had just dropped into boiling water.

She slid up to me in the kitchen, pressing my arm between her breasts as she reached over to cup my already hard dick. I turned to her and put my arms around her, rested my hands on her ass, and kissed her gently. I pulled back. "Hello."

My eyes drifted down to her breasts. "I'm not complaining about the view, but if you keep this up, the pasta will be mush."

She grasped me harder, then slid her hand up to my waist, released the button of my jeans, unzipped my zipper, and quickly slid her hand into my boxers. I moaned and grabbed her ass. Then reached around her to stir the pasta.

Her hips began to grind into me as she dragged her palm up over me. "As you can tell, I'm more than ready for you, but I need to get this pasta drained before our dinner gets ruined."

I sidestepped her to grab the potholders, and she bounced to the fridge with an evil grin. I finished draining the pasta and turned around. Her pants were off. *Fuck me.* I snapped my eyes back to the pasta and started counting as it slid back into the pot.

"Want a beer, too?" she asked. As I turned to her, she slipped her fingers down the front of her panties.

"Yes," I growled as I turned back to the stove, zipping my pants. I knew what she was trying to do. Anytime I tried to connect with her, she deflected with seduction and avoided all conversations of substance. She reached me at the stove, sat my beer on the counter, and lifted my shirt. "Zoey."

"What? If I'm going to watch you cook in my underwear, it's only fair that you cook in your underwear."

"Fine." I couldn't help a chuckle. She pulled my shirt over my head while I pushed my jeans off. As she walked away, I shook my head at her bare ass as she tossed my clothes down the hall.

That day, I'd been pumping myself up figuratively and literally to maintain my composure. I steeled my resolve to sit down and have dinner with her. As I watched her, my heart longed to connect, to uncover the secrets of her life over the past ten years.

She parked herself at the end of the counter jutting out of my U-shaped kitchen. Her ass tilted up as she braced her elbows on the counter and sipped her beer. I turned to face her, leaned my back against the counter, took a big gulp of beer, and searched her face for anything beyond the mischief sparkling in her eyes. She knew exactly how she was torturing me.

She rose up and down on her toes, bouncing her ass cheeks, and grasped the edge of the counter. How was I going to sit across the table and eat with her like that? I was about to explode.

As I stepped behind her, I set my beer down on the counter and ran my hand down her back. She giggled as I grabbed her hips. She knew she'd won once again.

I slid my hand up her spine, unclasped her bra, and let it fall to the counter. I reached over and cupped one of her breasts as I leaned into her neck and kissed her. She moaned and shifted her hips back into me. I gritted my teeth. "Dammit, Zoey."

"What?" she asked innocently. I pushed against her ass and squeezed her breast hard, pinching her nipple and gave her neck a nip. She moaned and turned quickly, grabbing my hip and thrusting me forward while she wrapped her hand around my neck, pulling me in for a hungry kiss.

Her tongue devoured my mouth as I reached around and grabbed her ass to bring her rocking against me. She moaned into my mouth, and I mumbled in response.

She pulled down my boxers and lowered herself down, palming me. I looked at the ceiling and tried to steady my breath. She settled on her knees and licked down my length. I moaned, "Zoey."

"Mm, hmm," she murmured.

I put my hand in her hair as she took me fully in her mouth, pulled out slowly, placed her hand along my base, and started bobbing in time with her hand. My seventeen-year-old self would never imagine that she would one day be on her knees in front of me, deep-throating my dick.

I lifted her up and turned her around onto the counter. She stepped out of her lace thong and opened her legs for me. I parted her, and as she gasped, I pushed into her, thrusting as she bounced against the counter.

We moved from the kitchen to the couch and were a tangle of legs and arms, chasing the release. She slid on top of me, riding me, and I was deep inside of her. When she finally shuddered and clenched around me, my head fell back. I thrust into her, and a moment later, I shook with my release.

She dropped her head onto my chest, panting. I wrapped my arms around her while we waited for our breaths to steady. She pulled back, and I studied her as I pushed her hair behind her ear. For a moment, I saw her wall cracking. She leaned over and kissed me quickly, and hopped off.

"That was fun." She looked over her shoulder and smirked at me as she shimmied to the bathroom.

I dropped my arms to my sides, slamming my fists onto the couch. As I got up to find my clothes, I rubbed my hand through my hair. I couldn't keep doing this. I'd fantasized about mind-blowing sex with her for what seemed like my entire life, but I had loved her just as long. And this didn't feel like love. It wasn't. It couldn't be, because this Zoey was a stranger to me. She wouldn't let me in.

I wanted more than anything for her to trust me, depend on me. For her to realize I would always be there for her, no matter what she had been through over the past ten years. The good, the bad, and the ugly. I wanted her to fall in love with me.

I heard her light footsteps, and I looked up to see her walking naked down the hall. She was just so *damn* beautiful and confident.

"I've got to get going, early shift tomorrow. I'm on at 6:00 a.m.," she said in a singsong voice.

"Can't you stay for dinner?" She turned away as she slid her panties back up and grabbed her bra. "It won't take long to finish; give me fifteen minutes?"

Her shoulders tensed as she took a deep breath. "I really can't."

"Can't or won't?"

She tilted her head and looked through me for a beat before walking over and grabbing her jeans. She turned around again, so she wasn't facing me while she pulled them on.

In my boxers, I stood in the middle of the room and watched her as she walked toward me and the door. She slid her hand up my arm, rose to her tiptoes, and gave me a kiss; she hesitated for a moment. I clenched my jaw.

"Won't," she whispered and stepped away. She picked up her shirt by the couch and put it over her head as she made her way to the door, barely getting her arms through the sleeves before opening it and walking through.

I stood there, stunned, but the sound of the door slamming shut snapped me out of it. "Dammit!" I turned and stomped into the kitchen to my now warm beer and looked at the half-cooked meal sitting there. I opened the trash bin and threw my beer into it, causing it to explode.

It didn't take long for me to learn that she had moved back here. When Andy texted me she was at Littles that night, I rushed over. That night exceeded all my expectations, and I was certain it was the start of our relationship. One I've longed for since high school. Frustration with her stubbornness churned in my gut.

I pivoted and opened the fridge to grab a cold beer, slammed it shut, and then opened it again and put it back. I needed something stronger to deal with what was to come.

As I stretched above my fridge, I grasped the smooth bottle of expensive bourbon. I pulled it down, poured a double serving into a glass, and chugged it. I slammed the glass down and filled it up again. This time I added an oversize ice cube to go with it. With my drink in hand, I stomped back to my bedroom to take a shower.

Sitting on the edge of my bed, I grabbed my phone from the nightstand charger. My hand shook as I took a sip of bourbon and unlocked my phone. I opened Zoey's texts and started typing.

I can't do this anymore. It's only dinner. Please.

I stared at it; my finger shook over the send button. I took another large swallow of my bourbon. This was her last chance. I erased the *Please.* And hit send. I gulped down the rest of my bourbon and got in the shower.

"Four years," Zoey starts. "I lived in Chicago for four years."

I hide my relief at finally getting some information from her, noting that's how long I've been back home. It's frustrating that this is the only way she's finally opening up to me. My anger that it's taking an incident of this magnitude for her to share her past with me is intensifying. The muscles in my jaw tighten and I rub it to release the tension and keep my cool. Raging under the circumstances isn't going to help anyone in this situation.

"Do you have any exes you think would be out to hurt you?"

"I didn't date anyone." Her eyes meet mine to see how I might react.

I swallow down my surprise. Four years without a relationship—that's crazy. Guys had to be after her all the time. I've had a few relationships in the last four years. I can't believe she hasn't even had one. My eyes rise from the notepad, and I stare at her.

"Any bad dates or creepy guys that seemed to show you too much interest?"

Zoey meets my eyes, holds it for a beat, and then looks down. "I went on quite a few dates." She jumps up. "I can look at my Tinder account and see if any stand out as total psychos."

"Great. That's a good idea." I fake confidence. Not sure I really want to see her Rolodex of screws. As she pulls out her phone, a thought comes to me. "Do you share that story about almost being kidnapped at the bus stop on your Tinder dates?"

She looks up at me, and the light dims in her eyes. "No. I don't. Dammit. *Dammit!*"

"It's still worth looking into. If we can get the data on your dates, we can run background checks on the guys, see if anything in their history is suspicious or criminal."

That will take time, and we will need to get resources from St. Louis. She messes with her phone and swipes through the app. I turn away. Not wanting to see the number of guys in her graveyard of one-night stands.

"Got it. Who can I email it to?"

"Email it to me, and I'll send it to St. Louis. They should be able to run background checks much more quickly than us."

She looks up at me apologetically, like she's sorry for what I'm about to see. I swallow hard, as reality sets in that she settles for meaningless relationships in her life. That she would stoop so low as to mess around with a married guy, a friend's husband.

My feelings are swirling. I'm disappointed with the decisions Zoey's made. Guilt chokes me that we grew apart. I want to protect her. My emotions are threatening to derail my focus. And I'm annoyed that I'm allowing it all to distract me from keeping this situation under control.

The computer lights up, and her eyes get big. I nod at her, encouraging her to answer. She turns to her desk and takes a deep breath.

"Nine-One-One. What's your emergency?"

CHAPTER 6

Zoey

"**I** thought I'd made it clear that I'm not interested in your scripts, *Zoey*," Ned sighs cruelly.

I turn to Jack and nod, confirming it's him again. As I turn back, I take a deep breath and close my eyes, forcing my mind to go blank. Madison's safety relies solely on me right now. My eyes open at the sound of feet shuffling. Jack's stepping closer to me. My eyes close again as I open myself up to my instincts.

"I'm sorry, Ned. I don't know who is calling until I answer." My heart is racing as I pray he doesn't catch the lie. We knew it was him when we saw the cell number come up on caller ID.

As I open my eyes, a shadow appears to my right, and the heat from Jack hovering behind my chair makes my palms sweat. I tense, and he must sense it because he takes a step back. I lower my shoulders, and then it hits me that Ned wants to be in control of our conversations. As much as I want to burst into questions, my gut says I need to wait until he speaks.

"How are you doing?" Ned's voice echoes in my ear.

How am I doing? I'm a wreck. My worst fear is becoming a reality for an innocent little girl, and I'm raging at my lack of ability to end this nightmare for Madison. My heart rate quickens, and I close my eyes again, trying to slow my breathing.

Thoughts form on how to handle this. Ned wants me hurting; he wants me in distress. The more I try to be strong and collected, the more he hardens. I need to give him what he wants to hear.

"I'm feeling very helpless right now."

"That must be a new feeling for you." His voice drips with disdain.

"Yes," I whisper.

Avoiding helplessness has been my obsession for the last four years. I've done everything, everything I could do to avoid this feeling again. My shoulders curl in, and Jack must notice my shift because he sidesteps so that I can see him from the corner of my eye. He wants to reassure me, but I can't bring myself to meet his eyes. I inhale and straighten again. My focus must stay on finding Madison.

"Good. It's about time that you feel how you make others feel."

I flinch. "Does Madison need to feel helpless too?"

"What makes you think she feels helpless?"

"You took her from her bus stop. She should be eating her lunch right now at school, not trapped with some stranger who picked her up."

"She is eating her lunch right now. Her mother packed her quite a lunch of treats; I'm jealous. I never got fruit snacks with my lunch for school."

At this, I finally look at Jack. He is studying his phone.

"What else is in her lunchbox?" I ask to clue him in to what I've learned.

He looks at me and then writes something on the notepad with *Joey Banks* at the top.

Got a hit on an Amber Alert. Someone thinks they saw Madison with a man near Bangs Lake. Madison did not look harmed.

"Does it matter?" Ned asks incredulously.

"No," I respond.

The pace of his conversation is excruciating. I just want to take control and start demanding information from him. As if he can read my thoughts, Ned drawls, "It must be taking every ounce of your control to not take over this conversation. Your restraint is unexpected."

My eyes close and a quick wave of relief hits me. I've assessed the situation correctly. He wants to be the one pulling the strings. "Yes. This is very hard for me. Is there anything I can do to get Madison back to her family?"

I'm so tense that I don't even notice I'm holding my breath until Jack's hand rests gently on my shoulder. I can't hide the pleading in my eyes. He squeezes my shoulder, conveying his confidence in me and encouraging me with a slight nod as he leans up against my desk.

My focus returns to the computer screen, and I wait. The waiting is all part of his manipulation. Whoever he is, he knows me well enough to remember that patience is not a strength of mine, especially under stress. I've spent the last four years staying in complete control and losing it again is crushing me.

"Hmm. Why don't we discuss how you gained that fabulous designer wardrobe in Chicago?"

What? Seriously. I can't believe what he's saying. My clothes? He kidnaps a little girl, and this guy wants to talk about how I filled my closet when I moved to Chicago? This is such a *mindfuck*. My chest tightens.

"I'm not sure I understand what you mean?" I ask and turn to Jack. He circles his hands to signal I need to keep him on the line and talking.

"*Zoey*, you *know* what I mean. And before you get your little wheels going, know I'm not interested in your spin. I will ask the questions and want to hear honesty in your answers," he demands.

My stomach churns with nausea. I place my hand on my stomach and close my eyes, desperate for this to end. "I stole it."

"Oh, *Zoey*, you know there is more to it than that."

My hands tremble as I look down at the keyboard, and I'm back at my first desk in the Pellman offices. I'm on my third day as a junior PR rep.

Anxiety rolled through me, informing me of how much of an imposter I was. A small-town Missouri girl entirely out of place in Chicago. I couldn't help noticing that the other girls were side glancing at me, laughing with each other, wondering how I made it through the interview process.

Their designer wardrobes were kindling to the building fire of my insecurities. Each Gucci purse and Chanel necklace caused the flames to jump.

"Hey, have you seen my AMEX card?" Pepper asked.

I looked up from my desk, realizing she stood before me. "Zoey, right? Have you seen an AMEX card lying around? You know what an AMEX card looks like, right, green and white? Have you seen it?"

This was the third time I'd heard Pepper asking around the office for her AMEX in as many days. Who loses a credit card that often? Isn't she worried about it getting stolen?

"No, sorry. I haven't seen it. If I do, I'll bring it to you." She pouted, and I noticed her Chanel necklace and matching earrings. Huffing, she walked away, and I saw the red bottoms of her shoes. That was probably why she took such little care with her credit card. Clearly, money wasn't a scarce resource for her.

I returned my attention to my computer and the list of media outlets I had been pitching about a top restaurateur and the charity he was promoting. In reality, he was just trying to deflect the rumors of his inappropriate behavior.

My fingers trembled as my anxiety rose. What was I thinking, going for a job at the top PR firm in Chicago? Did I really believe I could climb the social ladder and leave my disaster of a life in St. Louis behind? But St. Louis had changed me. Everything about this job was me trying to escape that life. I stood up, tried to shake off the fear, and headed to the break room for a coffee refill.

As I filled my Pellman office mug, I saw something green peeking out from underneath the corner of the creamer station. Was that ...? I reached and pulled it out. It was Pepper's AMEX. I found it; I perked up. This could help me get in with her, and she might invite me to join her and the other girls for their Thursday night drink date.

I held her AMEX as I walked back to my desk. I began planning on how to handle this to my advantage. As I sat down, it hit me. Pepper probably wouldn't find it significant that I found her credit card and returned it, because she seemed to lose it almost daily. The card warmed in my hand as I recalled her Gucci messenger bag that she'd drop this card in.

My insecurities were a raging bonfire. If only I could look the part of these girls, I could then fit into their circle. I knew Pepper's dad paid her credit card bills. In fact, I'd overheard several of the girls in the office talk about their credit cards, given to them and paid for by their rich dads.

I sighed, looked up at the ceiling, and started counting my breaths. In one, out two, in three, out four. As I reached ten, I turned back to the computer. I could use her card to order that Chanel necklace that seemed to be a uniform in the office, and the charge would probably go unnoticed by Pepper and her daddy.

Could I? My anxiety faded as my confidence emerged. I could try it. She would never learn that I found it. I could use it quickly and then put it back where I saw it in the breakroom. If a fraudulent charge got noticed, what would be the chance they'd investigate it? Adrenaline pumped through me. I couldn't help the smile forming on my face; this could be my way in. I needed to look the part, and once I did, they'd notice and include me.

With a few clicks, I ordered the latest version of the trendy necklace from the Chanel website. Then I took my coffee back to the breakroom, added some creamer, and slipped the card back under, letting it peek out more than before.

My heart was pounding with excitement as I made my way back to my desk. Now, I just needed to wait and see if this charge went unnoticed. In the meantime, I started making a mental note of each girl I heard mention that their daddy paid their credit card bills.

"I never took you for a slow learner, *Zoey*. Quite the opposite, actually."

I shrink into myself, and Jack steps closer again; I jerk away before he can touch me. His hand drops to his side. I don't turn to him, but I sense his gaze on me; his concern radiating around me.

"I stole the credit cards of the rich girls that worked at Pellman, and I slowly built myself a designer wardrobe."

The air around me goes cold as Jack steps away from me. I don't turn around to see where he's going. I raise my chin and refocus on getting information about Madison.

"Excellent. You see now how this is going to go."

He wants me helpless, distressed. "Ned? Can we get Madison back to her parents? Then I'll tell you every dark secret I have," I plead.

The sound of laughter echoes from the other end of the call. I count in one, out two, in one, out two, to push away the rising dread in my chest.

"*Zoey*, I already know every deep, dark secret of yours."

My mind races. "What do you want from me?" I whisper.

"I want all your secrets to become public record. Expect another call from me soon."

The line goes dead. I lean forward and put my head in my hands and hold in a sob. I can't lose control now. A throat clears behind me. I rise and straighten my shoulders.

As I turn, the faces of Jack and Sergeant Graves are staring back at me. My stomach is churning with dread. I need more time to collect myself. I've got to get away from them. My body launches from my chair. "I need to go to the bathroom."

They step back in unison, and I pass them as I head to the bathroom. "You're wasting time in our search for Madison," Sergeant Graves barks.

Anger and desperation are flooding me. That short fat-ass can shove it. I don't think Ned is planning on hurting Madison. He seems to only want to hurt me. I enter the dingy bathroom and lean against the sink, gulping in breaths.

"God dammit!" I turn to kick the dirty gray tile wall. That doesn't mean that Madison isn't scared to death. Every moment she's with this man, her terror must be growing. Joey keeps coming to mind. Could this be him? It doesn't seem right. I'm missing something.

I slam open the door and see Jack staring down Sergeant Graves with his arms crossed. They must not agree on the investigation. I head back to my desk, almost brushing into Sergeant Graves's chubby shoulder.

"Moore, go listen to the calls. That's an order."

As I sit down, there's a water bottle waiting for me. I'm sure it's from Jack. Sergeant Graves wouldn't show me an ounce of kindness. I watch the tense standoff between them. Jack takes a deep breath and steps toward me, rubbing his hand through his hair.

He leans over me, placing one hand down on the desk and one hand on the back of my chair. "Listen, Sergeant wants to question you, and he's right. I need to listen to the calls."

I can't turn to him; the kindness in his voice is destroying me. I don't deserve it. He should treat me like Sergeant Graves. Jack just heard me confess to credit card theft. He's a cop. I broke the law. He should be arresting me, not trying to comfort me. I open the water bottle and nod, taking a sip from it as I keep my face turned away. He stares at the side of my face for a moment longer.

"Alright, I'll be back as soon as I'm done reviewing the calls." He straightens up and walks away.

Sergeant Graves stomps over to me, replacing the sound of Jack's fluid steps. He stops at a chair against the wall and drags it up behind me. I'm suddenly grateful for my crappy desk because Sally can't see back here, and I don't think she has the nerve to interrupt Sergeant Graves.

"It's time for us to chat."

I turn my chair around and face him. Is his face always red, or is it just the day's events making him light up? My mask slips down and I aim to take control before he asks me a question.

"I want to do everything I can to help find Madison. We can both agree that we want the same outcome." I refuse to give this man the satisfaction of seeing me intimidated or distressed.

His eyes narrow on me, and he crosses his arms as he leans back in his chair. "Who is Ned?"

"I don't know. I don't know anyone named Ned."

Sergeant Graves doesn't believe me. He's trying to hold silence, to get me to talk more. He's wrong. I have every trick in the book to manipulate people and situations. The identity of this man is a mystery to me; otherwise, I wouldn't be revealing my most shameful moments on recorded 9-1-1 calls. I'd be sending Jack to arrest this psychotic *asshole*.

"He sure knows an awful lot about you," Sergeant Graves accuses.

I take a deep breath, swallowing my sigh. "I know, and before you ask, I don't know how he knows these things."

Sergeant Graves huffs and leans forward in his chair, placing his elbows on his knees. The effect makes him seem like a human bowling ball. He holds his stare and the silence for painful minutes. "Finding Madison depends on your cooperation."

CHAPTER 7

Jack

Dammit. As I approach Zoey's desk, I assess the standoff. She is sitting back in her chair with her arms crossed, and Sergeant is leaning forward, staring her down. My jaw clenches. He's distracted by his suspicion that she's involved in the kidnapping. He can't see that she's as much a victim in this as Madison.

I misjudged how others would perceive Zoey after listening to the calls. It doesn't seem like she's deserving of trust. She just confessed to credit card fraud. It's clear that my past with her gives me reason to look past her mistakes. Am I capable of proving myself impartial while working on this case?

My protective instincts toward her are clouding my judgment. I've known and loved her for so long that I can't just flip the switch and see her as a suspect. She was a Homecoming Queen. Loved by everyone. Zoey's eyes widened with surprise as they placed the crown upon her head. She was the only shocked one in the room. She had this magical way of including everyone.

I'll never forget how she approached the special education teacher at the school and organized a dance for her class at the end of the school day. Zoey decorated the gym and arranged for music. And even got a photographer from the yearbook committee to take pictures of the kids posing.

She was so beautiful and carefree as she danced with those kids like they were the most popular in the school. When I gave her a ride home later, I asked why she thought to do that. "I wanted them to experience a school dance without judgment and fear," she beamed.

I was crazy in love with her and wanted a way to make us more than just friends. It's hard to just forget all those feelings that resurfaced these last four months. The love I had for her never really left me. There's a harsh truth of what she's experienced, the pain she's felt, and how her life circumstances have shaped her, that she hasn't shared with me yet.

"Sergeant's right; we need you to help find Madison," I said, nodding at him. "You're one of the most resourceful people I know."

A flash of pain crosses her face, and I rub my hand through my hair. She must have found herself in a state of desperation that drove her to these actions. Sergeant's aggression toward her is only pushing her walls up further. I need to convince him to let me handle her. His presence is only hindering our efforts, and he can't even see it.

"Sergeant, a word?" I ask, motioning out of the room. He pushes up. "We're not done here," he barks.

My eyes lock on Sergeant as he turns down the hall. As she withdraws, my shoulders tense. I need to reach her. Not just because we need her help to find Madison, but because I can't stand the sight of her pain.

We head down the tight cubicle hallway. "This is really *fucked up*, Moore. She knows something, and she isn't telling us." He slams his hand against the door frame. "She is going to be held responsible if anything happens to Madison Pike."

I hold back a grimace and nod. Fighting with him is only going to hinder solving this case. My best bet is to get him on my side and agree to leave Zoey alone and let me do my thing. Then I can focus on getting her to open up and trust that I'm on her side.

"I agree it seems like she is holding something back, but going at her like this is only making her clam up." He grunts, so I continue. "Give me some time alone with her. Let me get her out of here for a bit. The caller, Ned, waited a couple of hours before calling a second time; he'll probably wait again. Let me take her out, away from the prying eyes of the station, so she is comfortable opening up."

He turns to me. "Moore, you have a soft spot for her. Everyone knows the two of you have been messing around since she got back in town. But she's a criminal."

"That gives me an advantage; she already trusts me," I respond, hoping he can't spot the lie.

He places his hand on his gun and looks to my right.

"The tip said Madison didn't seem in distress. The caller assumed they were related and skipping school to explore the lake."

"That doesn't mean she's still not in danger," he barks.

"I listened to the calls. This psycho seems more interested in hurting Zoey than Madison. I think he's using Madison as leverage to get to her."

"She isn't talking to us," Sergeant grunts.

I take a deep breath. "I think I can get her to talk. We need more clues into her past and who this bastard is. Can you give me a couple of hours?"

"You have until four, and if you don't get anything, then we do it my way."

"Understood. We already got a list of all her Tinder dates, and I sent them up to St. Louis so they could start running background checks."

He huffs incredulously and turns to head back into the station and to Madison's parents.

I put my hands behind my head and look up. One problem redirected. Now the one that won't be so easy to crack. Before I can start doubting my ability to reach her, I turn to walk back into the dispatch center.

As I round the corner to her dark desk, she's writing on the notepad and looks up. "Come on, let's go." I reach my hand out to her. She doesn't hide the shock in her eyes.

"What, why? I need to be here if he calls back." Desperation laces her words.

"You need to get out of this cave and clear your head. You haven't eaten yet today. He didn't call back for a few hours the first time. I think he'll wait a few more hours before calling again."

The uncertainty in her eyes turns into resolve. "I'm not leaving."

"I got Sergeant to back off, but only for a couple of hours. I need some fresh air, and you look like you need it too. Fifteen minutes. We will be back in fifteen minutes."

I'm holding her stare with my hand reaching out to her. "I have my radio; we won't be more than five minutes from the building."

"Fifteen minutes," she demands as she stands up, ignoring my hand. I glance behind her to see what she was writing. I only see random words.

Control. Knows everything. All my past. More than Chicago? Ex? St. Louis? Madison? Helpless.

We pass Sally's cube, and I turn back to give her my most grateful smile and a nod. Her cheeks flush, and she sits up a bit more, my charm working to subdue her.

"What were you writing?" I ask as we arrive at the dispatch room door.

"I was just trying to work through my thoughts. See if anything comes to me about who this guy is."

"Do you want to talk through it?" I ask as I open the door and let her walk out before me. She stops right outside and looks at me with her head tilted. Searching my face for where I stand. If I'm judging her or pitying her. I place my hand on her back and guide her right toward the tiny coffee shop.

I take a deep breath, and she stiffens. "We've known each other for a very long time. And so much has changed since those days when we were young and would hang out together. But I can't forget the way you made everyone around you feel so special back in high school. I can still sense that part of you here with me. No matter what's happened since then."

She stops and leans up against the building, looking at me skeptically.

"I was in love with you in high school. You *know*," I study her intensely, trying to reach the girl I knew at seventeen. She looks away and crosses her arms.

"And I'm sure you also know that each time we met on college breaks, I was hoping you would see me differently, and our relationship would move beyond friendship."

I take a step closer, and as she turns to face me, a tear rolls down her face. She wipes it away and drops her arms. "What do you want from me?" she whispers.

My emotions are in turmoil, a mix of sadness and disappointment, but also love. My feet root to the ground, my hands tighten into fists as I fight the urge to wrap my arms around her.

"I want you to trust me. Can you walk me through your thoughts on this asshole Ned's end game?"

She takes a deep breath and a look I can't place appears. Maybe a wave of relief? It's one I haven't seen before. I nod toward the coffee shop.

"This is only about me and not Madison," she says. I remain silent, hoping she'll continue. While I agree with her, I don't want to break her train of thought if she plans to keep talking. We walk in, and the place is empty. As we approach the cashier, she continues.

"He only talks about me and threatens me. He doesn't seem interested in the girl. It seems like it's more about controlling and hurting me."

I meet her gaze and give a short, affirmative nod, acknowledging her words. "Can we get two large coffees, two turkey sandwiches, and two bags of regular potato chips?"

After I pay the cashier, we walk to the counter and wait for the orders. Zoey is looking out to the street with desperation and defeat on her face. A sudden realization hits me, and the heaviness in her shoulders forms a new meaning. Over the last few months, I'd thought it was her ice-cold wall going up, but now I see it for what it is. Pain. Fear. *Shame.*

I grab the food, walk up to her, hand her a coffee, and stand right in front of her so I can meet her eyes. "I'm here for you. You're safe. You're always safe with me."

She nods slightly and turns back outside with urgency. The moment is over, and she's trying to get back to the dispatch center as quickly as possible. When I catch up to her, the chill of her resolve radiates from her.

"Please don't do that."

She snaps her head to me. "Do what?"

"Retreat behind that mask. The one that says you don't need anyone. You're pushing me away, and I really ..." I trail off. She stares at me in disbelief. I'm unsure if it's because I noticed the mask or I called her out on it.

"What should I do, *Jack*? Fall into your arms, crying, begging you to be my knight in shining armor?" I step back from her coldness. She sees the sting of her words and yet holds her glare, and I return it. She's breathing heavily. I won't relent, and I refuse to break the silence.

"Fuck," her eyes fall, and her shoulders turn in. "Fuck."

"I'm on your side. *Always.*"

"Don't say that. You don't know me anymore. Is that not abundantly clear after you listened to those calls?"

She turns to head back to the station. I grab her arm, almost dropping our food. She stops and looks at me with such sympathy my breath catches.

"I think you're right. I believe this lunatic is only looking to harm you. The Amber Alert tip didn't think that Madison was in any distress. They thought the two knew each other," I say as relief washes over her face. "Also, he hasn't taken Madison out of the area. Bangs Lake is like ten miles from her house. He isn't running off with her and hiding."

The wheels are turning in her head. "He's on borrowed time. There are not a lot of places for him to hide around here. He and Madison will not go unnoticed," I say.

My phone vibrates. I pull it out of my pocket and look down. It's an update from Sergeant.

Another sighting. This time at a Walmart in Mountain Grove. Buying Madison a toy.

"And now I'm convinced you're the target. Madison was seen with Ned in a Walmart in Mountain Grove. He was buying her a toy."

She's heading back into the station with long strides. "Is there a description of him? His car?" she shouts back at me.

I catch up to her. "They're working on it." I follow her back to the dispatch center and to her desk. She sits in her chair and stares at the brown cubicle wall. I sit our food down on her desk and turn to catch up with Sergeant.

"Jack?" she calls.

I turn back to her. "Yeah."

"She's going to make it home, right? Is Madison going to be okay? I'm not going to give her the trauma that ruins her life. I'm not going to kill her?"

Her eyes are filling with tears. I rush to her, get down on one knee, and grab her hands. I squeeze, reach up, put my hand behind her neck, and pull her into my shoulder. She shakes as a sob releases from her. Holding her tight, I realize she's been torturing herself with guilt for what's happened to Madison.

"This is not your fault." Her breaths are getting shorter, and I pull her in more. "You didn't cause this. You're not to blame for the kidnapping."

I rub the back of her head. "We're going to find her."

As I pull away, I put my hands on the side of her face and study her. The complete devastation that has taken over her breaks my heart. My thumbs rub her tears away. Is she counting? Slowly her breath is growing steady.

Her body relaxes against my shoulder as I hold her close, giving her time to catch her breath before pulling away. "I'm going to catch up with Sergeant and see what information I can get. I'll be back soon. In the meantime, eat the sandwich."

CHAPTER 8

Zoey

I side eye the bag of food. How the hell does he expect me to eat? My body betrays me as my hands shake, a physical manifestation of my emotional breakdown. Why can't Jack just back off? His kindness is overwhelming me; his compassion for me is too much to handle. I don't deserve it.

If I had known he was living here, I wouldn't have returned to this place. My plans were to disappear within this god-forsaken town. My life has been one major screw-up after the other. When I can't go any lower, I always outdo myself.

I drop my head into my hands as my self-loathing strikes. *Get over my damn self.* This isn't about me; it's about finding Madison. I scream silently in my head, and then I straighten my shoulders with a renewed determination to find Madison.

My attention returns to the notepad with my thoughts. As I study my list, I pray that we're right—that this is about me, not Madison. As I think back on my most disappointing experiences with Tinder, I take a sip of coffee.

Who is this lunatic? Before I spill the coffee with my shaking hands, I set it down. Welcoming the anger, the shame that's smothering me dissipates. As I let the burn of anger build in my chest, I close my eyes. I'm interrupted by the sound of hurried footsteps approaching.

"Great news. We have a description of the man, and they're working on getting the video from Walmart. No car details yet," Jack says, breathing fast and looking at me with hope. "He's probably in his early thirties and short. The witness said around five foot four or five foot five."

My gaze rests on the brown cubicle wall that holds so many of my thoughts. I can't meet his eyes while I'm confessing my one-night stands. "That rules out any of my Tinder dates. I never went on a date with anyone under six feet."

His footsteps stop, and when I turn, he's about to say something and then shakes his head. It's hard for me to make sense of why he's being so nice and considerate.

"Why haven't you arrested me yet?" I ask, my voice trembling.

"First, finding Madison is my only focus right now. Second, it's not our jurisdiction. Third, I'm finding it difficult to care about the mistakes of your past."

The compassion in his voice is too much for me. I turn away.

"I told you. This creep can't hide around here, and he isn't trying very hard. We're narrowing our search and pulling in the county sheriffs. He's on borrowed time," he seethes.

As his anger toward this situation grows, my shame multiplies, pushing down on my shoulders.

"What do you need?" I ask, forcing myself to project confidence.

"Can you think of any guy from your past that's shorter? Let's make a list of anyone you know: friend, ex, acquaintance. Doesn't matter."

As I turn to write names down on the paper, my computer lights up. A call is coming in. I snap to Jack, and he walks up and puts his hand on my shoulder, and this time I don't pull away.

"Hi, Ned." I try answering differently than before so as not to piss him off.

"Hi, *Zoey*. Isn't this a much nicer way to start a conversation?"

A shiver washes over me, and Jack squeezes my shoulder. I don't want to engage in pleasantries. I just want answers.

"Sure. How is Madison? Is she ready to come home yet?"

"No, not just yet. She is enjoying her new toy, though."

Ned was trying to be subtle, but the comment clarified that he's aware he's been seen. "So that was you in Walmart?" I confirm.

"Yes. I don't want to harm Madison. And if we continue having honest conversations, she'll enjoy this wild adventure with me."

I nervously smile up at Jack, slowly nodding my head to assure him that Madison is not the intended target and that he has no intention of hurting her.

"Which reminds me. I've wanted to ask if you've made a special video for Jack yet?" He asks with humor in his tone.

Shame is swallowing me. I jerk away from Jack's touch. My face is hot. Concern is radiating off of him. I refuse to meet his eyes.

"No," I say firmly.

"I'd hate for him to miss out on your talent." He pauses. "I think playing the video you created for Preston will be a great showcase for him."

I swallow hard. "It's gone. Deleted. Doesn't exist anymore."

My eyes close as nausea threatens to take over. Preston was the only guy I went on more than one date with in Chicago. I'd only been living there a few months when we matched.

Preston was handsome in that classic way. Clean cut, dark hair and eyes. He exuded arrogance and success. He always seemed to be in some version of a suit, like he was always just getting off work. Showing off that he was the most ambitious guy in the room. He worked at one of the big three consulting firms and traveled a lot.

He took me to the hippest restaurant on our first date, and I relished in the thought of bragging about it to the girls at work. When he asked me out on a second date, I immediately said yes.

We went to a bar that regularly had celebrity sightings, and we sat in the VIP area and had bottle service. I went home with him that night, and we had sloppy sex. He woke up at 5:00 a.m. and told me he had to head to the gym and asked me if he needed to call an Uber for me. I took that as my hint to leave.

I didn't care; Preston was going to be my ticket to the social elite. With him, I was planning to bury my unremarkable, desperate life in St. Louis so deep that the memories of my nightmare would disappear. As I slowly upgraded my wardrobe with designer staples, the girls at work admired my transformation. He was the next level in my rise to belonging.

On our third date, after dinner at the fanciest restaurant I'd ever been to, we walked over to Michigan Avenue and slipped into La Perla. He said he wanted me to try on some items for him and that he'd buy what he loved the most. I'd done nothing like that; it was thrilling and adventurous.

I first grabbed a red silk bra with black lace and matching boy shorts. Then I brushed my fingers over the sexiest slip in a deep teal. I looked up at him, and he nodded and then walked over and handed me a black lace garter belt and a matching lace corset top.

I took the items into the dressing room; he sat out front and then slipped in once the sales associate left to watch me try on the items. We'd only had drunken sex once, and it felt too intimate for me to undress in front of him. I swallowed down my discomfort and reminded myself what a relationship with him could mean.

He chose the garter belt and corset, and then asked me to keep them under my clothes. As soon as we got to his place, he pulled off my clothes and screwed me on his couch.

"I need a good night's sleep because I'm leaving for Japan in the morning."

I swallowed my shock. He hadn't mentioned that before. "How long will you be in Japan?" I feigned indifference.

"About ten days. I'll call you when I get back, and we can hit up that new restaurant in Lincoln Park."

I turned to him on the couch, studying him. "Will you have time to call or text while you're gone?"

"I'm really beat." He stood up. "I'll do my best, but I can't make any promises."

His standing there looking down at me made me uncomfortable, so I quickly got dressed. "Thanks for the lingerie. Enjoy your trip to Japan," I said as I walked out of his door, completely empty inside.

The next few days were a blur of trying not to think about him. I didn't want a boyfriend, but I also couldn't let go of the access a relationship with Preston would give me.

As I was getting ready for work on the fourth day, my phone pinged. Who would text me at 7:00 a.m.?

I can't stop thinking about you in that corset and garter.

A gasp escaped me and I smiled, sat my phone back down and tried to ignore the text. I finished getting ready and paced past my phone on the kitchen counter. I picked it back up.

What am I doing in the outfit?

I slammed the phone back down on the counter. What was wrong with me? Sexting? *Ping.*

I'm thinking about how hot your tits looked pushed up in that top. Send me a pic of you in it so I can study every inch of you while I'm gone.

My stomach churned with unease. What? No. I wasn't going to do that. I'd never taken a picture of myself undressed. Not going to happen. I needed to get to work. *Ping.*

I've had a hard-on for you every night thinking about you in that outfit.

My stomach swirled, and heat built in my core. I let out a breath and panic crawled down my spine. If I didn't respond, that might be the end with him. I didn't want that.

What have you done about that hard-on?

Eek. I slammed the phone down. What was I doing? *Ping.*

I'm stroking myself, thinking of you in that garter. Give me a pic. Please put me out of misery.

What was happening? My breath quickened. I was turned on. *Ping.*

Better yet, how about a video on how you spend your time thinking of me while I'm away?

He wanted me. My body reacted to his words with heat building in my core. No one had ever talked to me like this before. I felt desired and sexy. I pushed past my hesitation by remembering what dating him would mean. He could change my life entirely. That's why I moved to Chicago—to get as far away from my past in St. Louis as possible.

Shoving away my modesty, I headed to the bedroom and pulled out the lingerie. I slipped it on. And then I sat on my bed, held the phone up, did my best sexy pout with my finger next to my lip, and snapped a pic down my front.

I glanced at it quickly. Good enough. I sent it to him before I lost my nerve and set the phone facedown next to me. *Ping.*

You're sexy as hell Zoey. Are you wet for me right now?

Excitement and fear consumed me as I went for it. I wanted him to only be thinking about me.

Yeah, I'm soaked for you.

I watched the three dots appear.

Prove it.

Chewing on my lip, I wondered, am I going to do this? I set the phone on my dresser, propped up against books angled toward me on the bed, and did a quick test video of my angle—it's hot. *Ping.*

I'm so hard. I'm stroking myself, thinking of how wet you are. I need to see it.

After placing the phone back on the dresser, I hit the record button.

I laid back and spread my legs, so I was on display. My hands rubbed down over my breasts toward the garter. My fingers found their way down to my bundle of nerves, and I rubbed in slow circles. I continued rubbing, letting out a soft moan. Slipping two fingers into me, they went in quickly because *I was wet.* My other hand moved back up my front and I bit on my finger.

My hips raised as I pumped my fingers into myself and rubbed my palm over my sensitive spot. I squeezed my breast through the corset and my head dropped back. The naughtiness of the act turned me on. I pumped faster, and my moans grew louder, spreading my legs more as I hit my release.

I brought my head back forward and looked at the camera. The sudden realization of what I had just done hit me like a ton of bricks. I had just fucking recorded myself masturbating. *Ping.*

Why are you torturing me? Show me how you touch yourself when I'm not there.

I gripped the phone. I couldn't bring myself to watch it. My fingers were trembling as I pulled up the video into a text. I took a deep breath and hit send, then slammed the phone down and turned to scream into the bed.

The thought of waiting was unbearable, and I had to do something. I got up and got dressed again for work. My eyes kept darting to my phone, but there was still no response from him. It filled me with dread and regret. I was dizzy. What did I just do? I opened the text and got ready to delete the video.

That's the sexiest thing I've ever seen. I can't wait to watch you do that in person when I get back.

Six days went by before I heard from Preston again.

Want to meet me and some of my friends at Rally's for drinks? We're here now.

He was back. I'd been a nervous wreck, but thankfully, I was crazy busy at work, and the girls finally asked me to join them for drinks last night. The excitement of being included kept me from launching into a complete spiral.

Sure. I'll be there in about thirty minutes.

As I walked into the bar, I saw him with about five guys around him. They all seemed drunk. We locked eyes.

"Hey! Gentlemen, my star is here!" He raised his drink, and his friends all raised their glasses at me.

One guy turned to me, put his fingers over his mouth in a V, and shook his tongue at me. I turned away and looked at the bar. Crude. Another laughed, and I turned to see his hand go down to his crotch and he mockingly rubbed himself, dropping his head back and moaning.

I stopped before I reached them. What the actual *fuck*? Preston started walking toward me.

"Don't worry about these jerks; that's how they're trying to tell you they think you're fucking hot and talented too." He boasted with an arrogant swagger.

It was then that it hit me. All these guys had seen the video that I sent him. I froze and looked at him with daggers in my eyes. "Give me your phone."

"Oh no, I think she isn't excited about being so popular," he laughed back at his friends.

"Yeah, maybe she's one of those shy stars," someone said while he laughed.

I walked up to Preston and pushed him. "Give me your *fucking* phone."

"Okay, okay. I'm deleting the video." He pulled up his phone and showed me the video as he hit delete. "If you didn't want anyone else to see you masturbating, you shouldn't have recorded yourself." His words dripped with contempt.

Before I completely lost control, I turned away to hide my tears. "Wow, what a fucking uptight bitch!" I didn't turn around to see which friend said it.

I slam myself back from the memory. The cubicle walls are closing in on me, making it hard to breathe.

"Oh, that's where you're wrong, *Zoey*. Grab your phone and pull up triple X.com."

My hand shakes when I point next to Jack, signaling for him to give me my phone.

"Has the website loaded yet?"

"Not yet. I'm pulling it up," I respond, my voice shaking.

My hands tremble so much that it takes a few tries to get the address right.

"It's up," I whisper.

"Great. Hand it over to Jack."

The phone almost slips out of my hand as I give it to him.

"Go ahead, make sure you press play."

I reach over and tap my phone, starting the video as he looks down to see what I'm showing him. He slams the phone facedown within seconds. I flinch at the disgust I see on his face.

"What did he think? Does he agree you may be a rising star for OnlyFans?"

My limbs are completely numb. I can't take my eyes off his face. It's turning a deep shade of red, and his lips press together tightly.

"Oh no, he doesn't like it. That must be humiliating."

My body is heavy, and I can't find the strength to move or speak. The silence magnifies my shame.

"*Zoey? Zoey?* Are you still there?"

"Yes," I gasp.

"Oh no. It seems the day's events are finally catching up to you. Let's call it a night, and we'll speak in the morning."

With a jolt, I return to the present moment.

"Wait. Wait! What about Madison?! Can she come home tonight?!"

But the line is dead. "He hung up! He's, he's gone."

My throat is dry, and my vision is blurry. I drop my head into my hands. *What the fuck!* A sharp pain shoots through my jaw as my teeth clench. Is this Preston? Is he behind this? Who is this *asshole*? Did Cassie find out about this video? Is she still trying to ruin my life? *Fuck!*

CHAPTER 9

Jack

Zoey's screams finally register in my mind. "He hung up! He's, he's gone," she stutters.

She pushes back from her desk and puts her head in her hands, choking on her breaths. Rage blurs my vision. I can't get the image of her spread open on that bed out of my mind. My body is shaking, and it's then that I realize she is punching her fists into me.

"He still has Madison, and he said he won't call until tomorrow! She isn't going home tonight! She isn't coming back!"

Tears stream down her face. My hands clench into fists at my sides. My lungs are about to burst as I hold back the urge to scream. The impulse to throw my arms around her shatters my heart. All my thoughts are coming at me rapid-fire.

"Jack! Jack!"

Our eyes meet. I need to snap out of it. She needs me. She's unraveling. Madison needs me, needs her. "Did he give you any clues? Anything stand out?" I ask with forced restraint.

"I don't know, I don't know," she stammers. "Maybe. I need a minute."

There's a commotion coming from the front of the room. I turn as Sally and Sergeant are walking back to us. She is in no state to face them. I step around her and meet them in the cramped aisle.

"He called again."

"I know." Sergeant's glare almost destroys my resolve as he tries to walk past me. I put my hand up to him.

"Give her a moment. Let's go listen to the call. This one really shook her up. She can't remember any details." I glance back at Zoey, and she's sliding down the cubicle wall; she hits the floor, hands shaking in her lap. The pain radiating off her is too much.

"Go ahead and listen first, Sarge."

Suddenly, the room is impossibly small. I burst through the doors and step out of the station. My heart is racing with adrenaline. I bend against the wall, squeeze my eyes shut, and try to calm myself. Zoey appears in my mind, her eyes puffy and shoulders shaking in silent sobs. The humiliation of this game is putting her through–it's too much.

I rise, running my hands through my hair. That video of her, with her legs spread and her hand running down her front, is forever etched in my mind. "FUCK!" I slam my hand against the wall.

Feelings are crashing into me. Jealousy churns in my gut. Bitterness climbs my throat that it's online for others to see. Rage at that *asshat* for mortifying her. My urge to protect her and take her far away from all of this is agonizing.

Turning and pacing in front of the station, desperation threatens to unravel me. I must regain composure. There's a terrified little girl out there who isn't coming home tonight. I need to focus on what we can do for her. Then I can destroy him.

"Shit!" I've got to get back in there before Sarge tries to approach her again. As I rush through the building toward the dispatch center, I run right into Sergeant.

"We're running out of time, Moore." His lack of confidence laces his words.

"Believe me, I know, Sarge."

He pauses, taking in my current state. "I can't have you take the lead with her anymore." He turns to walk into the dispatch center.

I grab his arm. "Wait." I wince at the desperation in my tone.

"Clearly, you have a conflict of interest here, Moore. You look like shit and aren't thinking clearly. You're too focused on protecting *her* and not on finding Madison. Madison's parents are in my office, scared that they'll never see their little girl again."

I turn, lifting my hands behind my head, and let out a deep breath. "You're right, Sarge. I'm focused on protecting Zoey. She's a victim in this too."

Sarge turns and steps closer to me. "She's a criminal, Moore. And she makes terrible decisions. A complete *fuck* up."

It takes all my control not to step up into his face. Huffing, he turns back toward the dispatch center.

I jump in front of him. "Yes, she's a criminal, and she's proving that her judgment is shit. But this *asshole*, this *lunatic* Ned. He only wants to talk to her. We must keep her focused. She needs confidence. She needs to believe that she can lead us to Madison. We lose her, we could lose Madison for good."

He's contemplating my words. I've reached him. "Did you learn anything useful before the last call?"

"Yeah, that he can't be any of her Tinder dates. She never went out with anyone under six feet." Sarge's face reddens, probably because he's only about five foot six.

I continue before he can interrupt me. "This narrows down our suspects. Right before he called again, she was listing anyone that could match the description."

Sarge is staring at me, considering if this is actual progress in the case. "It's going to be a long night for everyone. Get your ass back in there and keep making a list of suspects. I want more to go on than the Amber Alert tips."

I let out a deep breath and nod. "On it, Sarge."

My relief is short-lived when I see Sally crouching next to her. Zoey is unrecognizable, her knees pulled up to her chest. She's curled inside herself and looks so tiny and fragile. My heart cracks open. An intense urge to come to her rescue takes over. I need to listen to that call, but I walk to them.

"Hey, Sally. Thanks for keeping her company. Think you can give us some privacy?" I coo. Sally looks up at me. I give her the warmest smile I can muster. "Yeah, sure, Jack. My shift is almost over, anyway."

I sit across from her in the cubicle and pull one of my knees up to my chest and squeeze to release the urge to wrap myself around her. "Zoey?" She shudders. "Zoey?" I don't know what to say. She looks completely empty of emotion. The lump in my throat grows as I turn away, trying to contain the feelings rising in me. Anger. Grief. Rage. Love.

"She's going to be spending the night with a stranger. With a *fucking* crazy person," she whispers. She hasn't raised her head off her knees. She's counting again because her breaths are steadying.

"Did you eat?" She doesn't move. Our bag of food sits untouched. Standing up, I grab the bag, pull out her sandwich, and put it beside her.

"I'm going to go listen to the call. I'll be back in a few minutes. Please try to eat a little."

As I reach an empty desk, I pull up the latest recording. Securing the headset, I take a deep, steadying breath, and click play.

Madison isn't his target. Zoey is. I hit pause. If we can believe this *motherfucker*. I clench my jaw and release the fists I've been pressing into the desk. I need to prepare myself for what led to her handing me her phone and hitting play on that video.

With as much restraint as I can muster, I remove the headset and push away from the desk. My stomach churns, and I might vomit. As my eyes close, I stop and snap them open before the video shows up in my mind. I need to move past this. She needs me. She looked so fragile against that wall. I long for the confident, playful Zoey. Strengthening my composure, I pull forward, put the headset on again and hit play.

I gasp for air, finally releasing the breath I was holding. She thought the video was deleted. Did this Preston put it online? We need to investigate Preston's role in the situation.

Dammit! I just want to go over there, pull her into me, and tell her I'm here for her. Nothing has changed. She is safe with me. I'll always be on her side. I don't care about any of the stuff he is making her confess.

But I *do* fucking care. What the *hell* was she doing? Making porn for a guy, and sending it to him? *Fuck!* She's smarter than that. My jaw clenches in disgust and my shoulders sag.

My head drops into my hands. I'm torn in two different directions. She's kept me at such a distance these last four months. Any expression of affection or care has pushed her away.

The priority is making sure Madison makes it home. I need to set aside my emotions and focus. As I rise, my fist slams against the desk as I release the anger brewing inside me.

Zoey hasn't moved from her position. Her sandwich is untouched. I grab mine out of the bag and sit down across from her. My stomach is like a brick, but I hope if she sees me eating, it will lead her to take a few bites.

He was clear he won't be calling until the morning. We're in for a long night. "Hey. You really need to eat a little," I say and roll my neck.

"You're right. This *asshole* only wants to harm you. Madison needs you to maintain your strength so we can identify Ned and find her."

She raises her head and sits her chin on her arms, staring into nothing on the floor. Her eyes are vacant. There is an eeriness around her, like he's taken the life out of her. I make a fist at my side. Releasing it, I take a deep breath.

"I can tell you're ashamed about that video, but your strength and smarts have kept Madison safe today. We've narrowed the search. Now we just need a list of suspects. Madison needs you to build that list."

She slides her hand over to the sandwich. She still hasn't looked at me, and it's crushing me. I want to comfort her, tell her she's strong enough to handle this. That she'll help us get Madison back. She opens it and blankly takes a bite and chews slowly. I can't get the words out, so I turn back to the investigation.

"Have you been able to think of anyone? Are you ready to build the list?"

She swallows hard and sits the sandwich next to her on the dirty floor. My phone vibrates and I dump my half-eaten sandwich in the trash. Pulling out my phone, I see the video from Walmart has come in.

"Alright. We have the video from Walmart. Are you ready to watch it?"

Silently, she puts her hand out for me to give her my phone. She taps the screen and squints in as she looks at it, sliding her legs out and dropping her hand and my phone in her lap. I see her catch her breath and swallow down a sob. A few moments pass, and she's counting again. Once her breath is steady, she pulls the phone back up again. She watches it a few times.

Zoey stands up slowly and hands the phone back to me. I'm desperate for her to look at me. She steps around me to her desk, sits down, and begins writing on the notepad. She writes a few things, pauses, looks to the side, and then writes some more.

As I watch her, longing takes over. I force my attention back to the video and, as I restart it for the third time, I hear the paper rip. She hands it down to me, then walks back to the cubicle wall and slides down.

Joey Banks

Preston Timms

David Slim - college hookup

Adam - lives in building in Chicago

Josh Cooper - a college friend

Justin Taylor - high school

I snap a picture and text it to Sarge. With the sheet in my hand, I study the list and then look at her. She's still far away, staring into space. I glance at the list again.

I know Justin Taylor. He's in the Air Force and, last I heard, stationed in Korea. I mentally cross him off the list. "Zoey?" She hasn't moved. She's holding her breath.

I review the list again and confirm my assessment. There are guys from here, college, and Chicago on the list. She said she lived in Chicago for four years. That leaves a four-year gap between college and Chicago. "Where did you live after college, before Chicago?"

She lets out a deep breath. "St. Louis."

My head throbs as I think about how little information I have about her life in the recent years. Regret is clinging to me. Why didn't she keep in touch with me? She wouldn't have stolen and made porn if she'd had me as a friend to lean on. I shake my head to clear my mind and remember that guy she brought home twice. Did they live in St. Louis together?

"No one from St. Louis looks like this guy?" I ask. She shakes her head. "What about that guy you brought home a few times? He wasn't that tall, was he?"

I recall seeing them at a bar one Thanksgiving, and she was wearing flats. It stuck out because I always noticed her shoes. She'd always worn heels and wedges; they made her legs look amazing. I remember noticing that if she wore heels, she would have been taller than him, and that's why she was wearing those ugly flats.

"Dead."

I flinch at the way she says it. Like it's a complete sentence. End of story. She rocks her head back against the wall and closes her eyes. Her breathing slows, and I think she's fallen asleep. I wait a few more minutes to make sure, and then get up to check in with Sarge.

As I walk out, I see Bob working the night shift. Thank God. He's practically a recluse; there's zero chance he'll try to get involved with what's happening.

CHAPTER 10

Zoey

I open my eyes and see that Jack is walking away. Finally. I've been pretending to sleep so that he'll just leave me the *fuck* alone. I can't stand his pity. His disappointment in who I am.

To prevent this exact moment from happening, I've been keeping my distance from him since I've been back. The way he longs for the high school version of me is overwhelming. He's trying to hide it, but he's horrified by that video I made.

I willed that video from my memory, put those assholes in a box, and shoved them deep within me. I can't even bring myself to think about how Ned got it. Desperate for a distraction, my determination to find Madison takes over.

Now that I'm alone, I can start getting myself under control. After a few rounds of counting my breaths, my mind is clearing. I grab my almost-full water bottle and chug it down to get rid of the dryness in my throat. As I put the bottle down, I review my list of suspects Jack left on the desk.

Joey Banks

Preston Timms

David Slim - college hookup

Adam - lives in building in Chicago

Josh Cooper - a college friend

Justin Taylor - high school

He saw it right away. I'm not shocked that he noticed. No one from St. Louis was on the list because I knew no one. Four years of my life are a complete void. A waste. My eyes close as memories threaten to emerge. I refuse to let myself shut down again. We need to find Madison.

I need to talk to Jack about the list of suspects. This is who I am now. Unfeeling, callous, and focused on results. He is wasting his time trying to get close to me. I'll never let my guard down with anyone. No man will ever have influence over my life again. Even someone as amazing as him.

The sound of footsteps brings me to my feet. Jack is approaching with two water bottles under his arm and two coffees in his hands. I stand up and reach for the coffees so he can set the water down on the desk. Handing a coffee back to him, I say, "You read my mind."

His eyes are full of skepticism. I'm a completely different person from when he left. Before he can say anything, I ask, "Want to walk through my relationship with each of the suspects?"

He takes a sip of his coffee as he contemplates how to respond. "And now you've read my mind. That's what I was hoping we could do. Sergeant has the list, and they're working their way through locating each person."

I hold his stare, knowing I can count on him to take my lead. He's scared of making the wrong move and that I'll pull away. Satisfied that I steered the conversation away from me, I lower myself back to the floor with the list in my hand. It's more private than sitting in the chairs around my desk.

"Justin Taylor is already out; I confirmed he's stationed in Korea," Jack informs me.

My mind is spinning as I nod my head, trying to make sense of this nightmare. Contemplating how a guy on this list could hate me so much that they would kidnap a young girl to get to me.

He is studying the list with determination, and I notice he has more stubble covering his jawline, which only makes his face more handsome.

As he lowers himself down to the floor, I notice he's only in his uniform shirt and pants. He's removed his belt and all his police accessories.

"So, you know about Cassie and Joey," I say with a forced confidence as my voice wavers. "It's hard for me to imagine that either of them would still care about me, but you never really know someone." A shudder passes through me. "And I was just a pawn in Preston's games."

An expression of apprehension passes across his face, and his lips draw into a thin line. It must be my swift transformation in demeanor. My eyes hold his stare as pain fills his eyes. I turn away and bite my lip. A lump forms in my throat, knowing I don't trust him enough to open up.

"I didn't put that video on that website," I mumble.

"Jesus, Zoey." He's standing up again, runs a hand through his hair, and drops it to his side.

He steps over to me, and before I can react, he slides down next to me. "Do you think I'm upset by that video? Of course, I wish it didn't exist. The thought of other guys seeing you like that ..." His jaw clenches and then he shifts to face me. "But I'm not upset with *you*."

It's impossible to turn to him for comfort. I steel myself, bringing my mask back down. He reaches out to put his hand on my knee. I flinch, and he squeezes, stopping me from creating distance between us.

"It's taking every ounce of my control to not hop in my truck," he says, almost growling, "and start speeding through the county looking for this *asshole*. All I want to do is destroy him." He sighs. "We all have things in our past that we regret, that we're ashamed of."

A bitter laugh escapes me. "Not like me."

Silence hangs heavy over us and as I finally meet his eyes, a muscle ticks in his clenched jaw. Why can't he just see me as the stealing, cheating whore I am? Why does he have to care so much about me?

"Jack." I lean into his touch and warmth. Shame sits heavy on my chest. I can't. *I just can't.* As I shift away, he removes his hand from my knee. "Can we keep working on the list?" I ask desperately.

He responds with a nod of defeat. "Yeah."

My eyes drift back down to the list in my hand. Did I get weird vibes from any of them? I close my eyes, trying to recall my last interaction with Adam.

"Zoey?"

I turn to him. He has one knee propped up with his arm hanging off it.

"I asked if you're sure there isn't anyone from St. Louis? I don't want to leave any gaps."

My eyes close as I'm overwhelmed by the memories that threaten to surface. I shake my head. Do I have the courage to talk about my life in St. Louis? A shiver runs down my back. *What if?* What if the answer to finding Madison lies in my memories of St. Louis? A lump forms in my throat. I need time.

"Why did you move back here?" My eyes plead for him to answer so I can get some space from the memories trying to surface. It's selfish, but I can't face it.

"My dad got sick, and mom struggled, so I moved back to help." Sadness overcomes his face.

"I'm so sorry." I lower my hand on top of his on the floor between us. "How's he doing now?"

"He died two years ago."

The bitter taste of guilt hits the back of my throat. How did I not know this? I'm such a selfish *bitch*. He senses my discomfort and turns his hand over and intertwines his fingers with mine.

"We haven't talked much about our time apart. It's not something I just blurt out during sex."

"That would be a buzz kill." I try to lighten the mood.

"Zoey," he pauses, squeezing my hand. "It's torturing me that you won't let me in."

"Why didn't you go back to Nashville after he died?" I continue to deflect. I can't do this with him right now.

Dropping his head against the wall, he sighs. "My mom hasn't handled his death well. I can't bring myself to leave her here alone."

Of course. He has always put everyone else's needs above his own. I stare at our intertwined hands and embrace his kindness through our connection. Suddenly, panic radiates through my chest. I try pulling my hand free, and he tightens his hold.

"Jack?" I rip my hand out of his grasp.

He lifts his hands to his head and leans back as he pulls at his hair. "Fuck!" He's standing up and pacing in my tiny cubicle. Stopping, he looks down at me, and his eyes are glassy.

"I can't give you what you want," I whisper.

"What is it you think I want?"

His tone leaves me stunned. I'm at a loss for words. What is it I think he wants from me? Annoyance runs through me.

"I don't know." I stand to face him. "But I know whatever it is, I can't give it to you."

We're standing face to face. My chest is tight with anxiety. He steps closer. I don't move away. The weight of the day, of Madison's kidnapping. It's rooting me in place.

"I only want you to trust me. That's all," he pleads.

He reaches for my hand, and I don't pull it away. Relief emerges at his touch. The promise of comfort is too much. He grasps my other hand and steps even closer.

We're sharing the air between us. His chest rising and falling, waiting for me to say something, do something. My heart wants to open. The desire to have someone to lean on, to share my burdens, startles me. My heart is racing, desperate for me to lighten the load. I don't want to be alone anymore.

"Grief is hard. I've been grieving for my dad for two years. I've seen how it can consume someone. My mom is slowly drowning in hers. Have you talked to anyone about it? That's helped me. Andy's been there for me."

I meet his eyes, skeptical. "Andy?"

"Surprised me too, but under all that yelling, he's a big softy."

He's raising our joined hands to wrap my arms around him. The movement brings back my focus. We're not the same. I snap back and turn around, breaking his grasp. It's not grief I feel about Sam's death. It's a relief, and that's an even worse feeling than grief.

I've never been so trapped. I can't leave this cubicle because I want to stay near in case Ned calls again tonight. Jack's presence is closing in on me. "Zoey?" His hand grazes against my shoulder. I jerk away.

"I've got to go to the bathroom." I rush past him, forcing myself to avoid his touch.

There's a loud thud. He must have kicked the bottom of the cubicle wall. I close the door of the bathroom and lean up against it. How long is he going to hold out? When is he going to just give up on me?

I see myself in the mirror. I look like absolute shit. Good. I slide down the wall and sit on the disgusting bathroom floor. It's what I deserve. That's what Sam would think right now. If he were alive, he'd be at the top of my suspect list. A tremor rips through me as memories of him threaten to emerge. He's dead.

As I took a sip of my cosmopolitan, I admired the décor of the hip bar until Cassie's laugh brought me back to the group. Her head dropped back, and I envied how carefree she was. I had been in Chicago for six months and I was still constantly surveying my surroundings for any signs of Sam.

When my eyes began their second sweep of the room, a wave of terror rushed through me, as my breath caught in my throat. There was Tony, Sam's drinking buddy from work. What was he doing here? Panic choked me. How can I leave abruptly without drawing attention?

As I gathered my jacket from the chair and tossed my purse over my shoulder, Cassie stopped me. "Do you know him, Zoey?"

I looked at her, my eyes wide. "Who?"

"Uh, the guy making a beeline for you from the bar," she laughed.

And before I could respond, Tony was right in front of me. I stood quickly and guided him away from the group as I dodged a hug from him.

"Zoey! What are you doing here? How are you?" Tony asked. Concern covered his face.

Oh shit. Oh shit. My words were stuck in my throat as my knees grew weak. He guided me over to the wall.

"I'm so sorry I didn't reach out after Sam's death. It couldn't have been easy handling all of his arrangements on your own."

The words echoed in my head. *Sam's dead? What? When? How?* My shoulders dropped, and I hysterically laughed and cried. *He's dead. It's over.*

Tony stepped back and looked around the room. His eyes were wild with desperation. I'm sure he was regretting his decision to approach me. All the terror, the guilt I had carried for the last five years, left me with every shudder.

Finally, my breaths evened out. His face was pale. I wiped the tears away and gave him an apologetic smile. "I didn't know."

His eyes grew enormous. "How?"

"I left him about six months ago. I've been living here in Chicago," I responded. Leaving out the part about how I'd blocked all of his numbers, social media accounts, everything I could so that he wouldn't find out where I'd moved.

"Wow." Tony let out a deep breath and rubbed his hands through his hair. "He never told us, but I also hadn't seen him much since, well, I guess since you left."

"How did he die?" I asked in a forced, somber tone. Relief bubbled up inside of me.

"Single car accident—he was drunk." He responded and averted his eyes.

I wipe the tears streaming down my face. That's the first time I've allowed myself to think about Sam in three and a half years. I get up to splash water on my face, close that box of memories, and shove it deep inside.

I see myself in the mirror. "Get over your damn self, Zoey. Get out there and focus on finding Madison. Enough of this pity party." Knowing my pep talk will do very little for me, I step out into the dispatch center and return to my desk. I will not fail her. She will make it home unharmed.

As I approach my cube, Jack is talking on the phone. "Got it, Sarge. Okay. No, we don't need you. Stay with Madison's parents."

With a glance over his shoulder, he crosses another name off the list. My back slides down the wall behind him and I don't bother slipping on my mask. It's losing its effect on him and I'm too tired to try.

Joey Banks

Preston Timms

David Slim - college hookup

Adam - lives in building in Chicago

Josh Cooper - a college friend

Justin Taylor - high school

A knot forms in my stomach as I see all the names that remind me of my lowest moments. Except for David. A deep sigh escapes me. Would my life have turned out differently if I'd chosen to date David instead of Sam?

Jack turns around in my chair. "We're making slow progress on suspects."

I nod in defeat.

"They're still tracking down the others." His tone is bitter.

It seems I've finally worn him down, too. The sooner he stops caring about me, the better. He should only be worried about getting Madison back. I drop my head back, and I can sense him watching me. This time, sleep comes, and I let it.

CHAPTER 11

Jack

Z oey's finally asleep. A weight lifts off my chest. She needs rest, and I need a break. What a *fucking* day. My body is exhausted. A lifetime has happened in twelve hours.

Doubts creep in about how much I care for her. She's kept her distance from me over the last four months and with what I've learned, I shouldn't be risking my career on her. Tension builds in my neck as I try to reconcile the girl from high school with the woman that has done these things. She hasn't earned my loyalty. I clasp my hands behind my neck and look up, releasing a deep breath. My head knows the facts, but my heart still aches for her.

I drop my hands. Maybe Sergeant is right. I'm too close to this. I need to get some space and clear my thoughts. If I keep watching her, my feelings are going to take control. I get up, head to the next cubicle, and pull up the calls.

I listen to them again and take notes.

He's trying to terrify her

He wants her to be helpless

Wants her humiliated

Knows technology—recovered a deleted video

He's stalking her—but for how long?

He's a wild card and I'm going to end him

This bastard has stalked her long a time. The tension in my neck travels down my spine. What kind of loose cannon is he? Madison better make it home safe.

Is Sergeant making any progress? I peek over and see her still sleeping. So I step out of the dispatch center and go check in with Sarge.

"Learn anything useful from her?" he barks.

"Yes," I say, not wanting to share any more about Zoey with him.

"I listened to the calls again, and this guy has been stalking her *for years*," I emphasize. "Maybe," he responds. "We've been able to locate the Banks—they're out of the country on a second honeymoon. We're down to three suspects."

With a nod, I sit at my desk and stare at my notes before I say something to him I'll regret. He walks away, and I look up and cringe at all the brown. The building is only a few years old, but the style reflects that of a small Missouri town. Nashville's stations were bright and filled with light. A familiar gnawing ache grows as I think of my promotion to criminal investigator.

If Dad hadn't gotten sick, I wouldn't be dealing with this ignorant know-it-all Sergeant. I'd be working for the Criminal Investigations Unit of Nashville. My head falls into my hands as I rest my elbows on the desk. I'd also be married to Sarah. Man, I was chasing all the wrong things in love.

I was home for a weekend checking in on him when Sarah called me from the *perfect* bungalow. Her excitement exploded through the phone. I couldn't bring myself to tell her I was moving back. After seeing how sick my dad was and how distraught my mom was, it was my only choice.

Long distance worked for a while. We created a plan for the weekends we would spend together, and she would spend the summer with me. We barely saw each other between the almost six-hour drive and my schedule. With the distance, we drifted apart. Asking her to move here was something I just couldn't do.

With Sarah, everything was comfortable. She was attractive in a way that only those who are always composed and perfect can achieve. Even after rough days teaching her rowdy second-grade class, she always looked as put together as she did when she'd left in the morning.

She'd be a fantastic mother. Taking care of me all the time, making meals, cleaning. She even did my laundry when I had double shifts. I never asked her to. It made me uncomfortable. I never wanted a woman to take care of me. I wanted a partner. Someone to experience life with. And the sex. It was dull.

She was always timid and shy in the bedroom. I tried to explore with her one afternoon when she got a little tipsy from an afternoon barbecue with friends.

"Sarah, are you drunk?"

Giggling, she admitted, "Maybe a little." A cute hiccup squeaked out of her. "This is my third White Claw."

"What would your students think?" I winked and headed to the kitchen to clean.

Her arms slipped around my waist. "Do we have to clean tonight?"

I turned around and hugged her. "Leave dirty dishes overnight? What has gotten into you, babe?"

Rising on her tiptoes, she gave me a kiss. I slipped down to grab her ass.

"Oh," she squeaked, and I walked her over to the couch as we kissed. She straddled my lap, and I didn't break our kiss as I raised her dress.

She pulled away. "The living room?"

"Yeah," I said, pulling her back into a kiss.

She pulled away and grabbed my hand. "Bed."

We walked down the hall to my bedroom. Sarah didn't turn on the lights as she entered and made her way over to her side of the bed. She slipped her dress down over her shoulders, dropped it to the floor, climbed into bed, and pulled up the cover. She shimmied out of her panties as I walked over, pulling my shirt over my head.

She'd maneuvered out of her bra while I pulled my jeans and boxers off and climbed into bed with her. I laid on top of her as her arms wrapped around my neck. Leaning down, I kissed her lightly on the mouth and then moved to her neck, tracing down to the middle of her chest. Her breaths quickened as she released her arms around my neck.

As I lowered my kisses down to her belly button, I longed to taste her. I was throbbing with the anticipation of her coming on my face. My tongue glided beneath her belly button.

"Jack."

Our eyes met, and she reached for my arms. Embarrassment covered her face as she tugged me up. I suppressed my urge to sigh with frustration, followed her pull and kissed her softly. As she pushed me onto my back, she climbed on top of me.

This was her way of apologizing; she'd never been on top. I looked at her, so delicate and pretty. Her eyes were closed, brow furrowed. She was uncomfortable. I lifted her and gently rolled her onto her back. As I held myself up over her, and I slid into her.

Her arms clasped around my neck, eyes still closed. I thrust into her, longing for passion, a moan, something that told me that this felt as good to her as it did to me. I wanted to please her, make her tremble with release, and yet she never would just let go.

After a few silent moments, I shook with release and rolled to her side, pulled her into me and draped my arm over her stomach. I held her until I heard her delicate snores, then I rolled over onto my back and stared at the ceiling.

"Moore, Moore." Sergeant is snapping in my face.

"You think you're some big-shot investigator from a big city, but let's remember—here, you're a patrol officer, and I'm in charge." His words jolt me back.

"What's our next move, then?" I ask, holding back my annoyance.

"There's more she isn't telling us. There's a sizable gap in her details." His face is full of suspicion.

"You're right. We need more to go on. I'll go back and see if I can get her to be more forthcoming about her life in St. Louis. I don't want to overlook anything."

Notes in hand, I walk through the corridor as new turns to old before he can give me any resistance. As I approach, Zoey looks up at me, anguish in her eyes.

"How terrified is Madison right now? Is this going to ruin her life?" A tear rolls down her cheek. I go down on one knee in front of her as she pulls her knees to her chest. I raise my hands to place on her shoulders, hesitate, and then drop them to my sides.

"No good can come from playing out worst-case scenarios."

Her shoulders sink down deeper, like she's trying to disappear. "This type of trauma ruins people's lives."

"We don't know what she's going through. I'm holding on to the facts. The two tips both confirm that she isn't in distress. She doesn't seem afraid."

She winces and looks away. I sit back in the middle of her cubicle. I can't push her anymore. The sight of her switching between her mask and despair is painful. I won't cause any more agony for her.

"What time is it?" she asks.

"It's 5:00 a.m." Her body jerks upright. "What? How long was I sleeping? Did I miss a call?"

"You've been out for a few hours. No, he hasn't called. I've been up monitoring. They located a few more guys on your list. We are down to three. Adam, from your old building. It's taking a bit more time because we don't have a last name, so we have to deal with property management to get information."

She nods. "Who else?"

"David Slim and Preston Timms."

"It's hard for me to see David as a viable suspect. We hung out during the first semester of my junior year. We parted as friends." She shakes her head.

"It's still a lead. We're getting closer. But we need to prepare in case these three guys end up being dead ends." I take a deep breath. "Which means talking more about St. Louis." She nods, reaching out for the old coffee on her desk.

"I know, it's just ..." She releases a deep breath. I cross my legs in front of her as she grimaces after sipping her cold coffee.

"Want me to get a fresh one?"

"No, it doesn't matter," she mutters.

"This man has been stalking you. For quite some time."

She rocks against the wall and seems to take in what I just said about a stalker. I hold in my shock when she makes eye contact.

"I moved to St. Louis with Sam. My college boyfriend. He's the guy you saw me with. The one I brought home a couple of times." She's trying to gather composure to discuss this part of her past.

"And he died?"

"Yeah, a drunk driving accident," she says flatly.

I'm shocked by the news and her lack of emotion relaying it. "Oh my God, Zoey." I lean forward to touch her, and she shakes her head.

"Don't. He was the driver." She studies a spot on the floor. I'm at a loss for words. It doesn't matter if he caused it; death is a loss, and it still hurts. All the air has left the room. The silence is closing in around me.

"I really didn't know anyone in St. Louis. I worked from home. My world was very small and isolated. It was just Sam and me."

Each additional detail I learn about her past, the more I'm on edge. Why didn't she try harder to stay in contact with me? My jaw tightens. I would've been there for her.

"Jack?" There's compassion in her eyes. "It wouldn't have mattered."

"What do you mean?" I ask, studying her eyes.

"Having you in my life. It wouldn't have changed what's happened."

"How can you know that? I would do anything for you, then, now. *Anything.*"

She shakes her head. "I moved home once before. About two years after I moved to St. Louis."

I hold back my surprise that she's sharing more. She nods and has a small smile. "I was here for about three months. I asked around about you."

Two years after she moved to St. Louis, that was eight years ago.

"I was living in Nashville, a year out of the academy."

"Yeah. I was so proud of you. Living the dream that you always talked about in high school. I thought a lot about that. It made me happy that one of us could make our dreams come true."

She averts her eyes downward. I shift to sit next to her and bump into her shoulder. "We still have time for dreams. We're only thirty."

"My life is a total clusterfuck. I'm sure I'll be arrested as soon as this is over."

I reach around to put my arm around her and squeeze her close. A sigh of relief escapes me when she doesn't pull away. The thought of what will happen when this is over is too much. The idea of her enduring more pain, even if it's because of her own actions, is agonizing. I pull back and shift the focus to learn more details about her time in St. Louis.

"Why'd you move back to St. Louis?"

"Sam. We were in a bad spot, so I moved back home. He came and got me. Promised me the world, a ring, a wedding."

"You were engaged?"

"No, he lied. There was no ring."

There's a long silence as I take in that information, trying to make sense of it.

"Why are you still here?" she asks. "You didn't want to move back to Nashville?"

"I'm not really sure." I sigh. "I kept thinking about moving back, but never actually put any plans into action."

If I'm being honest with myself, I hate it here. I'm stuck. I've bailed on any relationship that was getting serious for fear of them wanting me to settle down and build a life here. Staying here is keeping my mom stuck in her grief. We're in the cycle of her needing me and me supporting her. It gives us some purpose in our life. When I can't sleep, I wonder if I left, maybe she could heal.

"Do you like it here?" she asks.

I shift, not wanting to talk about myself, but this closeness with her is fragile. I want to hold on to it as long as I can.

"No, I hate it."

Nodding, she pulls away and turns to face me. I turn so we are looking at each other. She leans her head against the wall.

"I hate it too," she whispers.

I reach out to hold her hand, and she doesn't pull away. She closes her eyes, and all that she shared is swirling around me, settling into a realization.

"Why did you feel isolated in St. Louis?"

Her breaths quicken, and she looks at me. There is a depth and openness to her I haven't seen before. I push down my anticipation so that I don't spook her.

The computer lights up, and we both turn. "He's calling again," we say at the same time.

CHAPTER 12

Zoey

"Hello, Ned."

"Good morning, *Zoey*. How was your night?"

"Difficult." I push away what I was about to share with Jack so I can focus on getting Madison back.

"I'm sorry to hear that. I wish we could have spoken, but I needed my rest. We have so many things to discuss today."

I suck in a breath, steadying myself. "Okay. But first, can you tell me if Madison is okay? Can she come home?"

"She is doing well. But, sadly, no. She can't go home yet. Maybe by tonight, if we get through all that we need to cover today."

Bile rises in my throat, knowing that she is going to be spending another day away from her family. I close my eyes to focus.

"I'm glad she's doing well, and I'm ready to do exactly what you want so that she can make it home tonight," I respond for Jack's benefit.

He's leaning up against the wall outside my cubicle. I'm grateful he's keeping his distance. I need to focus on giving Ned what he wants—a helpless, mortified woman.

"Glad to hear you're growing comfortable with our conversations. I wasn't sure how this morning would go after our last one." He lets out a deep, menacing laugh.

I refuse to take his bait. My determination to bring Madison home is the only thing I care about. I'm done feeling sorry for myself.

"What, what would you like to talk about today?" I stutter, playing into the despair he wants to hear.

"I'm sorry you're struggling. I wasn't sure where to start today." He pauses again, continuing his control of the conversation. My leg is bouncing as the silence is getting to me.

"How about how you got an A in statistics?"

My leg stops. I hold my breath, waiting for the crushing weight of shame to come over me. I have no physical reaction. The past twenty-four hours have turned me numb. I wait for a reaction that never comes as I release my breath.

"I slept with my statistics professor to get an A," I say firmly.

After all that Jack has learned about me during the last day, I'm sure he isn't the least bit surprised to hear this. My hands grow clammy, and I force down the memories.

"Tsk, tsk. You're making it seem so straightforward." Condescension is dripping from his voice.

He's right. It wasn't simple. That summer, that class, changed the course of my life.

Jack steps up behind me and leans over; his breath is hot along my neck as he drops a paper on the desk. I close my eyes, and it's Professor John Bradley's breath along my neck as I'm working through a statistics problem at my desk.

"No, you have the mean and midrange flipped," Professor Bradley said as he squeezed my shoulder.

The warmth and anticipation of his touch shocked me. He walked back up to the front of the class. I looked at him more closely. He was older, maybe in his fifties, but fit. He was attractive in that old man, silver fox way. I'd seen him in the campus gym a few times, now that it wasn't so crowded.

Sticking around that summer was a last-minute decision I was grateful I'd made. I was dreading the stats course, but the summer course had a reputation for being easier. I couldn't imagine taking it in a full semester because it was *fucking* hard.

Even more so, I was grateful that Professor Bradley always stopped by my desk to check my work. Anticipating his attention was something I looked forward to. Each time, his hand lowered down my back and rested for a little longer. The heat between us grew, and the tension was thick.

One day when he leaned over me to discuss my graph, I noticed a wedding band. How did I not see that before? I recoiled at his touch. I couldn't bring myself to attend the next class, disgusted with myself for the attraction I felt. A professor old enough to be my father. He must have sensed my discomfort because he stopped checking in with me during class.

I'd been nervous about how I did on our first exam. I was lost attempting the problems. Professor Bradley dropped my test on my desk with a big D on it. *Shit.* I needed to get at least a B in this class, so it didn't tank my GPA. I thought if I went to his office hours, maybe he'd let me do corrections or extra credit.

The next day, I knocked on his door, and he looked up. "Zoey, come in." I sat in the one and only chair in front of his desk in the small, messy office.

"What can I help you with?" he asked.

I opened my bag to bring out the test as he got up and shut his door. The test was in my lap when he turned around and leaned over me. Breathing heavily, he reached down along my collarbone, and picked up the test from my lap. My stomach churned at his touch.

"Professor Bradley."

"John, please," he interrupted me. I took a deep breath. "John, I was hoping we could talk about my exam. Is it possible for me to do some corrections or extra credit?"

He was holding my exam in front of him, studying it, then placed it on his desk and looked at me as he tapped the paper. "Why don't you come around here, and I'll show you where you made your mistakes?"

I swallowed hard. Despite the uneasiness I felt, getting a D in this class was not an option. Slowly, I rose from my chair and went to stand next to his desk, gazing down.

"Come closer, here." I stepped closer, tension gathering in my stomach. "Come on, I want you to see this graph here."

He reached for my hand and pulled it over my exam as I noticed a picture of him with his wife and teenage sons. The sour taste in my mouth made me hold my breath, fearing I would puke any moment.

"Zoey, I wish you would relax," he cooed.

As I released my breath and tried to steady my racing heart, he began rubbing his thumb up over my hand that he was still covering.

"I've been watching you in class. You bite the side of your bottom lip when you are thinking? It's like you're trying to tease me. Playing a little hard to get."

The room spun, and my stomach's churning was becoming unbearable. I pulled my hand away and headed back to the chair to get my things and leave.

"I just want to get to know you a little better. You intrigue me," he said. His words dripped with disappointment.

I was unsure of what to say or how to say it. Panic replaced my unease. What if I pissed him off, and he failed me in this class? It was too late to drop a summer class.

"I do?" I asked sheepishly.

"Yes, your smile is beautiful. Like it holds the keys to happiness."

I laughed nervously. Was he being serious?

"Why are you laughing?"

My hands rubbed on my thighs. "I'm just flattered, that's all." I tried to act calm, but all I wanted was to get out of this office and think through what to do about this class.

"We can take care of this exam. I just want to spend a little time with you first."

Bile was fully coating my throat now. I was stuck to the spot on the floor in front of his desk. "Okay?" He spoke with such ambiguity that I couldn't discern his true meaning.

"Zoey, you and I can have special study sessions." I watched as he rose from his desk and walked over to me. My body was so heavy. I turned to grab my bag and get out my stats book.

"No, not that kind of studying."

Shit. My heart pounded so hard I heard it in my ears. Panic paralyzed me. It seemed like he was moving in slow motion as he stepped in front of me. I took a step back and fell into the chair. He was standing so close to me now. I was trapped.

I'd only wanted to improve my test grade. Get help with corrections or some extra credit. This was not what I had in mind. I froze, watching him undo his belt and unbutton his pants.

"You see, if you're open to spending some special time together to study *each other*, I can help you with your exam grade." His voice slithered down my back.

I just blinked at him as he pulled down his pants right in front of my face. Did people do this? Is this what I had to do to pass this class?

"I'm serious. This is how we can study together to improve your statistics grade."

His pants were down around his ankles, and his slender dick was sticking up. It looked like a fucking pencil. My mouth was completely dry. Time stopped.

My options were racing through my mind. If I ran out of his office, he would fail me for sure. If I did this, I'd hate myself. An F would kill my GPA, but honestly, I was more afraid of him. What else could he do to me? If he thought I might ruin his career, it might mean more than just my grade.

"A girl like you must be an expert at giving head." His cruel voice echoed in my mind.

"My test grade?" I looked up at him for the first time. "You'll change it to a A?"

He nodded. The churning in my stomach crested as I wrapped my hand around his small girth. I swallowed my shame as I lowered my mouth and sucked him off.

The next day, he sent me roses and a card that said, *Looking forward to our next study session.*

I didn't get out of bed. When I returned to class, he gave me my exam back with an A. I stared at the grade, and I thought about reporting him. I made it to the student affairs office with the note he'd given me on the flowers and stared at the door. I couldn't go in. My shame and fear were paralyzing. I couldn't stomach the idea of saying out loud what I did. I resolved to keep going to class for the next two weeks and put this entire situation behind me.

A week later, when he sat the next exam on my desk and I saw the F, he whispered into my ear, "Let's do our next study session out at the lake tomorrow at 8:00 p.m." I nodded slowly as a knot formed in my throat.

I couldn't sleep. I tossed and turned, worrying about whether I should go. At the end of the night, I told myself my only option was to play along with Professor Bradley. I woke up and everything was heavy. I'd lost a piece of myself with my decision.

It was the longest day, and I just wanted the 'study session' to be over with. My stomach turned, and I couldn't bear to think about it all day. I threw up my breakfast and lunch.

When I showed up, he had a blanket for us off to the side, protected by dense trees. He had champagne and pillows. If I hadn't been numb, I would've laughed at the absurdity of the scene. He was trying to take me on a date. I chugged champagne to get a buzz as he tried to have a conversation with me.

"We're out of champagne," John told me.

"Uh oh," I hiccupped.

"Why don't you take off your shirt for me?"

As I lifted my shirt over my head, I completely dissociated from myself. I don't remember anything except him standing over me, pulling up his pants. I headed back home and drank vodka until I passed out.

Next class, he returned my exam with an A. I stared at the grade and told myself, one more week and this would all be over. I was a zombie, just going through the motions. I didn't even attempt the homework anymore. It wouldn't make a difference in my grade; that's not how I was earning it.

Finally, the ever-present nausea subsided the day before the final. As I was leaving class, John stopped me.

"You need to study before the final. Meet me in the garden at midnight." It was not a question, it was a command. The garden was this special sunken area in the middle of the quad that students liked to claim they'd had sex. It would be empty during the summer.

I was so numb by now that I didn't even contemplate not going. At 9:00 p.m., I started drinking cheap vodka to help me get through the hours leading up to midnight. When I showed up, he had his blanket down again. I was already buzzed and swaying, but I still welcomed his cheap champagne.

John tried kissing me, but I was sloppy drunk. I sensed his frustration and pulled down my pants to speed this along.

"Get on your hands and knees," he demanded.

I was happy to not have to see him when he fucked me from behind. Everything else from the night is a blank spot. I barely even remember the rest of the summer.

"Wouldn't you call it an affair, *Zoey?*" My anger explodes. This was not an affair.

"No. I'd say it was a sleazy old professor taking advantage of his position and forcing a student to perform sexual acts for grades." The sharp tone of my voice shocks me.

My breath comes in quick, shallow gasps, as if my lungs are racing to keep up with the frantic pace of my thoughts. After that summer, shame took over. I was so depressed. I was gaining weight and not going out. My best friend, Jackie, forced me out the night that Sam hit on me. I was so desperate for a distraction and attention. There was no stopping me from falling in love with Sam. Out of the corner of my eye, I see Jack walking away.

"*Zoey.* I'm disappointed with your tone. You need a little time to cool off. I'll call you in a couple of hours."

I slam my fists on my desk. "Fuck!" I lost control and gave him exactly what he wanted. We don't have enough info to find Madison, and now we must wait for him to call back. As I push away, I turn and Jack had walked back to me. He stands in my cubicle opening, his hair completely erratic.

"He's calling back in a few hours. Nothing on Madison."

Desperation is threatening to take over my thoughts. It's my fault Madison is still out there with this lunatic.

Jack nods. "Zoey?" He steps forward, and I step back; I immediately regret it when I see his face. *Shit.* I turn away from him.

"Zoey?" His voice is gentle as his hand lands on my shoulder. He turns me to face him. I meet his eyes, and I release the breath I was holding. I fall into him. He wraps his arms around me. I wish for time to stand still and fast forward all at once. This nightmare needs to end. Madison needs to come home.

"I'm not sure I can do this anymore," I whisper.

Jack's embrace tightens. "You've got this. There isn't anyone more determined to succeed than you."

He pulls back and wipes at the tears rolling down my face.

"I'm not leaving your side. We will get through this together," he says with determination.

I nod in surrender. I pull away, wrapping my arms against my stomach.

"Did you report the professor?" Jack asks through gritted teeth. My head shakes as I push down my shame. I took part in his demands. I let him use me to get that A.

He senses my remorse. "Look at me." Grasping my face between his hands, he pulls me forward and holds me tight. His breaths are shallow and fast.

"That professor is a predator. You're a victim."

"I let it happen." I say, as my body trembles in his arms. "I did what he asked."

He then wraps his arms around me again, and they're keeping me from dropping to my knees. He lays his cheek on the top of my head. His chest rises with a deep breath.

"You are not to blame," he says slowly and firmly.

The rise and fall of his chest calms me, and my legs steady. He slowly pulls away and his hands are resting on my arms. A small part of my shame falls away. A sigh escapes my lips, and a small sense of relief hits me.

"Could Ned be this professor?" I shake my head. "He's too tall."

He pulls me close again like he can't bear the distance between us. I welcome his strength around me, allowing myself to accept Jack's support and, with it, a crack in my defenses.

"How old was he? Did he have a family? Sons?"

I step back. "Yeah, I remember a picture of his family on his desk. He had two teenage sons," I respond.

"Great, Zoey. That's really good," Jack says.

I can see he's conflicted. He doesn't want to leave me to go share the information with Sergeant Graves.

"Go. We need to know if one of them has Madison. His name is John Bradley. Professor of Statistics."

CHAPTER 13

Jack

I t's torture to turn and walk away from Zoey. The things I've learned are threatening to choke me. What she's been through, what she's done, what she's *survived*. Hate and rage are a familiar energy that fuels my movements.

As I burst through the doors, I yell, "John Bradley, Professor of Statistics. We need to find out who his sons are, and we need to locate them."

Sergeant looks at me.

"Now!"

"Moore, you're not in charge here," he commands.

"Fuck, Sergeant. I know. He called again, and we have a new lead. John Bradley. His sons. We need to find them." I cringe at the desperation in my plea.

"Calm down, Moore. This is exactly what I knew would happen. You're too close to this."

I stare Sarge down. No *fucking shit*. I'm too close to this. But there's no way anyone is going to keep me from Zoey. My hands lift to the back of my head as I turn away from him. My sense of guilt and loyalty towards her intensifies as more aspects of her past come to light.

A professor offering her grades for sex. That kind of abuse of power can cause irreparable damage to a girl's sense of worth. The victim training I had in

Nashville informed me that victims often don't report these incidents because of shame and fear of judgment.

I drop my hands. Zoey was all alone for the last ten years. She mentioned being isolated in St. Louis. No doubt she was trying to cope with what this predatory professor did to her. I need to get back in there and keep digging into her life in St. Louis. It's the one part of her life that has remained a mystery to me.

"Have any new tips come in?" I turn and ask Sarge.

There's too much to do. Find Madison. Convince Sergeant to let me stay by Zoey's side. Protect her. Save her. *Fuck!* My jaw clenches.

"Only wackos. Wherever this fucker has kept Madison overnight, it's well hidden."

"He's playing games with us, just like he is with Zoey," I warn.

"No shit, Moore. Seems you're getting played by him and her."

The urge to punch Sergeant has never been greater. "Did you find Adam or Preston Timms?" I grit out.

"Property management company opens in an hour. The after-hours service was shit. Preston is in Asia for work."

I turn and slam my hand against the wall. "What about David Slim?"

"Can't find him. David graduated two years after Zoey and then moved to St. Louis. He wasn't at his last known address; he hadn't lived there for at least two years. We're trying to find family members to locate him."

Pride is oozing from Sergeant. This is basic fucking police work. Tracking down people and confirming their whereabouts. My fists squeeze with frustration. He didn't realize there must be a connection.

"Did you say he moved to St. Louis?" I ask.

"Yeah, did you ever find out what kind of shit Zoey was up to there?"

My head shakes. "No. She was about to open up to me, and then that fucker called again."

Sarge is contemplating if he believes me. "Dammit, Moore. Get back in there and see what you can do!"

I hide my relief and nod. "On it. Find this Bradley and his kids." I walk out before he can bark at me about how he's in charge. His raging ego is the last thing this investigation needs. Making my way back to Zoey, each step is too heavy. All her secrets are sitting like a brick in my stomach.

The video. The stealing. The cheating. This professor's manipulation. Her life has been painful; my neck stiffens with the anger. How could she not have come to me? As I approach her sorry-ass cubicle, she's back on the floor, her forehead resting on her arms, hugging her knees. She hears my approach and turns her head to the side, resting her ear on her arms, and looks up at me.

"Any new tips?" she asks in a small voice.

I study her for a moment. She seems different. Lighter? Relieved? I shake my head and lean up against the wall across from her. Disappointment and fear cover her face. I need to get her talking about St. Louis. Especially now that the one suspect we can't find lived there too.

The reality of how heavy her life must've been these last ten years, carrying around these secrets, sets in. I squeeze down my sorrow for how lonely she's been. To have a professor use her like that. My jaw clenches. Some people are just a burden on the world. I would do anything to wipe away all that she's been through, take her far away from here, and give her the life she deserves, not this shallow existence.

The last four months replay in my mind. My anger is becoming uncontainable, along with a growing sense of unease. How has she not realized how great we could be together? I've just kept welcoming her into my bed. Playing along and letting our relationship just be sexual. I should've been proving to her she means so much more to me than that. Instead, I've allowed her to use me as a distraction. A way to pass the time in our miserable hometown.

"What's wrong, Jack?"

The urge to kneel in front of her, beg her to let me in, and tell her how amazing she is, threatens to overpower my focus. I avoid meeting her eyes, take a deep breath and then step toward her. "They still haven't located Adam, but we learned David moved to St. Louis after college."

She nods as the realization hits her of what I will ask next. "I need to tell you about St. Louis," she states coldly.

"Yes." With another step, I close the distance between us and reach down to her to see if she'll take my hand. I want to get her out of this place. We need fresh air. It's been a long night. I'm relieved when she takes it, and I pull her toward the exit. My heart swells as she doesn't let my hand go. Once we make it outside, the early morning sun shocks my senses.

"It's bright," I comment, shielding my eyes.

"It feels nice. Like a new day, new possibilities. Madison is coming home today." Her eyes are closed, and her head tilts up.

The conviction in her voice sparks faith in me. I didn't realize how desperate I was for hope. Hope that the Zoey I loved is still inside her.

"We don't have much time." I lead her to the side of the building for privacy. I sit down on the curb, stretching out my legs. She joins me, releasing a deep breath. She wipes her hands down her thighs.

"Earlier you said you were isolated in St. Louis. When I asked you about it, you seemed like you were about to tell me something." I rub the back of my neck. "And then he called."

"Sam was broken. I was broken. I *am* broken."

I'm lifting my arm to pull her into me as she stands up and keeps her back to me. As she turns to me with pain-filled eyes, I stand and take a step towards her. It hits me. I don't know all her secrets yet. How did I miss that?

"Zoey." I raise my hands to her arms, rubbing. "Were you with him when he died?"

She folds her arms across her stomach and looks down. "No. He was alone. Single car accident."

I release my breath, relieved that she wasn't harmed. "Does his family blame you for the accident?" I'm grasping at straws.

"His parents died when he was young. His grandma raised him, and she died when he was in college." She drops her arms and steps away from my touch. "He was alone. I was all he had."

Her ice-cold tone disturbs me as I see anger flash across her face and settle into pain. I'm slowly realizing that her relationship with Sam wasn't healthy. I pace in front of her. She must sense my suspicion because her words stop me.

"I was stupid."

"Don't say that, Zoey. Don't ever say that."

"I was ... I was such an idiot. I should've ended it in college. My friends hated him. Not at first. They were happy I seemed to get out more, and then I kept coming home at night crying. They tried to tell me and get me to break up with him."

Her words are coming out in a rush, a flood of emotion. The dam has broken, and she can't contain them anymore.

"I just thought that it would get better. When we were done with college, we would grow out of going out all the time, he'd drink less, and we'd build this wonderful life together. That we'd get married, have kids."

She walks over to the curb and sits down, pulling her knees to her chest. Her face grows red and tears fall down her cheeks.

"I can't believe I was so *fucking stupid*, such a cliché. I was weak. It was my fault, all my fault." Her words tumble out between sobs.

She is rocking and shaking, her body trembling with emotion. I've never wished someone dead, but *dammit*, I'm filled with satisfaction that this guy is dead. I just want to hold her and have her unload all that Sam did to her. Take away her pain and be the one to show her what love is.

I drop behind Zoey and pull her into my lap. As I hold her tightly, I hope that deep inside, she can sense my love for her. I'm running out of time. We must get back inside and bring the focus back to the investigation. But I need to hold Zoey for a few more minutes. The warmth of her body is what I need to soothe my guilt of losing touch.

I can't start down the path of what-ifs. For ten years, I've longed for the chance to be near her again. But not like this. Her entire world is falling apart, her secrets forced out for all to know and judge.

"Hey," I say cautiously. She shudders as a sniffle escapes her. "We won't talk about Sam anymore."

"But what if I'm holding back something that could lead to finding Madison? What if there is a clue hidden in my memories?"

"Well, Sam's dead, and doesn't have any family, right?"

"He always said I was the only person he had. That if I left him, he'd be all alone. That he wouldn't be able to go on with life." She sighs.

I try not to stiffen, holding space for her to continue. "It's stupid now. He died anyway."

I pull her closer. "Did you go to his funeral?" I ask.

Zoey leans back and meets my eyes. "No, he didn't have one. I actually didn't find out until about six months after he died, when I ran into one of his friends in Chicago." Her head drops into her hands after the admission.

I pull her back against my chest and an uncomfortable feeling hits my gut. Could Sam still be a threat? "What was Sam's last name?"

"Sam Coleman. Why?" Zoey mumbles into my chest.

"I just want to check out his background. His friends. See if anything suspicious turns up," I say calmly. I don't want to alarm her, but Sam needs to be confirmed dead.

"Let's get some food and go back inside," I say.

She climbs out of my lap, reaches out to help me up, and pulls me into a hug. "Thank you."

"For what?" My heart swells.

"For being you. Being here. Listening. Not leaving me."

"I mean it when I say I'm not leaving you. Not today, not when this is over. I'm not letting us grow apart again." I release her and grab her hand.

That spark of faith emerges at our continued touch. We walk toward the station; I stop in front of the door, glancing down at the coffee shop. It's crowded with the morning rush.

"You can head inside." I nod. "I'll get us fresh coffee and bagels."

I squeeze her hand as she's considering leaving my side and the look in her eyes is like a punch in the gut. I see the tiniest spark of Zoey. With a clenched jaw, I will myself to march toward the coffee shop.

I'm growing frustrated while waiting in the line, tapping my fingers on my legs. All I want to do is get back to my desk and start researching Sam Coleman. My gut is screaming that there is more I need to know about this guy.

"Two large coffees and two plain bagels," I bark out.

"Room for cream?" the cashier asks.

"No."

"Bagels toasted?"

"Nope, in a hurry. Just sliced, please."

As I grab my order and head out the door, tension builds in my shoulders. The outcome of today relies on him. Zoey's reliving her past and it's torture. I'm ready for this to be over.

The sun warms my back as I walk toward the station. *Damn.* It is a nice day. Zoey's right. We're getting Madison back home today. We're going to arrest this *asshole*, and then I'm not going to leave her side. She's finally letting me in, and the connection between us is growing.

CHAPTER 14

Zoey

Jack walks into the dispatch center and looks around the room. "Who's on this morning?" he asks.

"Sally again." I huff as my eyes rise to the ceiling in disdain. "She went to go talk to Sergeant Graves for a briefing."

"Don't worry, I'll keep her away from you," Jack reassures me, and I hold his gaze with an expression of appreciation as he hands me a hot cup of coffee.

"Eat a bagel, please," he says as he shoves the bag toward me.

"I will if you do," I challenge.

"Fine."

As I open the bag and hand him one, I pull off a chunk of the cold plain bagel and stuff it into my mouth. He bites into his and grimaces.

"These aren't good," I mumble with a full mouth of the dry bagel.

"I was going for as fast as possible," he shrugs.

"I've been thinking about David Slim," I say and notice the dark circles forming underneath his eyes.

"And?"

"He seems like a stretch. My junior year, the first semester, the few times I went out to parties, he and I would end up together at the end of the night."

I take a sip of my coffee, as I recall my time with David.

"I never slept with him. We would just end up talking. We'd talk about everything. My childhood, his. What we were going to do after college. He was such a tech wiz," I say with admiration.

"What do you mean, a tech wiz?" Jack asks, leaning up against my desk next to me.

"Well, there was this accounting class I was really stressing about. I sucked at the exams. And then David hands me the answer keys to all the exams in the class. He'd hacked into the professor's account and downloaded them for me."

He's lost in thought, arms crossed. The stark contrast of my memories of David, a gentle, meek guy, to that of Jack, strong and commanding, standing before me, makes me chuckle.

"What's funny?" Jack asks with a stern face.

"Nothing, it's just ..." I look up at him. "He was sweet and cute. We made out a few times, and I'd stay in his room. He never pushed me further, but one night he asked if he could put his hand down my pants. I'd been dreading that moment. I knew it would lead to more, and a friend had told me she hooked up with him and that he had the tiniest dick. It's shallow, but she was like, it's the size of your pinky, hard."

Jack chokes on his coffee. "Yeah. I wasn't sure how I'd react if it was true," I say with a grimace.

"What'd you do?" he asks.

"I told him no, that we needed to go on a proper date if he wanted to go further. I wouldn't just be his drunk hookup."

"Did you ever go on a date with him?" My shoulders sink a little. "No, I turned him down. I was dating someone else by the time he called and asked me out."

"Sam?"

"Yeah," I say, dropping my eyes. A past with different choices haunts me.

The computer lights up. I sit tall and put my headset on. "This is it. Madison is coming home."

"Hi, Ned," I say in a soft tone.

"Hi, *Zoey*. I see you've calmed down."

"Yes. I'm sorry about that. You were right." I'm determined to give Ned what he wants. I'm not getting off this call until he lets Madison go.

"That you're a homewrecker. A thief. A *tease.*" His tone is dripping with disgust.

"I'm a terrible person. I've ruined a lot of lives." My jaw is clenching with restraint.

"I've known that, and now everyone else does, too." His laughter is sharp and cold.

I remain silent, my mouth sealed shut. Closing my eyes, I take in a deep breath and steady my nerves with the silence as I play into his need for control. He didn't need me to share all this shit to help me understand how awful I am. I'm a cold-hearted bitch.

My heartbeat is quickening as I try to imagine what he's going to bring up. What else will Jack learn about me? He's already brought up all my worst moments in life.

"Madison is still unharmed, *Zoey*; you should be proud of that."

"Yes. I'm happy Madison isn't hurt." I turn to Jack and nod. "Can she come home?"

"Maybe." Ned's cruel voice echoes in my mind.

My hands are sweating. His slow pace is excruciating. My leg bobs under the desk. I shake my head no to Jack, and his shoulders drop.

"First, I want everyone to understand what a tease you are." Hate fills his words. "You lead guys on, give them your attention, make them feel like there's a chance with you."

Ned's words pierce my heart as I glance at Jack. He's held on to the scraps I've given him like they mean something. I almost gave him more. I close my eyes to squeeze away the pain.

"Fancy meeting you here," Jack drawled as he jogged up beside me.

"Are you stalking me, Jack Moore?" I gasped.

"Ha, this is my running trail. I was here first. Remember? Me, four years, you," he pointed at me, "four weeks."

I chuckled. "Fine."

"When did you start running?" I asked.

"The academy. Turns out I like it; clears my head," he responded as he turned to the side, doing a side shuffle run facing me. "You?"

"Chicago. The trail along Lake Michigan lured me in," I responded, as a smile formed at the memory of running along the lake.

"Do you like to listen to music or silence?" I asked.

"Silence."

"Me, too," I chuckled.

"Worst run?" he asked.

"October. Windy, sleet, along the lake."

"You?"

"July, ninety degrees, humidity."

"Races?" I asked.

"Rock n' Roll Marathon, Nashville."

"Impressive." I gave him a side eye, and he finally turned and we jogged side by side.

"You?"

"I signed up for the Chicago Marathon, didn't do it."

He laughed. "Favorite TV show?"

I thought for a minute. "Too many to choose from. You go first."

"*Breaking Bad.*"

"Ha, typical." I elbowed him.

"You, what's yours? *Sex and the City*?" he said while mock flipping his hair.

"Rude. *Sex and the City* is a great show. But I've been binging *The Walking Dead.*"

"Zombies, huh? Interesting." He brought his hand up to his chin.

"Whatever, you're such a cop."

"Hey, want to come over for pizza?" Jack blurted out as we approached downtown.

I bit my lip. I had successfully kept him at a distance. That run, our banter, it was too much. Spending time with Jack rekindled our friendship and reminded me of why I always loved his company. He sensed my hesitation.

"Come on; the first one to my door gets to pick toppings."

Not fair. I never backed down from a competition. "I don't know," I responded as I burst into a sprint. Laughing, I heard him take off behind me. "Ha, I won!"

He smirked at me, knowing he'd actually won. I stuck my tongue out at him and swung open the door. "Losers first." Laughing, we made it up to his apartment.

"Okay, what's your order?" Jack asked as we entered his apartment.

I followed him to his kitchen. "Black olives, pepperoni, and mushrooms," I deadpanned.

He turned around. "Are you serious? Olives, mushrooms?"

"Hey, a deal's a deal," I said as I placed my hands on my hips.

He leaned over his counter. *Damn*, he really turned out to be hot. The sweat on his T-shirt clung to his back muscles. I walked over to grab a bottle of water from the fridge.

"Ordered–will be here in about forty-five minutes. I'm going to jump in the shower. Make yourself at home."

I raised the bottle to him. "I'll do just that. Can't wait to find the secrets you've hidden in this fancy place." I smirked.

"I'm an open book for you. Explore." Jack waved his hand above his head and his muscles flexed in his back as he walked away.

As I chugged my water, I knew I didn't really want to explore. The idea of getting to know him better made my stomach flip. My chest tightened, and I exhaled deeply. I needed to make sure I was in control. This relationship needed to stay superficial.

As I walked over to the couch, I looked down the hall. The bathroom door was open a little. My heart skipped. I needed a distraction from my thoughts. My feet took me on a detour from the couch and I walked down the long hallway to his bathroom.

I pushed open the door and leaned against the doorframe. He was ripped. I admired his powerful back muscles and his adorable ass as he tilted his head back with his eyes closed and let the water wash over him.

"Enjoying the view?" he chuckled.

I hadn't realized he'd seen me. My cheeks warmed with desire. The confidence he'd developed only increased his appeal.

"Feeling grateful I don't have to smell you while I eat." I didn't move; the moment was intimate and natural. I soaked in the comfort of Jack's presence.

"Can't say the same for me." He waved his hand in front of his nose.

"Ha, I stink?"

Dipping my head into my armpits, I looked up and grimaced at the smell. He laughed and turned to grab the shampoo. *Fuck it.* When he closed his eyes and started scrubbing his head, I quickly slipped out of my sweaty clothes, and I slid between him and the water.

"Hey, I was using that."

"And now I am," I quipped.

He opened his eyes and watched me dip my head back to get my hair wet. His eyes dropped to my exposed neck and then lowered to my breasts. I watched the rise and fall of his chest quicken as he took me in all the way to my toes. I peeked down and saw his hardness between us.

He reached around my waist. "I guess I'm to blame. I said you stink."

As I closed the distance between us, I wrapped my arms around his neck. He poked me just above my belly button. "You did," I said into his mouth as I kissed him.

Each time his lips touched mine, a rush of excitement sent flutters to my stomach. It differed from that sloppy make-out session on our only date. It was so bad that I just pretended like the entire night didn't happen. Now, I couldn't get enough of making out with him.

"I need to rinse," he mumbled into our kiss. He then grabbed my ass with both hands and turned me, so I was out of the stream. I raised my hands and ran them through his hair to help the soap rinse.

"It's cold on this side," I whined.

"So demanding." He turned us so the water fell between us, and he plunged down and kissed me deeply. Exploring my mouth with his tongue, igniting warmth between my legs. I moaned and pushed into him. He was hard against my stomach. I rose on my tiptoes to create friction. He moaned, and I grinned.

"We need soap."

"We do," he growled. He reached around me, not breaking our kiss, and grabbed the soap. "Hold out your hand," he demanded.

After he squeezed the soap into my hand, he pulled away, grabbed his loofah, and squeezed some into it. I rubbed the soap between my hands and began rubbing my breasts; he looked down at my hard nipples.

"*Fuck.*"

"What?" I innocently asked and lowered my movements around my stomach and in between my legs.

Jack scrubbed his body quickly as I kept my slow pace, bringing my hands around to my ass, and arched my back, so my breasts bumped into his face as he scrubbed his leg. He took my nipple into his mouth, sucked it in, and gave it a nip.

"Hey." I playfully slapped his head.

"You pushed them into my face," he said and grinned up at me.

He grabbed my ass and pulled me back into him to rinse the soap off of us. "Good enough." He turned off the water and grabbed my hand to pull me out.

"I didn't wash my hair!" I pouted up at him.

He leaned back in and kissed me, tugging on my lower lip. "You can do that later."

"Fine." I feigned annoyance as he tossed a towel at me.

He tried to dry himself off with the hand towel. I pushed him out of the bathroom and toward his bedroom. Once we were inside, we were a tangle of kisses. Warmth and desire flooded my senses. Kissing him was carefree and safe.

He tugged the towel away from me and tossed it in the corner as he led me to the bed. Jack turned us so that I fell onto my back as he climbed on top of me, kissing my stomach and gently kissing one breast and then the other. He made his way up to my neck and then reached my mouth.

"Jack," I moaned, consumed with want. I wrapped my arms around his neck, slid my hand down his back, grabbed his ass, and pushed our hips together.

He gasped into our mouths and began following his path back down my neck and down further to my breast. He was not as gentle this time, pulling my breast into his mouth and teasing my nipple with his tongue. I raised my hips into him as he kneaded my other breast.

Jack's touch heated my skin as he kissed down my stomach. He looked up at me as he trailed his tongue down my front. He stopped and teased my bundle of nerves. My hips bucked, and he placed his palm on my lower stomach and slid his tongue down into me.

Holy shit. He knew what he was doing. How did he learn this? Shaking my head and dropping back as he kissed, tugged, and licked in all the right places. "Shit, Jack," I gasped. My hips pushed against his palm as I trembled with the release.

I was in complete bliss, consumed with his warmth, as he gently climbed back up to me and kissed me. I rolled him over onto his back. When I sat up, I looked down at his handsome and caring face. And then I dropped my breast into his face, and he took it in his mouth as I slid against his hardness, slow and steady.

As I rose onto one foot, I positioned him to enter me. With my foot planted next to him, my other knee was against his hip. I rocked back and forth on top of him. "Zoey," he gasped and reached up to cup my breasts. My head dropped back and took him in deeper, completely rocking in rhythm with his heavy breaths. "Fuck, Zoey," he shook with the release.

I fell to his chest and kissed him, rolled to his side and rested my head on his shoulders, draping my leg over his waist. His arm held me tightly as our combined breaths slowed. My emotions took over me. I was safe in Jack's arms, content and loved. Dread rose in me. I was too damaged.

He deserved someone better than me. I wasn't worthy of his love. The room was closing in on me. Panic came to the surface. It could never last with Jack.

"Oh shit! I forgot I promised my mom I'd be home for dinner." I blurted out the lie.

"What?"

I rose. "I need to go. My mom expects me for dinner."

"Really? You can't text her and tell her your plans have changed? I already ordered the pizza." He pulled me closer to him. "And I'm so comfortable right now."

I was too. That was the freaking problem.

"No, she'll be pissed. It'll become a whole thing. I really need to go." He dropped his arm away from me.

"Fine. I don't like it, but I get it." He grabbed my hand, and I looked back at him. "I'm saving this pizza for you because there is no way I'm eating it with black olives and mushrooms." He grimaced.

I leaned over and kissed him quickly. "Thank you."

I made my way to the bathroom and cringed as I pulled on my sweaty clothes and left without saying goodbye.

"And poor Jack, he believed you would choose him. That he could build a life with you." Ned's bitter laugh brings me back.

My hands are ice cold. He's right about me.

"Don't worry, *Zoey*. I've ensured he won't want anything to do with you anymore."

The familiar blanket of shame comes over me. I'm such a piece of *shit*.

"Aren't you going to thank me?"

"For what?"

Fatigue is slowly settling in. My thoughts are getting muddled together.

"Getting Jack out of your life, of course. It's what I do."

"Thank you."

"I'm glad you're seeing my importance in your life. The things that I do for you. I really hope you're grateful."

My leg bobs again. I'm anxious to get more information about Madison. To get her home.

"Yes. I'm grateful. Jack needs to leave me alone." I cringe as I play into his game. Jack steps closer to me, and I raise my hand for him to stop.

"I'm excited about our future," Ned says enthusiastically.

My instincts scream in warning. I force myself to focus.

"It's time for Madison to go home. She's waiting for her parents to pick her up at Forks Park," Ned says.

I scramble to grab a pen, reach for the notepad, and scribble. Adrenaline pumps through me.

Forks Park. Madison is there.

Jack is running out of the room, and I barely hear Ned.

"Don't forget, *Zoey,* I'll always help you remove the wrong men from your life."

"Is she there, Ned? Ned? Is Madison at Forks Park?"

The line is dead. I slam down the headset and run after Jack into the station.

CHAPTER 15

Jack

Zoey bumps into me as Sergeant is announcing over the radio all available units to head to Forks Park. I can't contain my smile when our eyes meet. She's beaming at me as I put my arm around her and pull her in.

It's over. It's finally over. The longest twenty-four hours of our life has ended. Madison will be with her parents soon.

"You think she's there?" Zoey asks, panting.

"Yeah, I'm going to believe she's there."

I turn to her, gripping her arms. "You did it. You *freaking* did it." My adrenaline is surging. I pull her in tight and lift her off the ground.

"Calm down, Moore. No one has eyes on her yet," Sergeant warns.

"She's there," I whisper to her. I refuse to consider any other options. I can't. If I do, I might lose it.

"Yes!" Sarge screams. "She's there. They're loading her into a squad car and taking her home. We fucking did it!" He slaps me on the back.

I bite my tongue and fight the urge to correct him. Zoey and I did this, but I don't want to ruin the moment. I pull her in again, this time spinning her around.

"Was Ned in the area? Did they get him?" Zoey asks the room.

"No sign of him," Sarge answers.

The smile slips from her face.

"Hey, I won't stop until we find the bastard. I mean it. I'm going to arrest him myself."

"Woah there, Moore, you're off the case. I told you, you're too close." He's looking at Zoey and me.

Pain radiates between my eyes. How does he expect me to sit on the sidelines when he is out there *fucking* with Zoey's life?

"It's okay, Jack. Sergeant Graves is probably right," she says, grabbing my hand. As she touches me, I concentrate on the warmth of her hand. I'll let it go for *now*.

"We need to get your statement, Zoey," Sarge demands.

My jaw clenches so tight at his tone I may crack a tooth.

"Can it wait? She's been up for twenty-four hours," I bark back at him.

"No, I want it fresh in her mind. Willy will take her statement." The scowl on Sergeant's face makes him look like a troll.

As I release Zoey's hand, I step toward Sarge to inform him she is not a suspect but a victim, and this is not how to treat victims. Her hand lands on my chest after my first step.

"It's alright. I want to do it now. I don't want to forget anything."

Her hand next to my heart stops me. When I meet her eyes, my chest warms with pride.

"Moore, you look like shit. Go home, take a shower, and take a nap. Eat," Sarge commands.

I struggle with the decision to leave her. My hand covers hers on my chest and I squeeze. *Fuck*, I love her.

"He's right. You look like shit. Go home. I'll text you when I'm done."

My eyes narrow at her skeptically.

"You can pick me up and take me home. Will that get you out of here?" She lets out an exasperated sigh.

I'm ripping in two. "Fine. Promise me you'll text me when you're done."

"Promise." She pulls me into a hug. "Now go, you stink." She shoves me toward the door.

As I walk outside, I knead the tight muscles in my jaw. Madison is safe. She's home. And Zoey is letting me in, *finally.*

On the drive home, I beam with pride, tapping my hands on the steering wheel to the beat of the music. When I reach my apartment, my relief fades. This *asshole* is still out there. He's the only thing standing in the way of our future together. He needs to go.

As I stomp up to my apartment, anger brews at Sergeant. He better take the threat to her seriously. As I step through the door, fatigue strikes. Shower, then food, then Zoey. As I enter the shower, I can't help but smile, recalling the sound of her laughter as she joined me after our run.

It'd only been a few weeks since we'd reconnected. I'd just started sensing she was keeping me at a distance. Now, with Zoey's walls down, we can finally move forward and build a stronger connection.

After the shower, I'm like a new man and head to the kitchen. Eggs and bacon sound amazing. I get the coffee started and start whipping up a quick breakfast.As the eggs are cooking, I lean up against the counter and run my hand through my hair. Man, it's like I've lived a lifetime in twenty-four hours.

I plate my food, pour coffee, and sit on the couch. Zoey has left an imprint on this place. There isn't a spot I don't see her. The last time we screwed was on this couch. I told her I wouldn't settle for what we had any longer, that I wanted more from her. I'd do anything for her, even stand by her as a friend. How did I let myself slip right back into that lovesick teenager again?

As I force myself to take a bite of food, my eyes are drawn to the kitchen. That *damn* counter where I lifted her up, pushed her dress up and pulled down her panties. I devoured her right there on the counter, the taste of her so sweet. Another forkful of eggs goes into my mouth. I'm getting hard underneath my plate. I've got to get myself under control. The last thing I want Zoey to feel is that I only want her for the sex. She means so much more to me than that, despite what my dick won't let me forget.

After I sit my plate on the coffee table, I lay my head back. The buzzing of my phone catches my attention. I take a minute to realize where I am; I dozed off. Looking at my phone, Zoey's texted me three times. *Shit!*

I'm done. You can pick me up now.

Are you sleeping?

You're sleeping.

Hey, on my way, and yes, I fell asleep

I respond, knowing she would razz me until I admitted it.

I slip my feet into my boots and head out the door. My heart is pounding with excitement as I anticipate taking her away from that building.

When I get out of my truck at the station, I act calm, but I'm dying to run into the station and carry Zoey out. *Shit.* My hands run through my hair. I'm in deep.

As I enter, I almost run right into Sergeant. "Moore, come to my office for a minute."

My fingers curl in frustration as I follow him into his office. "Sit." I sit down in the chair too quickly. Trying to keep cool is not working out for me so well.

"News on Ned? Zoey's stalker?" I ask.

"No. Listen, I know you believe this Ned is stalking her. But our primary focus is finding out who is responsible for Madison's kidnapping and charging them."

I grip the arms of the chair, turning my knuckles white.

"Ned is responsible. We know that. He's confessed on the Nine-One-One call," I respond with a forced, calm tone.

"It seems so, but we are keeping all options open to see if he has any accomplices."

I hear the words that he isn't saying. He hasn't ruled out Zoey. He's such a stereotypical egotistical cop. Dismissing the threat of stalkers. It always pissed me off when I'd hear cops in Nashville minimize a woman's concerns over a guy they believed was stalking them.

"Understood." I'll play along with his power trip if it gets me to Zoey sooner. "When are you going to talk with Madison?"

"That's none of your concern, Moore. You're off the case," Sarge barks.

"Is she free to leave?" I grit out.

"Yes, she's free to go. But she can't leave town."

He really didn't need to say that last part. *Asshole.* "Great," I respond and stand up. "I'll make sure she knows to stay in town."

With a nod, I walk out the door and see Zoey sitting at my desk. I smile down at her. "Let's get out of here."

"You look better," she beams.

"I wish I could say the same to you." I rock into her and wrap my hand around hers.

We walk out hand in hand, and I'm full of hope. "I can take you back to your place, but do you want food first?"

She pauses as she climbs into my truck, uncertainty on her face.

"Actually, can we go to your place? Mine's a dump. I don't have much. After being stuck in this hellhole for twenty-four hours, I need some Jack Moore luxury."

There's a bit of trepidation about her. Is it about coming to my place or fear about a stalker? Laughing, to reassure her, I say, "Whatever you want. Do you want to pick up some clothes first?" I grimace playfully at her.

"Nope. I'm just going to steal some of yours." She shrugs and climbs into the truck.

I'm down for that. No complaints from me about her in my T-shirts. My grip tightens on the steering wheel and I let go of the thoughts of taking her to bed. We ride in silence to my place, and I soak in every moment of this short-lived victory. My focus must shift to locating Ned and guarantee that he poses no threat.

She's already nodding off as I pull up to my place. "We're here."

"Oh," she jolts. "I'm fucking exhausted."

"I know the feeling," I respond as she slowly climbs out of the truck.

We go up to my place, and she heads toward the bathroom. "I need a shower, then sleep, then food. Maybe food first," she mumbles as she closes the door.

My phone vibrates in my pocket. Adrenaline surges through me as I grab my phone, followed by a wave of frustration when I realize it's my mom.

"Hey, Mom," I answer and walk into the kitchen.

"Hi, Jack. Are you okay? I heard there's been quite the commotion at the station."

"It's been one hell of a day. I'm sorry I haven't checked in."

I roll my neck as I pull out ingredients to make Zoey eggs and bacon.

"I heard about the kidnapping and all that stuff Zoey did from Barb. You're not still seeing her, are you?"

My shoulders tense at the mention of Sarge's loudmouth wife, Barb. "Mom, it's complicated."

As I beat the eggs, my grip on the bowl tightens, and I set the phone down and put it on speaker.

"I'm not sure how it could be. I mean, stealing credit cards? And messing around with married men? A porn video? Her parents must be mortified."

My patience thins as anger builds. Mom's always been in the middle of all the town gossip. I've been avoiding checking in with her for this exact reason.

"It's still an open investigation. I really can't talk about it."

"Oh, you're on the case? Is that hard because of your history?"

As I turn to grab milk from the fridge, I see Zoey is standing by my kitchen table, frozen in place in my towel. *Shit.* The ashen color of her face makes it clear she heard my mom. I shake my head slowly.

"Mom, listen, I really can't talk about this. Please understand," I plead.

As I turn to pick the phone up and turn it off speaker, I hear Zoey's rushed footsteps down the hall.

"Okay." She lets out a sigh. "I want to have dinner with you this week and catch up. Love you."

I push away the guilt she's trying to put on me. "Sounds good. Love you too."

As I rub my hands through my hair, exhaustion presses down on me. Dread guts me at my mom's judgment, and Zoey heard it all. With a deep exhale, I head to my bedroom.

When I arrive at my door, I give it a soft knock and open it. Zoey is sitting on the edge of my bed in her towel, staring at the wall. "Hey," I say softly.

"I need some clothes." She shrugs and doesn't meet my eyes.

My mouth opens and then closes. Words are stuck in my throat. What could make what she overheard better? Instead, I nod and pull out an old T-shirt and boxers from my drawer.

"Thanks," she says as she takes the clothes out of my hands.

"No problem. I'll just head back and finish cooking." She nods in response.

As I close the door behind me, I clasp my hands behind my head and silently scream *Fuck!* I quickly make my way to the kitchen and pick up where I left off.

The pan sizzles as I pour the eggs in. As they cook, I reheat some bacon in the microwave and drop some bread in the toaster. As I load up her plate with food, I hear Zoey approaching. When I turn, I'm hit with the sight of her in my old T-shirt and boxers. My body betrays me as my dick hardens in my boxers.

"Yes, please." She grabs a slice of bacon off the plate. "After not feeling like eating for the last day, I'm starving."

I'm doing my best not to stare, but her demeanor is shocking. She's acting as if she didn't just learn the town gossip circuit is featuring her. The tension in my shoulders is growing heavier with each silent minute that passes.

"This is great. Exactly what I needed." She looks at me and smiles as she stands. "And now I'm ready for sleep."

I take her plate and head to the kitchen. "Take my bed. I already got some rest." I glance over my shoulder at her and wink. As I turn back to the kitchen, her footsteps fade away down the hall.

As soon as the plate clatters in the sink, I decide to deal with the dishes later. With a sigh, I finally make it to my couch and collapse onto it.

"Jack?" I rise and see Zoey standing in the hallway. My cock twitches. *Damn.* She looks sexy in my clothes.

"Yeah?"

"Can you lay with me? I don't want to be alone." Her voice trails off as she tugs on the hem of my shirt.

I'd planned on giving her space, but I'm relieved she wants me with her. The distance is killing me.

"Of course, whatever you need," I respond as I rise off the couch.

By the time I get to my room, she's already snuggled under the covers. "Do you care if I take my jeans off? I have this weird thing about jeans and blankets and beds."

"No." She laughs. "It's your bed, your rules."

As I climb in and lay next to her, I clasp my hands behind my head and stare at the ceiling. My mouth opens and then closes. Guilt is choking me. I want to ask her how she is. My body wants to roll over and pull her close to me. I don't do anything.

Zoey rolls over next to me and lifts her head onto my chest. My breath catches as I lower my arm around her, and she slides her leg up over my waist. As her breathing slows, my muscles relax, and the tension melts away.

"Thank you."

"It's nothing."

"No, Jack. It's everything."

I kiss her forehead as she falls asleep, and a few minutes later, I follow her.

The sun is setting as I wake up to my phone buzzing. Somehow, we've stayed touching. I'm now snuggled up behind her, my arm cradled over her body. I roll silently to grab my phone and see what I've missed.

It's a series of texts from Sarge. All just updates, nothing requesting that I come in. Not that I expected him to ask me to.

Madison is fine. She wasn't harmed.

She doesn't have a good description of him other than small, kinda young, and nice.

Located Adam; he's been in Chicago.

David Slim is like a ghost; no one knows where he is–his family hasn't heard from him in years.

Bradley boys are too tall.

I ignore my rising panic. We still have no solid leads on his location. I need to listen to the last call. In all the excitement of finding Madison, I didn't check it out.

Thanks for the updates. Did you listen to the last call?

I replay what Zoey has told me about the calls as I wait for Sarge to reply.

Yeah, nothing of importance other than Madison's location.

Bullshit. I need to listen to that call.

Zoey stirs next to me. "Hey," she says sleepily.

"Hey. How are you feeling?"

"So much better. Hungry."

"Me too."

She glances at my phone in my hand. "Any updates?"

"Madison wasn't harmed, but no solid leads on Ned's identity."

Her body collapses back on the bed as frustration covers her face.

"How about burgers? I can do a pickup order at the brewpub down the street."

"Burger sounds perfect. Fries, too," she mumbles.

I just want to hold on to her for a little while longer before reality sets in and she tries to pull away again. Reluctantly, I sit up in bed and place the order on their app.

"It'll be ready in fifteen minutes. I got a double order of fries; I'm starving too." I set my phone down on the nightstand and lay back down next to her.

We lie in silence for a few moments. Zoey stretches her arms above her head and climbs out of bed. Her hair is disheveled, and it somehow makes her sexier. My eyes follow her as she heads to the bathroom, cursing my body's response to her, and then I get up, pull on my jeans, and head to the brewpub.

"Hey, I'm heading to grab the burgers. I'll be back in fifteen."

"Okay," she says through the door.

I jog to the brewpub and then rush back to the apartment. When I enter, Zoey's leaning up against the arm of the couch, her knees pulled into her chest. My stomach drops. This is how she spent most of her time in the dispatch center.

"You okay?" I drop the food on the kitchen table and head to her quickly.

She stands. "Yeah, I'm good. Just still tired." Her arms cross and she avoids eye contact. She's withdrawing again.

We go to the table and dig into the fries and burgers. Clearing my throat, I break the silence. "I'm going to head back to the dispatch center, listen to the last call, and see if there are any clues." I'll also do some research on Sam Coleman, but I leave that part out.

"Okay." She continues to avoid my eyes and looks around the room. "Can you drop me at my place before you go? I know it's out of the way, but I need to go home."

"Why don't you just stay here? We still don't have any solid leads on who Ned is, and we don't know where he is. You're still in danger. Stay here," I insist.

She bites her lip as she looks at me. She isn't sure.

"Really, hang out here. I'll know more when I get back, and then I can take you home."

"Fine, but I'm going to make you take me home tonight," she says as determination steels her face.

CHAPTER 16

Zoey

Reality sets in as I watch Jack close his apartment door. What am I doing here? Why did I ask to come here? Because if I went to my place, I'd get lost in my head. I glance around at his place. It's masculine but cozy. The brick wall and old wood floors give it a rustic vibe, and his oversized leather couch warms the space, unlike my black metal futon from Walmart.

When I learned Madison was on her way to her parents, the adrenaline that had been driving me faded. I crashed hard and couldn't stand the thought of being alone. I can't help but feel safe and at home here. It's nothing like my dingy place, my cream laminate cabinets straight out of the seventies, a stark contrast to his dark green kitchen cabinets. There's a reason I've never had Jack at my place. An image of my mattress on the floor flashes in my mind.

"Dammit!"

I push away from the table, dragging his chair on the floor. I'm pacing behind his couch, chewing on my thumb. Why does he have to see my damage and still want to look out for me? I brace my arms on the back of the couch, remembering the last time Jack and I were on it. I was pushing him too far that night. Stripping while he was cooking, teasing him by slipping my hand into my underwear.

I don't mean to shut him out, but I can't stop it. I've carried the shame of my past for so long I don't know who I am anymore. My heart won't let me open to him. I won't be shattered into a million pieces again.

Things would be so much easier if sex with Jack wasn't so amazing. That first night, I'd only slipped onto his lap to avoid talking, but it quickly turned intense. It only took a few more hookups, and I was addicted to his touch, kisses, and cock. The distraction became a bonus.

I crave Jack's bed, his warm flannel comforter. Entering his bedroom, I take in his dark wood bed and remember being on my knees, hands braced on the top of his headboard. He thrust into me, his hands gripping my hips, my breasts bouncing with the movement. He reached around and teased my bundle of nerves, and the sensation exploded in me with release. Jack came right along with me. No guy has cared as intently about my pleasure as he does. I climb into his bed, his smell comforting me, and I sleep.

I jolt up, not recognizing where I am. My eyes dart around and let out a breath. Jack. I'm in his bed. Madison made it home. It's over. Wait. Where is he? Panic surges when I see how dark it is outside. What time is it? I reach for my phone. It's 3:00 a.m. My heart races. Is he still out?

As I scramble out of bed and turn into the hall, I see the TV is on. I let out a breath, peek over the couch, and he's out cold. I reach to put a blanket over him as my annoyance builds. Why didn't he wake me up? He was supposed to take me home. And why is he sleeping on the couch? He needs rest, too. He should be in his bed.

When I walk to the kitchen to pour a glass of water, I hope to wake him up so I can unload my irritation. Jack doesn't stir. And then my heart warms as I watch him for a minute, peacefully sleeping with his arms crossed across his chest.

I can't bring myself to wake him. Rolling my eyes at him, I go back to his room and climb into the comfort of his bed. It's too empty without him. Why didn't he come and lie with me? I was at peace with him earlier, falling asleep in his arms. My anxiety is rising, and I count my breaths: in one, out two, in three, out four, in five. Two rounds clear my mind.

He's on the couch because it's over. He was staying by my side to keep me focused on finding Madison. Jack was only doing his job. Disappointment settles in my chest. Was I hoping that Jack would still care about me after all this? I've done nothing but push him away for the last four months and now he learns about my disgusting past.

Even worse, the entire town knows all my secrets. A wave of nausea hits me as I recall the conversation I overheard with his mom. I curl up into the fetal position, my breaths growing rapid. She's right, Jack should stay away from me.

Tears fall down my face as I remember being on my knees, sucking Joey's dick. It was wrong, but I couldn't stop myself. I had to prove that I wasn't worthy of friends who cared about me.

I turn to the side, choking on my breaths. Who am I kidding? I'm a criminal. I could never ask Jack to protect me, not allow me to be charged. He can't compromise his values for me. I'm sick of carrying around the guilt of stealing those girls' credit cards. I sold everything before I left Chicago, so I'd have some savings when I moved here. As soon as we find Ned, I'm going to turn myself in.

As I release my knees, my breaths calm, and I'm determined to do the right thing for once. A stack of books on his nightstand catches my attention. And I remember how I'd propped up my phone to take that video for Preston. I roll over onto my back and slam my hands into the bed, silently screaming *FUCK!* I'm such a fool.

Of course, Jack's avoiding being close to me. I was the one that asked him to lie with me earlier. He was going to stay on the couch. He could never want to be with me again, knowing I'm on display for the entire world to see. My eyes squeeze shut as the desperation for Preston's attention resurfaces. I fell right into his game. I open my eyes and stare at the ceiling as I remember that night in the bar with Preston's friends. Desperation turns to shame, making it difficult to breathe.

I count my breaths, in one, out two, in three, out four, in five. In the middle of my third round, my thoughts drift back to why I can't let Jack in. I promised myself I'd never lose myself to a guy again. I'll never fully trust anyone, ever. And I sure as hell won't be helpless, afraid, vulnerable, and controlled again.

I count again, in one, out two, in three, out four, on and on until I smell coffee. Opening my eyes, I see Jack sitting on the edge of the bed.

"Hey, I brought you some coffee," he says, looking at me tentatively.

"What time is it?"

"Seven."

I nod and sit up as I reach for the coffee. The silence in the room is closing the walls in. "You were supposed to take me home." My words come out with an unintended edge.

"You were out cold. You needed the rest; I couldn't bring myself to wake you."

"Can you take me home now?" I huff.

Glancing at him, I see his damp hair and the familiar smell of pine and spice surrounding him. He's already showered.

"How about breakfast?" He grins at me.

I take a sip of the coffee. All I want is to leave. I need space. Being this close to him is bringing up feelings I'm desperately trying to avoid.

"I already made a batch of eggs and bacon." He reaches his hand out to me.

My hand rubs along my thigh as I take another sip of coffee. I stand up, avoiding his hand. Every muscle in my body aches like I've been slammed into a wall. The hangover from all the adrenaline of the last day is brutal.

"Sure. If I eat, will you take me home?"

"We'll see," he says coyly.

I whip my head around and glare at him. His mischievous grin annoys me as he puts both hands in his pockets and follows me out to the kitchen.

I grab the plate he's made and sit on the couch. As he refills his coffee mug, anger rises as I realize how much I want to spend the day with Jack. I struggle to breathe, as the reality of leaving his place and going to my cold, lonely apartment sets in. Which is ridiculous. He hasn't even asked me to stay. He turns to face me, leaning up against his counter.

"I listened to all the calls again last night, a few times," Jack says with an intensity that tightens my stomach.

My cheeks grow hot and I sink into the couch and turn to study a magazine on his coffee table. Rising shame is making my hands sweat. Out of the corner of my eye, I see him approaching.

"Did you uncover anything?" I turn to him.

He pauses halfway to the couch, dropping a hand into his pocket. "You're in real danger, Zoey. Sergeant is focused on Madison's kidnapping, but I can't shake how he talked to you. It's like he thinks he owns you, like you're his."

I swallow hard and take that in.

"What about finding any of the other guys on my list? Any leads?"

"That's the thing." He comes to sit next to me on the couch. "No actual progress. David's like a ghost. Three years ago, he just vanished. We have Adam's last name, Marks, but they haven't located him yet."

I contemplate what I remember about David. Shaking my head, it's hard for me to see David as a threat. He was kind. His small stature emphasized his thoughtfulness. It drew me to him; he felt safe.

"Do you believe Ned is David?" I ask.

"I'm not sure what to think, and until he's located, he's still a suspect." Jack looks away and takes a deep breath. There's something he's not telling me. "And I researched Sam, and some things don't add up."

My entire body tenses. *No.*

"I didn't want to mention that I was investigating him, because I wasn't confident I'd find anything. Thing is that the funeral home listed on his obituary doesn't have a record of him." With a calm, measured tone, he moves closer to me on the couch.

As he sits next to me, he takes the plate from my hands and sets it on the coffee table. My body trembles as the information settles over me.

"What does that mean? Is he not dead?" Fear paralyzes my body.

"Well, I can't confirm it yet. I'm still trying to get a copy of his death certificate from the county. Until I see it, we can't be sure he's dead." His voice was heavy with regret.

No. I refuse to believe that Sam's not dead.

"Zoey." Jack places his hand on my thigh. "I want you to stay here until we know more."

"What? No. I can't do that. I don't need to do that."

I stand. The instinct to run is overwhelming. I can't allow myself to rely on him. Fear will no longer control me. I won't lose myself like I did in St. Louis, never again. Jack follows me and reaches out to my arm, sliding down to my hand. My eyes drop to our hands joining, and he drops his away, confirming that this request is about the job, not us.

"I need to get home. Fear won't control me." I say, inhaling deeply and fix him with a firm glare. "I won't live a life like that again. It's time for me to go home and get back to some normalcy. I have a shift tomorrow."

With my legs spread wide and arms tightly crossed, I stand strong, determined to hold my ground. It takes all my strength to push away the terror that threatens to paralyze me. I'm not budging on this. There are too many confusing feelings and if I care even more for Jack—my stomach churns. I can't be this close to him when it's over. I'm going home. When I'm alone, I'll allow myself to cry about leaving him. The exasperation on his face makes me turn away.

"I'm worried about your safety," he says coldly.

"You said Madison was unharmed, right? If we look at the *facts*, Ned isn't violent. There's no evidence that I'm in danger. He wanted to destroy my reputation, humiliate me, and push you away." I take a deep breath and wiggle my toes so I don't start crying. "He succeeded."

I turn back to Jack as he raises his hands behind his head and lets out a deep breath.

"He's still out there. Until he's locked up, I'm not going to consider you safe." He drops his hands into fists at his side.

I turn my back to him, taking a steadying breath. "I'm not going to change my mind," I whisper. He approaches me. As he reaches out to touch me, I swiftly turn and block him with my upraised hand.

"I'm not going to change my mind. The only thing I have left is my independence. I won't let him take that from me."

Jack flinches and then shoves his hands in his pockets.

"Fine." Defeat covers his face. "You ready?"

"Let me grab my stuff," I say with forced resolve.

The ride in his truck is unbearably quiet. I focus on counting my breaths: in one, out two, in three, out four.

"You said you're on tomorrow? You're going back to work right away?" Jack's tone is bitter.

"Yeah."

His knuckles grow white on the steering wheel.

"I want to keep moving forward. It's what I do. I just keep going."

He grunts as he pulls up to my place. He opens his door.

"I don't need you to walk me up."

He glares at me.

"Jack, please."

He slams his door shut.

I take the steps up to my apartment two at a time. As soon as I shut the door, I slide to the floor, drop my head into my hands, and sob.

CHAPTER 17

Jack

I stare at the empty stairs of Zoey's shitty apartment complex. *"FUCK!"* I scream, beating my hands into the steering wheel. I throw my truck in reverse. She needs time to process all that happened. I just wish she'd let me be there for her. This is not what I wanted, but when she makes up her mind, there's no changing it.

The quiet of the farm road only amplifies the hollowness settling within me. The past day has been a complete nightmare for her, but Zoey not needing me anymore guts me. Finally, she's trusting me, and I'll do whatever it takes to maintain that trust. My need to protect her is relentless. This guy, he's a wildcard. This isn't over until I find him.

I pull up to my apartment, hop out of my truck, and walk up the stairs to my door. My chest tightens, knowing Zoey won't be inside. My mind is a chaotic mix of emotions, with no clear direction. Exhaustion lingers over me, but I won't be able to rest in this headspace.

If I go for a run, it will help me make sense of my thoughts. With rushed steps, I enter my bedroom and change into my running gear. In just a few minutes, I'm on my way.

Out on the trail, I let the steady thuds of my feet hitting the dirt clear my mind. I dissect the calls and all that I know. Despite what Sarge thinks, Zoey's had a stalker since college. He's had access to her phone for the video and her computer for the stealing. How did he know about the professor? That was a surprise. I burst into a sprint, my frustration pushing me forward with every step.

Did Zoey keep a journal? She doesn't seem like the type to tell her friends about her dirty deeds. I'll need to ask her how he might've learned about those acts. The sense that I'm running out of time increases my urgency. My feet stop, and I bend over with my hands resting on my knees, trying to catch my breath. I need to focus on investigating the suspects.

The depth of his knowledge of Zoey's past shows their history goes beyond St. Louis. My instincts are pushing me to direct the focus on David and Sam. My breathing calms, and I rise and continue back to my apartment.

I need to get my hands on Sam's death certificate, confirming he's not a threat to her. I put in the request with the health department last night. Anger increases my pace. Since Sarge won't let me on the case, I can't use the investigation to expedite the request.

As I reach my building out of breath, I walk up and down the street to cool down. Sarge gave me the day off, but I'm back on tomorrow. So, I need to use my time wisely. I stop and place my hands behind my head. Today, I'll focus all my efforts on finding everything I can about David Slim until I hear about Sam's death certificate.

As I climb the stairs to my apartment, I start mentally making my to-do list. *Research everything about David. Find out if Zoey kept a journal or told anyone about what Ned knew. Convince Sergeant to investigate Ned.*

I'm sharp and ready, but it doesn't last long. As I step through my door, I see Zoey everywhere, and usually naked. I head to the fridge to grab water, and I go hard remembering her bent over the counter watching me cook.

My head tilts to the ceiling as I chug the water. Not thinking about her is more challenging than I expected. I needed to give her more time, not push her into a relationship. The water bottle crumples in my hand. I drop it in the recycling and head to the shower.

Walking into the bathroom doesn't help. All I see is Zoey torturing me by washing herself. As I step into the shower, I need to clear my mind of all distractions. Turning my attention to my throbbing dick, I stroke myself. The image of her covered in soap, rubbing her breasts, consumes my mind. With a few intense strokes, my fist slams against the shower wall as I hit my release.

When I step out of the shower, a sense of calm washes over me. I dress quickly and head out to the kitchen. Hastily, I throw together a sandwich and take it over to my table.

With the sandwich disappearing quickly from my hand, I boot up my laptop. I pull out my notebook and start reviewing my notes. I'm going to figure out what I've missed about David Slim. Once I'm finished, I'll know where this guy *shits*.

Three hours later, I sit back and assess what I know.

David's from a small-ass town in Iowa, smaller than West Plains. He started college a year after Zoey and graduated two years after her. He worked part-time to pay for college and switched to full-time after she graduated. No record, not even a parking ticket during college.

After college, he moved to St. Louis; I suspect to follow Zoey, which confirms the timeline that he started stalking her at least eight years ago. He bounced around jobs, always part time for the first year. Then he started his own cyber-security consulting business. That's the last detail I can find about him.

Zoey and David lived in St. Louis for two overlapping years. I can't find any connection between them during that time though. It's possible that it's a coincidence. However, my instincts are firing warning signals. It's like he's a ghost. My jaw clenches as my frustration grows. I force myself not to panic and focus on social media.

There is no trace of him on any social media. He probably has an account under a fake name to stalk her accounts. It's a risk, but would she let me examine her social media accounts? Investigate any followers that she doesn't know in person?

I don't know a lot about technology, but his company in cybersecurity could give him the access and tools to hack into her accounts. Didn't she say he hacked into a professor's account? Tension is building in my neck. I try to rub out the knot that's forming.

If I look at this as an investigator and build on the theory that David has more planned, then he must have assumed a fake identity when he disappeared. And if he had been stalking her, he could've moved to Chicago at the time he vanished, following her there. Who knew she was moving to Chicago?

That's my working theory. I can't prove it yet, but I will. Which means he was stalking Zoey while she was in Chicago. And now, he's here in West Plains, tormenting her. There would be a pattern of him following her. He must have been here for at least a couple of months to know about my relationship with her. That last call, where are my notes?

"Aren't you going to thank me, Zoey?"

"For what?"

"Getting Jack out of your life, of course. It's what I do."

"Thank you, Ned."

"I'm glad you're starting to see my importance in your life. The things that I do for you. I really hope you're grateful."

"Yes, Ned. I'm grateful. Jack needs to leave me alone."

He thinks he can keep her from me. My shoulders go tense, thinking about his shift in motives. Well, I'm not leaving her. He can go to hell. My hands slam on the table. I get up and start pacing.

Do I have enough information to show that he could hack into her devices to gain info on the video and credit card fraud? His business website is vague. He doesn't outline his company's services. And how did he learn about the professor?

Zoey's actions don't have a viable connection with David. I can place David at her college, but how could he have known about the dirtbag professor?

The knot in my neck is growing unbearable. I roll my neck and massage it out the best I can. Unless I find out the alias he's using, I won't be able to place him in Chicago. I shove my chair to the ground. I've hit a wall. Zoey and I need to talk. Quickly, I grab my notebook and jot down the questions I have for her.

Can I have access to her social media to investigate her connections, messages?

I doubt she'll agree to that.

Who knew about her move to Chicago?

Could David know about the professor?

I grab my phone to call her, and she doesn't pick up. She's avoiding me, thinking I'm checking up on her. I text her.

I have a couple of questions for the investigation. Call me when you get a chance.

Pacing as I wait for her to call, I glance at the clock. It's late enough for a beer. As I make my way to the fridge, I hear someone at the door. I pause and listen. Who could be here? No one else lives up here. It's silent.

I grab a beer out of the fridge, pop it open, and continue pacing. My phone sits on the table, and I stare at it, wishing for her call. I inwardly groan and shake my head at myself.

My steps slow, and I listen. There is someone outside my place. I perk up. Maybe it's Zoey, and she's changed her mind. I set my beer down on the table, head to the door, and swing it open.

The hall is empty. Huh? When I step out, no one is there. From the top of the stairs, I see the bottom door closing. Was she here and then changed her mind?

I run down the stairs to catch her before she leaves. "Zoey? Zoey?" I step out onto the sidewalk. I turn both ways. "Zoey?"

She's not here. Her car isn't on the road. Disappointed, I run back to see if she's called. My phone is buzzing as I enter the apartment.

"Hey," I answer breathlessly.

"Hey," Zoey responds.

"How are you doing? Do you need anything?" I can't stop myself from asking.

"I'm fine, Jack. You had some questions about the investigation? Sergeant Graves changed his mind and put you back on it?"

"Yes. I mean no." I sigh. "Yes, I have questions; no, I'm not on the case. I'm just doing research on David Slim."

"Ah." I hear her chuckle. "Well, what do you want to know about for your unofficial investigation?" Her tone is mocking me, and I smile that she's got a little of her spunk back.

"Are you good at answering over the phone, or do you want to meet up?"

"Out with them; I want to get back to *The Walking Dead*."

"I see ... zombies over me. At least I know where I stand."

"Jaaack," she draws out my name in mock annoyance.

"Okay, fine. First, college. Was it widely known about that professor trading sex for grades?"

The line goes silent. My hands run through my hair. I should've waited until we were together. I don't want to upset her more.

"Zoey?"

"Yeah, I'm fine. I'm just thinking. It was a long time ago, and I didn't talk about it with anyone." She pauses again. "Sam knew," she whispers.

"Okay, anyone else?" I ask trying to encourage her to continue.

"The professor wasn't very discreet. I'm sure I wasn't the only student. Jerks like that can't get enough of their power over women."

"I agree with you there. What I wouldn't give to beat his ass and then arrest him," I growl.

"Not helping."

"Sorry."

"I guess it's possible I told someone else when I was drunk, and I don't remember. After it all happened, when I got drunk, I got *really* drunk. Blacked out a lot."

I punch the sofa in anger at myself for not being around.

"At some point, I started calling the whole thing a *lay for an A*. I'm not sure where it came from. Maybe I told someone drunk, and that's what they called it?"

"That's good," I said, processing. "Didn't you say you talked a lot with David when you were drunk? That you stayed the night with him a few times?"

"Yeah, I did. I mean, I guess I could've told him and not remembered. Some of our conversations were deep." I hold the silence to see if she recalls anything else.

"I mean, yeah, it's totally possible I confessed it to him. The secret was crushing me that fall semester when I was hanging out with him."

"Great, this is great. I'm trying to connect the info with Ned," I explain, containing my anger, "the secrets he made you confess with evidence that David had knowledge of them."

"That's smart. Ever think about being an investigator?"

"I was, in Nashville."

"What? You were? That's awesome."

"Yeah, I was promoted before moving back here." I can't mask the regret in my voice.

"Well, I'm glad you're unofficially investigating Ned." I smile at her, trying to make me feel better.

"Next missing connection is in Chicago," I let out a breath, "and the bathroom with the husband."

"Oh, not the stealing?" she says lightly. She's trying to mask her unease.

"No, I think he hacked into your computer and probably your phone. Before David disappeared, he started a cybersecurity consulting business. How was Sam with tech?"

"Hacked into my phone?" Zoey's breaths are heavy on the other end of the line. "Sam was resourceful, but I don't think he could hack into anything."

"Okay. We probably need to get you a new phone, but we could also use it to our advantage to draw him out. But I'm getting ahead of myself. I want to link Ned to the holiday party," I clear my throat, "incident."

I can't say blow job; not wanting to bring her more shame around it all by being crass.

"It's a mystery to me how he could have found out about that. I've lost track of how many hours I've spent trying to figure out how Cassie found out. Nobody was near the bathroom, from what I can remember. I didn't tell anyone. I'm certain Joey wouldn't tell anyone. It's not something he would want people to think about him."

"What? That he's a cheating *asshole*." I cringe at my anger escaping.

"Yeah, that."

"Do you keep any online journals?"

"No."

"Paper journals?"

"Nope. I'm not one to memorialize my life with words. More of the shove everything down so deep that I can pretend it didn't happen kind of girl."

I don't like her disdainful laugh. "Zoey."

"Don't. I'm happy you're looking into this. Grateful really. But you can't fix me." My grip on my phone tightens, knowing I've reached my limit with her. Asking about her social media accounts will have to wait. I'll have to settle for connecting one missing piece.

"Okay, I'll keep digging to uncover what David's been up to these last three years. I think Ned has access to your phone and computer. It's best if we call versus text."

"Jack Moore, are you going old-fashioned on me?"

"I'm serious. You should assume nothing on your phone or computer is private anymore."

"Okay, I've got it. Computer hacked, phone hacked. No texts, calls only."

I sigh. "Zoey, please take this seriously. Otherwise, I'm going to camp out in front of your place."

"Enough said. I will." She lets out a breath. "I mean it."

My lungs fill with a deep breath. I hope this doesn't backfire on me. "One more thing. Can you look at your connections on social media and see if any profiles are unfamiliar or stand out?"

I can't just ignore the possibility that the key to finding him could be in her social media accounts. If she builds a list, I can research the accounts.

"Do you think Ned is following me or a friend on one of my accounts?" Zoey's voice has a slight tremor.

"I'm not sure, but it's important that we exhaust all options for leads," I respond in a firm tone. My fingernails are digging into my palm as I wait for her to agree.

"I'll start working on a list."

"Thanks. I'll stop by your desk tomorrow and grab it."

"I'll see you tomorrow. Get some rest," she murmurs.

"Same to you," I respond and set the phone on the kitchen table and pick up my beer. That went well, but it could've been better. I got some good info, but I can tell that Zoey is trying too hard to act normal.

I need to eat, review my notes again, and assess the threat. Could Sam and David be working together? The idea sends a chill down my spine.

It's possible. Until we can confirm David's whereabouts and I set eyes on Sam's death certificate, I'm keeping all options open. My stomach grumbles.

What do I have for dinner? There's a frozen dinner that will do. I pop it in the microwave and start reviewing my notes. I bring the food to the table and assess this asshole's mindset and how dangerous he might be.

Does he have any weapons? He was so desperate to get to Zoey that he would commit a kidnapping. He's in the area and escalating. Although he hasn't directly threatened to harm her, his coming out of the shadows is concerning. We must be on alert.

What is that? My hands grasp the edges of the coffee table and look around. *Shit.* It's my phone. I scramble to grab it in case it's Zoey. My alarm. *Dammit.* Last night, I sat down on the couch to organize my thoughts for the meeting with Sarge and ended up falling asleep.

After a quick shower, I fill my mug with yesterday's coffee and head out the door.

When I pull up to the station, just in time, my stomach drops. And as if my day couldn't start off any worse, I see Sarge as I walk in.

"You're on school duty today, Moore."

School duty is the worst. Sitting outside the schools and watching to ensure parents and teenage kids follow all traffic laws. He's punishing me.

"Really, Sarge?" My voice is full of frustration.

"Really, Moore. I don't want you hanging around the station and sticking your nose where it doesn't belong."

I clench my jaw to keep my mouth shut. It's going to be hard to convince him. I better play nice, so I don't piss him off more. "Alright. School duty it is."

There isn't time to stop in to see Zoey. I'll have to do it between school drop-offs and pickups. After getting into my patrol car, I head to the middle school.

CHAPTER 18

Zoey

When I arrive at the station, I take a moment and count my breaths to calm my nerves. My heart picks up, knowing I'll see Jack soon. My hands grip the steering wheel. He's going to be annoyed that I didn't research my social accounts, but I haven't logged on since I left Chicago. There's so much I'm not ready to face about what I left behind.

With a deep breath, I push forward and take the first step out of my car. I close my eyes and recite what I'm grateful for: Madison is home, and Jack. Since I left his place yesterday morning, I've longed for his presence and the security it brings. I open my eyes. The heaviness of failure weighs on me.

I'm intercepted by Matt, my supervisor. "Hey, Zoey, before you head to your desk, let's have a chat." He pauses and does this annoying short cough. "… In Sergeant Graves's office."

As I silently follow him into the station, my shoulders tense as my concern grows. This can't be good. Sweat pools in my palms.

"Come in. Sit," Sergeant Graves demands. I rub my hands on my thighs and look around at his brown office illuminated by overhead florescent lights. Brown floors, brown filing cabinet. Matt's short cough interrupts my thoughts.

"Sergeant Graves suggested we place you on suspension while Madison's kidnapping investigation is still open," he says, coughing, "and I agree."

He pauses, and I realize Sergeant Graves is waiting for me to say something. "Okay. For how long?" I'm at a loss for words. What am I going to do if I'm not working? My leg bounces in the chair, and I push my hand down on it to stop the nervous tick. This nightmare just keeps continuing.

"Until we find this Ned character and charge him," Sergeant Graves barks. My eyes shift to Matt, and he won't make eye contact. I'm not going to grovel to Sergeant Graves. He won't get the satisfaction of seeing my desperation.

"I understand. If there is anything you need from me, let me know."

"We will," Sergeant Graves responds with a tone laced with skepticism.

It almost seems like a threat. Heat climbs up my neck, and I wiggle my toes so tears don't explode out of me. I stand up and leave his office, not even saying goodbye.

As I make it to my car, I swallow hard, as tears well up when I open my door. This is just great, *fucking* great. The last thing I need is to be stuck sitting around my apartment all day wallowing in self-pity. I turn up the music, so my thoughts don't destroy me.

As I pull into my apartment, I'm filled with a sense of determination to come up with a plan. My steps are steady as I climb the stairs. When I step in and take in the depressing sight of my place, my resolve deteriorates. Tears stream down my face as my knees give way and I fall to the floor.

Slowly, I'm able to count my breaths to gain control. My breathing steadies and I rise to my feet and walk over to my futon. Collapsing on the hard cushion, I sit staring at the wall. As I wipe away the last tears, I remind myself to be logical and make a plan.

First, I need to check my finances and rework my budget now that I don't have a job. I open the laptop, do some calculations, and realize I can make it at least three months before finding another job. I'd like to believe the investigation will be over by then, but Sergeant Graves seems more ego-driven than competent.

I collapse against the futon as I stare at my laptop and think about what I need to do next. My chest tightens and I cross my arms at the thought of opening my social media accounts. The computer screen stares back at me, and I avert my gaze. The dismal sight of my place reignites my determination. If I can identify Ned, Jack can arrest him, and I can put this entire nightmare behind me.

I reach forward and pull the laptop onto my lap as I cross my legs. My eyes close and I take a deep breath. As I open my eyes, I move the cursor to the address bar and type in Facebook. As the page loads, I refuse to look at the feed and see all that I've missed out on.

With a quick movement, I click on my friends list. First, I search for David Slim. Nothing comes up. Hmm. Everyone has social media these days. The only time I didn't have it was when I was with Sam.

My head shakes as I try to block out thoughts of Sam. There's a red circle over the messages. Instead of reviewing all of my friends, I click on my inbox. The first message is from a Max Payne. Who is Max Payne? His parents must have a sense of humor, poor guy.

When I click on the message, my heart skips a beat, and a small gasp escapes my lips.

Sorry about what happened in Chicago. Things will be better for us in West Plains.

A shiver runs down my spine at the cryptic message. Straining my eyes, I examine his profile picture. It's a guy outside with dark hair and sunglasses. I can't tell where. Am I friends with him?

As soon as I click into his profile, my heart races. Where do I know this guy from? I scroll his feed. There's a weird post about lost love and tons of pictures. Lake Michigan, Chicago skyline. I must have known him in Chicago. Probably a Tinder date, one of my many one-night stands. I cringe and swallow down my shame.

I scroll past another weird mumble about lost love and another stream of pictures, this time from St. Louis. The arch, Busch Stadium. Looks like he lived there, too. St. Louis and Chicago are big cities. Someone living in the same place as me is not unexpected.

Scrolling back to the top, I stop cold. My palms grow slick with sweat. *What the hell?* That's the street I lived on in Chicago. That's the building I lived in.

My adrenaline spikes and I slam the computer closed so that I don't freak out. My heart is slamming against my chest. I hear a rattling. What is that? I turn to my door.

Shit. My doorknob is jangling. The thudding of my heart grows so intense that my ears are ringing. *Jack.* I need to call him. I grab my phone and call him. It's ringing. Please pick up. The doorknob shakes more. Pick up, pick up.

"Zoey?"

"Can you come over?" I whisper out.

"Huh? To the dispatch center?"

"No, no. I'm at home. Someone's trying to get in." My breaths are rapid, my hands sweating, and my vision is growing blurry.

"Okay, I'm on my way. Stay on the phone with me. Where are you?"

"I'm on the futon. The doorknob is shaking."

"Go to the bathroom, lock the door. I'll be there in ten minutes, hopefully less. Just stay on the line with me. It's going to be okay. I'll be there soon. Nothing is going to happen to you."

"Okay, I'm in the bathroom. Thank you." My heart is calming, knowing he will be here soon. "No problem. I'm not going to let anything happen to you."

"Zoey? Zoey? Are you home?" I hear a gruff man calling out.

"Wait, someone's calling my name."

"Don't leave the bathroom. Wait for me to get there."

"Zoey? I'm here to fix your bathroom sink. You said it was slow?"

"Oh *shit.* It's just the property manager." Heat climbs up my neck in embarrassment at my overreaction.

"Just wait until I get there so I can make sure."

I open the bathroom door, completely mortified, hanging up on Jack. "Hey, Ed. I totally forgot about that."

"Did I scare you? I didn't think you'd be here. You said I could just come in while you were at work."

"I remember. My plans changed. Please, here, go ahead and fix the sink."

I step out of the way and walk to the futon. As I sit down, I drop my head in my hands and count my breaths: in one, out two, in three, out four. My hands are shaking. Despite my attempts at ignoring the possibility that someone is stalking me, it's time to face the reality. I drop my head in frustration.

"Zoey?! Zoey?!"

Jack's voice echoes into my near empty place as he runs in. My eyes meet his in my doorway. My breath catches. Why does he have to look so good in uniform? The urge to run into his arms is overwhelming. *Dammit.* I turn away.

"I'm fine. It was just the property manager. I forgot that I'd asked him to fix my bathroom sink." I cover my face with my hands. Jack sits next to me.

"So you're okay?" He looks me over.

"Yeah, I'm fine. A little embarrassed?" I shrug sheepishly. Instead of the shame I've been carrying, I'm now consistently embarrassed. Humiliation is becoming a familiar state for me.

"Why aren't you at work?" Jack asks. "I was just making my way back to the station to say hi when you called."

My hands rub against my legs as I try to act unbothered. "I got fired or suspended, whatever."

"Shit. I'm sorry. That's bullshit. You're the best dispatcher this town has ever had."

"Well, Sergeant Graves doesn't want me there until the investigation is over."

"Bastard." Jack's eyes grow dark.

I fall back against the futon. Fatigue is hitting me like a wave now that the adrenaline has passed. Jack's hand covers mine. "Zoey?"

My eyes meet his, and I steady myself for whatever he's about to say.

"Come stay at my place," he pleads. "My place is in the central part of town. There are always people around, coming and going downtown. This place is in the middle of nowhere."

The tension leaves my body as relief washes over me at not being alone. I close my eyes and all the doubts echo in my head as I consider all the reasons staying with Jack is a terrible decision. He squeezes my hand. "Please."

When I open my eyes, I study his handsome face, the care in his eyes. The fear still running through me wins out over my better judgement. I want the safety of Jack's presence.

"Okay."

His face brightens. "Okay?"

"Okay, but I'm sleeping on the couch," I say, pointing at his chest. "Not you. It's your place I'm crashing."

"We'll see." Squeezing my hand again, he stands and looks around. "What do you need?"

"I can pack my bag." I head to my bedroom to pack a bag with a few essentials. In the bathroom, I sidestep Ed to get to my makeup bag, toothbrush, and deodorant.

"I'm heading out, Ed. Can you lock up?"

"You bet. See you later," he says cheerfully.

Jack's waiting for me by the door. "Ready?" he asks with a triumphant smirk. Before I answer, my head turns to scan my place. When I turn back, his arrogance is replaced with concern.

"Yep." As I step up to him, he reaches for my bag, and I pull it back and throw it over my shoulder. "I got it." He mumbles something undecipherable under his breath. I ignore him and walk ahead of him down the stairs and out to my car.

As we reach our cars, he glances at his watch. "I have just enough time to drive with you back to my place before I need to be at the middle school," Jack says casually.

I open my car door and toss my bag into the passenger seat. "Sounds good." He turns and opens his car door. "Jack?" He turns back and leans over the top of his open door and meets my eyes. "Thank you."

As we drive into town, I turn my music up loud so I can't think my way out of this decision. When we arrive in front of his place, I hesitate. My eyes squeeze shut as I grip the steering wheel. My door opens, jolting my attention back to the present.

"Ready?" Jack asks as he reaches his hand out to me.

As always, I ignore his chivalry and grab my bag and step out of my car, forcing him to take a step back. He ignores me too and heads into his building and up the stairs. I follow him up.

"Make yourself at home. I wish I could stay and help you get settled."

"It's fine. I'm fine. I promise." He tilts his head and looks at me, contemplating if I'm okay.

I plop down on the couch, ignoring the tightening of my stomach at the sight of Jack in his uniform, looking at me like that. "Just going to watch *The Walking Dead* all day. I'll see you later."

He stands at the door with his hands in his pockets. "I'm doing my best to be here for you." He looks up at the ceiling. "I wasn't around when all this shit went down in your life." Jack's tone was heavy with resentment. "But if I was, I sure as hell would've been a voice of reason in your life."

He meets my eyes and my stomach churns at what he's left unsaid. That if I'd had a shred of self-respect, I wouldn't be in this dangerous situation.

"And now you have a stalker out there, tormenting you, and I'm not going anywhere until he's behind bars." And with that, Jack abruptly turns and slaps the door frame as he closes it behind him.

As the door shuts, I stare dumbfounded at the space where he was just standing. I lay down and scream into a pillow on his couch. What am I doing here? I roll over and stare at the ceiling. There is no future for Jack and me. He's just doing his job.

A tear rolls down my cheek. Did I ruin my chance of being with him? I didn't mean to shut him out or push him away. Everyone's words are an empty promise to me; my past is always haunting me.

My eyes scan his place, trying to figure out what to do. The dishes are piling up in his sink, so I head over to wash them. The repetition of washing dishes calms me, and I get lost in a memory of walking in on Jack, shirtless, at his sink washing dishes. I bite my lip, remembering his back muscles flexing with each movement.

I was so turned on that I walked up behind him, slid my hands down his pants, and stroked him in time with his scrubbing. My mouth nipped at his back, and he turned quickly and started kissing me, running his wet hands through my hair. A deep, passionate kiss, filling my mouth with his tongue. I pulled back, tugged on his lower lip, and reached down to unbutton his jeans. He growled as I lowered myself to my knees, pulling his jeans down.

Jack dropped his head back, grasped the counter behind him, and moaned my name. I covered the base of him with my hand, sliding up and down as I teased his tip with my tongue. I glanced up at him, and the pleasure on his face heated my core. He filled my mouth, and I bobbed in rhythm with my hand. As he hit the back of my throat, he shook with release.

I smiled up at him, enjoying the pleasure I was giving him. He pulled me up and told me I was beautiful, then lifted me onto the counter, lifted my dress, pulled down my underwear, and returned the favor. My stomach tightens as the memory of Jack in between my legs surfaces. He knows how to please a woman.

As I look down and see the running water, my face grows hot with the realization that I've been washing the same dish. I snap back to the present, finish the dishes, and then head to the couch to watch some of *The Walking Dead* to kill time. After the third episode, I get up to stretch and glance at the time on my phone. Jack will be home soon.

What does he have that I can throw together for dinner? I explore his cabinets. He has some pasta and marinara sauce. Does he have any meat in the fridge? Ground beef. Not ideal, but it'll add more flavor to pasta and sauce. I pull out the pots to get dinner going. The silence has my mind overthinking, so I turn on some music on my phone.

My head is bopping to the music as I pour out the pasta, mix in the sauce and ground beef. It'll do. I smile to myself. Look at me, making dinner again for a guy. As I grab a beer from the fridge, I hear a door shut, and the full beer drops out of my hand. It shatters everywhere. I turn and see Jack by the door.

"Oh my God! I'm so sorry; I'll pick it up right now. I didn't mean to waste a beer. You startled me. I mean, it's not your fault. I'm such a klutz. Can't do anything right."

CHAPTER 19

Jack

I can't move as I watch Zoey's eyes fill with terror as she continues apologizing for dropping a beer. As she bends down to clean it up, tears fall down her face. The sight of her trembling hands trying to pick up the glass snaps me into action.

"Are you okay? What happened? Did Ned contact you again?" I ask as I rush over to her.

When I reach her, she looks at me like a deer in headlights.

"Zoey, Zoey, are you okay?" Her silence has me on high alert, the hairs on the back of my neck standing up.

"Yeah, yeah," her voice shakes. "I'm just so sorry I dropped the beer. I'm cleaning it up."

Her hands tremble as I gently grasp them. "Hey, don't worry about it. I startled you. Let me clean it up." I squeeze her hands. "Please."

She stands, rubs her hands against her thighs as she turns away and cradles her stomach with her arms. I busy myself picking up the large pieces of glass. She's terrified.

"I'm going to go grab my broom. You okay?"

"Yeah, yeah. I'm okay." She responds softly as she glances back at me.

Her face does not match her words. *Dammit.* I'd meant to call her, but I got so busy with school duty, the moms trying to chat with me, then I had to pull over a teen for speeding. My hands grip the broom tightly. I shouldn't have barged in.

As I walk back to the kitchen, my shoulders tense at my carelessness. "Hey, I'm sorry I scared you. I should've called you when I was on my way home. You would've been expecting me."

Understanding reaches her. "No, Jack. No, it wasn't you. I'm sorry. I just ..." Zoey pauses, releasing a breath. "I just forgot where I was for a minute."

Her words fall around me. As I look around, I see she's made us dinner. Did my dishes. *Sam.* Would he get mad if she dropped a beer or didn't have food ready for him? My knuckles turn white around the broom. Is this why she is so reluctant to stay here? I finish cleaning up the broken beer bottle and walk over to her.

"You made me dinner." I smile, keeping my distance.

She shrugs. "I got bored."

"Well, I'm starved. Can we eat? Want another beer?"

I reach into the fridge to grab a beer for myself.

"Maybe wine?" she responds sheepishly.

"Of course, red is behind you, or I have some white open?" She reaches for the red as I hand her a glass and then some bowls.

We head over to my little table and take bites in silence. My mind is drifting to what her life was really like with Sam. Ideas of Sam's reactions to a spilled beer fill my mind as I grip my fork tightly. The terror on her face will stay with me for a long time.

The sooner I can confirm the bastard's actually dead, the better. Because if he's not ...

"How was your day?" Zoey asks, interrupting my spiraling thoughts.

"It was fine. School duty was Sarge's way of putting me in my place." I smirk at her, trying to ease the building tension.

"He's just threatened by you, you know that, right?" She reaches out and places her hand on top of mine.

Our eyes meet, and I'm overwhelmed by the warmth of her hand as I search for something deeper. She's still the most beautiful woman. I shrug. "Maybe."

"Definitely. You're talented. You've got instincts." The smirk on her face reminds me of the last time she was in this kitchen. I need some space before I bust the zipper on my pants.

"Thanks. This is great. You did a great job with the few ingredients I have." I rise to place my bowl in the sink. "I'm going to get in the shower. Leave the dishes for me," I say, looking back at her and pointing at her with my beer in hand. "I mean it."

As I walk away, I hear her heavy sigh, and I'm filled with relief knowing she's safe here. *Dammit.* My dick goes instantly hard when I walk into the bathroom. The sight of Zoey in my shower is permanently etched in my mind. I twist the faucet all the way to the left so that icy water cascades over me as I take a quick shower.

As I enter my bedroom, I stop and grab a pair of sweats to warm myself back up. When I walk out to the living room, I see Zoey curled up on the couch, her back against the arm, with a fresh glass of wine. I smile at how relaxed she looks. It's about damn time. I grab another beer and sit next to her, throwing my arm over the couch toward her.

She places her arm over mine. "Thanks for earlier. I'm sorry I freaked out a little."

My arm lifts over hers, and I run my fingers over a jagged scar on her forearm.

"You know how you said I had good instincts?" I meet her eyes. "Did Sam give you this scar?"

She's holding her breath when she nods. In response, I reach forward and trace a smaller scar on her upper arm.

"And this one?"

She nods silently again as her shoulders sink down. I shift closer, reaching up to trace a scar above her eye. A tear falls.

"And this one."

She pulls her lower lip in and nods. I rub away the tear. "No one is ever going to hurt you again. I promise."

She releases a deep breath as I place my arm back on the top of the couch and take a drink of my beer. We sit in silence.

"It didn't start out bad," Zoey explains.

I see shame in her eyes. "It never does."

"You must think I'm just a dumb girl since I went back to him."

My hand lowers on her arm that's hugging her legs. "I could never think you're dumb. It's never the victim's fault in domestic violence."

Zoey flinches at the mention of domestic violence. Clearly, she was in an abusive relationship, and she blames herself. I've had enough victim training; I should've noticed it earlier. A guilty shudder runs through my body as I take another sip of my beer. I'm the idiot.

She stretches her legs across my lap, and I lower my hand across them. The moment is fragile. My chest tightens as I hope Zoey will open up. This time, I'll be sticking around. No matter what happens. I make a silent promise to always protect her.

"Sam was abusive," she says. I nod and hold space for her. "I've never said that out loud before."

My hand gently squeezes her leg, and the tension releases. "I didn't realize I was in trouble until it was too late. I was in St. Louis alone. I had no friends. No money."

A strand of hair falls loose, and I reach out and tuck it behind her ear. "I don't mean to be guarded with you."

"It's okay. I realize now all the things you've been carrying on your own. The things you've been through, what you've survived. I'm here for you always. I mean it. Promise me you'll always call me if you're scared, in trouble, no matter what. I'll always come to you."

Zoey bites her lip nervously, her expression full of trepidation. She wants to protest, but I shake my head at her. I will not let her push away how I care about her. We sit in silence, sipping our drinks.

"The first time he hit me, I thought it was an accident. We were drunk and fighting. I tried to lighten the mood, and it was the wrong thing to say. He pulled back his arm, and before I knew what was happening, he'd punched me in the jaw."

I force myself to keep my jaw relaxed. The last thing she needs is to deal with my anger. I study her, and she's looking down. I steady my breath and study the coffee table as I wait to see if she continues.

"None of my friends in college ended up liking him. They tried to tell me he was bad news many times. I couldn't see it. I was desperate for his attention. It was all I cared about. I tried to be the girl he wanted, the one he wouldn't get mad at."

Zoey takes a drink of her wine, keeping her eyes on a spot on the floor. While I wait and listen, my chest tightens. Why didn't I try harder to stay in her life? *Pride.* My grip intensifies on my beer bottle.

"When we got to St. Louis, it got bad quick. He insisted I take a job as a copywriter and work from home. I had no reason to leave the house. No way to make friends. I'd burned all the bridges with my college friends. He changed all my social media account passwords and deleted them."

My anger is rising. To distract myself, I focus on the rhythmic motion of softly kneading her foot.

"I wanted to leave. I wanted to leave for so long, but I had no money. He made me use my paycheck to pay all the bills, leaving me with nothing at the end of each month. I was trapped."

I drain my beer in one gulp, trying to wash away my guilt. Never again. I'll prove to her she can trust me to be there for her from now on.

"About two years before he died, I started saving money. It wasn't much. Sometimes only twenty dollars a month. I'd transfer whatever was leftover from our bills to a secret PayPal account. I was always afraid he'd find it, but he never did."

She had to deal with his abuse and plan her escape for two years. Her strength and perseverance leave me in awe. I can't comprehend what Zoey has been through.

"Then one day, I took a train to Chicago and found a shelter. I had fifteen hundred dollars. On that train, I decided I would never live a life like that again. That's why I was so desperate. I couldn't get trapped again."

The urge to tell her I wish she would've called me is overwhelming. My neck tenses. One call, and I would've come. Taken her far away from him, protected her. But, right now, that won't help ease what's she's been through.

"You're the bravest person I know." My hand reaches up and cups her face. She laughs into my palm. "It doesn't feel brave. I feel desperate."

"No, Zoey. It's courage."

She contemplates my words as I hold my breath to see if she'll allow herself to believe them.

"You know what's crazy? What haunts me the most? It's guilt, because I'm glad he's dead."

She studies me to see how I'm going to react. "Then we're going to hell together because I'm happy that asshole is dead, too." *I hope.*

She relaxes then, and I can see she's getting tired. I take her wine and set it on the coffee table. My hands make their way back to her other foot, and I drop my head back as I rub. My heart warms at the possibility of more nights like this with her. Cuddled up on the sofa, talking about life. I hope for better topics, but we must get through the bad stuff to get to the great stuff.

The delicate rhythm of Zoey's snores calms me. As I take in how peaceful she looks, I debate moving her to my bed. I don't want to face the wrath of her in the morning.

I drape a blanket over her, and my heart skips at the spark of hope. She let me in tonight. Allowed me to listen and support her. On light feet, I turn and head to my room. When I enter, I toss off my T-shirt and fall into my bed.

The sunshine pouring into my room wakes me up. Sounds of Zoey up and moving about is the best way to start the day. The intimate moments from last night are making my heart swell. And then immediately anger at her *fucking* ex hits me. I take a few deep breaths to calm down. I'm only looking forward.

But first, coffee. As I walk down the hall to the kitchen, I notice Zoey on the couch. She freezes when our eyes meet. She seems uncertain. *Shit.* She's having second thoughts about confiding in me last night.

"How'd you sleep?" I ask casually.

"You let me take the couch." She gives me a sly grin. "You're finally listening to me."

"I've surrendered." I hold up my hands. "Coffee?"

"I've already had two cups, but there's still some left for you." She nods over to the coffee maker.

As I walk over to grab a mug and pour myself a cup, I can feel her watching me. My eyes drift down my front quickly to check if I'm sporting a morning wood. No. But I also didn't bother throwing on a T-shirt. Am I making her uncomfortable?

I turn around and lean up against the counter. She's biting her lip suggestively. These sweats aren't going to hide her effect on me.

"How long have you been up?" I ask and walk past her quickly to sit next to her on the couch. I grab a pillow and place it over my lap.

"About an hour."

I give a stiff nod. There's a tension in the air. I've got to get out of this house before I do something stupid like pull her on my lap. "Feel like a run?"

"Yeah, too much coffee made me jittery. I could really use a run to burn it off."

"Great, let me finish this, and I'll get dressed. You can use my bedroom to change. Leave in fifteen?"

"Perfect." She bounces down my hall.

My head drops back against the couch. How am I going to keep myself under control around her? At least a run will help for now. It's the perfect distraction from what I want to do with her this morning. A warm smile spreads across my face as I recall our last run together. Chatting about nothing, just enjoying each other's company.

My bedroom door opens and I stand up to see her walking down the hall. She is cute as hell in leggings, an oversized T-shirt, and hair piled in a messy bun on top of her head.

"Give me five minutes, and then I'll be ready." I walk past her quickly so she can't spot my hard-on. When I enter my bedroom, I look down at myself. *Okay. Get it together Moore. Don't ruin this.*

After my quick pep talk and a stop at the bathroom, I'm all set. As I walk down the hall, I see she's sitting waiting for me on the couch. I plop down beside her and knock her leg with mine. "Ready?"

"Let's go," Zoey responds as she stands and grabs my hand, pulling me up.

As we walk out, I turn to lock the door and then watch her bound down the stairs in front of me. In a matter of minutes, we arrive at the trail opening and jog in silence for a while until she breaks it.

"Favorite movie?" she asks.

"Hasn't changed."

"*Top Gun?*"

"You remember?"

"Of course."

"You? Is it still *Mean Girls?*"

Zoey laughs. "I grew out of that phase."

"So?"

"It's cliche."

"Don't care, tell me."

"*The Notebook.*" I'm thinking for a moment, trying to recall that movie.

"I know, lame, right?"

"No, no, I was just trying to remember it. Not sure I've seen it." She huffs and moves on.

"Favorite food?"

I laugh at her changing the subject. "Pizza, always pizza."

"Do you like Chicago-style pizza?"

"No," I respond, shaking my head. "Give me the traditional thin crust."

"You? Chicago or regular?"

"Either is fine for me." She shrugs.

"Well, what's your favorite food?" I ask and turn, shuffling sideways next to her.

"I can't just pick one."

My eyes narrow at her. "Name a few."

"Sushi, pasta, burgers."

I chuckle and jog back alongside her. "That's quite a lot of things."

Silence fills the space between us again. The lighthearted banter is soothing, but my desire to go deeper is building. How is she feeling? Does she regret telling me the details about Sam?

As I'm about to open my mouth, Zoey interrupts me. "Have you had any serious girlfriends?"

My words catch in my throat. I'm stunned by the level of intimacy of her question. "Yes, Sarah."

"Tell me about her."

And again, I'm rendered speechless. Uneasiness fills my stomach. It wouldn't be fair of me to not talk about my past with her after all she shared last night.

"We dated in Nashville for a few years. She's a second-grade teacher. Almost moved in together."

She nods in response. "Did she not want to move to West Plains?"

My throat is dry. If Sarah had moved here, Zoey and I would never have reconnected.

"I never asked her to," I respond solemnly.

She doesn't ask any more questions and my anxiety eases as we turn onto my street.

"Race you to the door!" She yells back at me. Already sprinting off in front of me.

When I arrive, just on her heels, I wrap my arms around her and lift her up. "You're a cheater, you know that?"

"And you're a sweaty animal. Put me down." She laughs as she hits the tops of my shoulders. I drop her on her feet, and she turns and opens the door, heading up the stairs to my place.

Zoey waits for me, tapping her foot as I unlock the door. Ignoring her, I walk in and to the fridge to grab water. I turn around, and she's stretching in a downward dog. *Dammit.* I rub my jaw as I turn back to the fridge.

When I finish chugging the water, I crinkle up the bottle and drop it in the recycling. She's finally standing upright, and I walk over and hand her water. "Mind if I shower first?" I ask. My need for a cold shower is growing. I'll be taking a lot of those while she's staying here.

"Yeah, I was actually going to run back to my place. I forgot my shampoo and conditioner and a few other things."

I smirk at her skeptically, not liking the idea of her going there alone.

"Sorry, but your Head and Shoulders isn't going to cut it for me. I'll go straight there and come right back, promise."

"Can you wait fifteen minutes, and I'll drive you over?"

"Jack, I know I freaked out yesterday, but I can't completely hide out. It'll destroy me." She rubs the scars on her arm, and I know she's thinking about Sam, how controlling he was with her. "I'm coming right back, promise."

She's determined and isn't willing to hide like she did when she was with Sam. I understand that, and if she leaves, I can take a proper shower and take the edge off.

"Okay, but call me if anything seems off. No matter how silly it seems."

CHAPTER 20

Zoey

I close the door to Jack's apartment and lean against it, dropping my head.
Thank God I got out of there. Jack looked so hot this morning in those gray
sweatpants. If I didn't leave, I would've tried to join him in the shower again. My
hands cover my face. *That* would've been an epic disaster.

His ex is a *second-grade teacher*. My arms are suddenly heavy, and they drop to
my sides. He wants a woman who exudes warmth and kindness. Not someone
who is damaged and reckless like me. Embarrassment heats my face as I try to
process the weight of rejection.

I drive to my place feeling hungover and raw with vulnerability. His actions
were so kind and tender; it brings me an immense sense of security. I replay all I
shared about my relationship with Sam last night.

Jack was patient and didn't rush me. He allowed me to go at my pace. For the
first time in a long time, something stirred in my chest, like I was no longer alone
in carrying my past. Last night I fell asleep easily and slept better than I have in
years.

I screwed up things with Jack. It's torture being so close to him. I just want
him to hold me and distract me with his kisses. My hands grip the steering wheel
tightly in frustration. My life is such a mess. As soon as Ned is arrested, I'm
getting out of West Plains. I'll turn myself in and then rebuild my life.

When I walk through the doorway of my apartment, a wave of determination fuels me, and I am certain of my plan to leave West Plains. This *shitty* apartment. What was I thinking trying to build a life here? I grab another set of pajamas and realize that I stink. I'll just take a quick shower here. Then I can shave. I hiss as my hand slides along my prickly leg.

After my shower, I'm refreshed and finish packing quickly. I head out of my place and walk down the stairs to my car. "What the hell?" I inspect my car closely.

Is my tire flat? Just what I need. I stare at it for a moment and glance around to see if anyone can help me. Empty parking lot. *Dammit.* Why do I always have to call him to rescue me? As I unlock my phone to call Jack, I let out a groan.

"Zoey? Is everything okay?" There's unease in his voice.

"Yes, I mean no. Yes. I'm fine, but I have a flat tire." My bag thumps against the asphalt as I drop it next to my car in defeat.

"Are you still outside?"

"Yeah, I'm getting ready to get my spare out and figure out how to change it. I just wanted you to know it will take longer for me to get back."

"No, don't. Get back in your apartment and lock the door. I'll be there in fifteen minutes."

His seriousness puts me off. "What? Don't be ridiculous. I can change a tire." At least, I think I can. That's what YouTube is for, right?

"Zoey, please. I don't want to take any chances. You don't know how your tire went flat. Ned could have done it. Please, just get back to your apartment and lock the door. I'll be there soon. Already climbing into my truck."

My fingernails dug into my palm as I kept myself from outwardly expressing my annoyance. "You're being paranoid."

"Maybe, but you could also be in denial. *Please.*" His pleading sends a chill down my spine. My breath quickens and instinctively I count as I pick up my bag.

"Zoey? You okay?"

As I reach my apartment door, I choose irritation over fear. "Yes. I'm just trying not to rant about what an overprotective pain in my ass you are."

"Well, clearly, you didn't try very hard." He laughs.

As I enter my place, I let out an annoyed sigh. "Okay, I'm in. The door is locked."

"Thank you." The controlled and firm tone in his voice leaves no room for argument.

"Sure. Call me when you're here. I'll make us breakfast."

"Just stay on the line until I get there."

"*Jack*," I groan. "I'm fine. I'll burn the eggs if I'm talking to you."

"Fine. Ten minutes. I'll be there soon."

I shake off the fear threatening to take root. As I open my fridge, I grimace, knowing I don't have much. Well, eggs and toast will have to do. It's all I have.

Just as I finish the eggs, quick knocks thump on my door as my phone buzzes on the counter. Knocking and calling. I roll my eyes as I go let him in, spinning in a circle. "See, I'm fine."

"Yeah, because you listened to me." He smirks as concern clouds his eyes.

I hate that smirk. It's too damn adorable. I turn to put our eggs and toast on plates. I'm starving. "Here, eat first. Then we can change my tire."

Jack looks at me skeptically, and I huff in response. I can help him. I'm not totally useless. He scarfs down the eggs, eager to get out of here. I don't blame him; I am too.

"I'll get started on changing your tire. You have a spare, right?"

"I think so? It's not something I've ever gone searching for."

He rolls his neck, turns, and then walks out of my place with a heavy sigh. Whatever. I clean up my shitty kitchen, grab my bag, and head down to watch him work.

Which is a complete mistake. How can he be sexy changing a tire? I should turn away, but I don't. He's so cute when he's serious. His back muscles flex under his movements. I bite my lip and force myself to focus on what he's saying.

"I know you don't want to hear it, but I don't have a good feeling about this. Ned could have done it," he says, looking up to me for emphasis, "to keep you here."

A deep sigh escapes me as I lean against the car, watching him tighten something in the spare. Jack is being Jack; he is a cop, after all. It's his job to be suspicious, but I can't be always looking over my shoulder.

"I could've run over a nail."

He pauses, shakes his head, and looks up at me. "I looked through the tire, and there isn't a nail anywhere to be found. I can't be certain of what caused it, but if we can take your car to the tire shop, they should be able to tell us the cause and if it can be repaired."

"Can we drop this entire incident until we know more if I agree to go to the tire shop?" I ask as he's loading the tire into my trunk, his arms flexing through his shirt. I turn away so he doesn't catch me staring.

"Yes, until we know what caused it." He slams my trunk and wipes his hands together. "I'll follow you there in case there are any issues with your spare."

I resist the urge to roll my eyes, and hold my gaze steady. "Okay."

As he walks over to his truck, I open my door and slide behind the wheel. I place my hands on the steering wheel and a wave of emotions crashes over me. Fear of Ned, relief at Jack's support, anger at myself. *Shame.*

With a deep breath, I pull out of the parking lot and into town. I turn my music up to drown out my feelings of helplessness.

When I arrive at the tire shop, I pull into a bay behind a couple of cars. Before I can get out, Jack is already walking into the lobby. Naturally, he has to be the one in charge. Is he ever not in cop mode? A vision of him makes my stomach clench. I force the thoughts of screwing Jack out of my mind.

"Hey, they can't get you in for a few hours. It may even be tomorrow. They said they'd try to check out your tire today and get back to me with the cause."

"Looks like you get to be my driver for the day." My shoulders tense as I respond with a shrug, trying to conceal my uneasiness. He walks over, puts his hand on my lower back, and turns me toward his truck.

"Hey, I don't mind. My only plans were to hang out with you at my place."

That's true. We were going to be together all day, anyway. My chest constricts. What the hell are we going to do at his place?

"You're quiet. Are you feeling okay?" Jack asks.

"Yeah, I'm good. Just seems like I can't catch a break." I shrink down in my seat.

He reaches over and squeezes my hand. I can't tell him what I want to say. That I wish we could return to how we were before the calls, that I might be ready to trust him if he's patient with me. I stare out the window as we enter downtown.

He pulls into the parking spot, turns the truck off, and grabs my bag. My body is heavy and drained, so I accept his help. I slowly follow him up the stairs and when we reach his apartment, he opens the door for me. "After you."

When I take my first step in, I hear a splash and I look down. I stepped into a puddle. "What the hell?" There's water all over the floor. I can hear water running. "There's water everywhere."

"*Shit.*" He pushes past me into his place, and I stumble against the door. "The pipe is busted in my hall. Here!" Jack throws my bag into my chest. The force knocks me off balance and I fall to the floor in the building hallway.

"What the actual *FUCK!*" There's a loud bang that follows his yell. "All my stuff is getting ruined!"

As I sit on the floor, my body trembles. His intensity has triggered my body to ready itself for survival, my heart racing with adrenaline. In one, out two, in three, out four. My eyes close as my counting continues. Jack isn't going to hurt me.

As I open my eyes, I stand and step into his place to look around. There's water everywhere. What a mess. I set my bag down on the couch and head to his bathroom to grab towels to soak up the water.

"It's going to take a lot more than the towels I have," he barks out at me, and I flinch. "Right, I know, I'm useless," I mutter as I drop the soaked towels on the ground.

He storms past me into the building hall. He must have turned the water access off because the pouring water ends. As he walks back in, face red with anger, I'm frozen in place.

"I'm calling the landlord to see if we can get a plumber out here to fix it and a restoration crew to clean up the water."

Jack paces behind the sofa, his hand opening and closing into a fist. He seems like he's about to explode. Fear and adrenaline course through my body. We can't stay here. I rub the scar on my arm. We'll just have to go back to my dumpy place.

"The landlord is sending over a plumber, but the restoration guys won't get here for a few days." His tone is brimming with frustration.

"My bad luck is rubbing off on you," I say as I fall back against the couch. "We can go back to my place. I'll take the futon. It's cheap. I don't want you to have to sleep on it. You're already doing so much for me."

His hands land on my shoulders, and I hold back a wince. "We're not going to your place. It's not safe. We can go to the extended stay hotel."

"What? No." I stand up to face him. "Don't be ridiculous; my place is fine." Jack looks at me with pity.

"Zoey, it's scary to think about, but until we learn what happened to your tire, it's not safe at your place."

I sit back on the couch and cross my arms, knowing I'm not going to win this argument. "Fine."

I hear him muttering something as he splashes down the hall to grab his stuff. I wait a few moments and take in all that's happened. Jack isn't going to hurt me. The apartment is trashed; he can be angry about it. My breaths even out. I rub my hands on my legs, rise off the couch, and walk down to his room to grab my other bag.

"You ready?" he asks.

"As ready as I'm going to be," I respond, shrugging.

"That's my girl." That *damn* smirk on his face. I let out a breath and try to ignore the anxiety squeezing my chest.

We splash down the hall and out to his truck. We sit in silence all the way to the hotel. When we pull in, I turn to him.

"Listen, I'll stay here, but why don't you stay with your mom? There's no reason for both of us to stay at a crappy hotel."

He gets out of the truck and doesn't respond. I jump out after him as I watch him walk into the lobby. *Dammit.* Why is he so stubborn? I catch up to him as he approaches the front desk.

"I'd like to book a room for five days." He skips all pleasantries and the front desk clerk busies herself looking at the computer.

Five days? I grab his shoulder to turn him to me as he's putting his credit card down.

"Five days? Really?"

"I'm factoring in a couple of extra days for my repairs. My landlord is always slow to get projects done."

I drop my hand and sigh. He's determined. I'm not going to be changing his mind. I'll play along, so I can rub it in his face when we find out it was a nail and that he is, in fact, being an overprotective ass.

As I follow him to our room, I cringe at the musty smell. He unlocks the door and follows me in. It's old but has a bit of space. A small kitchen, an old couch, and then one bed on the other side of a half wall. Of course. My shoulders tense. I'll be sleeping on that dirty couch. Jack takes my bags and drops them in the closet.

"Not bad for West Plains, Missouri," he says.

Really? I watch Jack plop on the couch and cross his ankles on the coffee table.

"Sure." Dropping my head in defeat, I walk over and sit next to him, only because there is nowhere else to go except the bed. "Now what?" I ask.

He lifts his hands behind his head, contemplating. "Want to stock this place with some booze and snacks?"

"I think this is your first idea that I've actually liked, Jack Moore," I say, elbowing him in the stomach. "Let's go."

I can see his irritation, and I ignore it as I grab my purse and head to the door. He hasn't moved.

"Are you actually going to let me go outside *alone*?"

He drops his feet to the floor and leans his elbows on his knees. *Shit.* I've struck a nerve.

"You think I'm being an overprotective ass?" He says and then takes a deep breath. He's irritated. "But I can't tell if you actually think I'm overreacting, or you just don't care about your own safety."

His words slam into me, and I step back against the door. I watch as he stands up and starts walking toward me. "Do you value your life, Zoey?"

I'm rooted to the spot, too overwhelmed to say a word. Jack is standing right in front of me. "I want to believe you do, but the fact you keep trying to minimize what's going on ... it's like you don't care if anything happens to you."

"I ..." I mumble, releasing a breath. "I don't know." My eyes drop to the floor. I can't look him in the eye. His words are swirling in my head. Is he right? Am I that defeated? His hands cover my shoulders.

"I'm going to do whatever it takes to keep you safe, even if you believe you don't deserve it."

There's a fierce resolve in his eyes. The room is closing in on me. I need to get out of here, away from this conversation.

The muscle in his jaw twitches and he goes still in front of me. My hands are sweating, and I want to run, but I have nowhere to go. I step into him, reaching my hands for his belt and rise to kiss him. He leans into the kiss, exploring my mouth with his tongue.

"Zoey, Zoey." His voice is low and heavy.

Heat rolls up my neck, and my face turns red as he pulls my hands away from his pants and takes a step back. Shame crushes my chest. What is wrong with me?

"I'm sorry. You're here because of your duty, your job. I crossed a line. I'm sorry. I won't." My hands cover my face.

"Jesus, *Zoey!*" His words are like a slap that makes my hands drop.

His hands are behind his head as he turns away from me. I'm paralyzed with humiliation. I watch in slow motion as he turns back to me.

"Is that what you think? That I'm here with you because it's my job?"

My throat is dry, and I can't get any words out, so I nod.

"Fuck."

He paces away from me, hands in his pockets. Panic hits me. I don't know what to do, what to say. I watch as he does a few laps in the small space.

"Zoey," he pauses, and then keeps pacing. My toes wiggle as the tears build behind my eyes. My heart is pounding as I wait for him to speak, afraid of what he might say.

"I don't want to say the wrong thing. You're dealing with a lot right now. I don't want to add more complications to your life."

He pauses and my throat constricts as our eyes meet. "I'm just going to lay it all on the table, okay?" He takes a step toward me, waiting for me to respond.

"Okay," I whisper.

He continues moving toward me. "I've been trying to give you space. Time to process everything. I don't want you to think ..." he swallows, "to think that I only want you for sex."

He's so close to me. We're sharing the air between us. I break eye contact. The silence is deafening as I struggle to respond. I can't make sense of the emotions swirling in me. His hands rise to my face, and he turns my head to face him.

"I love you."

My eyes drop away from him. "No." I can't keep the tears away. They fall down my cheeks into his hands. I shake my head. "You deserve someone better, less damaged." My voice is a low rasp, completely defeated.

His thumbs rub my tears away. "No. I love you. I choose you. Please look at me." Reluctantly, I meet his eyes. "I might not understand how you did those things, but I don't have to. I've accepted what happened in your past. I accept you as you are."

My breath catches. He leans in to press a kiss gently into my mouth. My eyes close. I can't open up to him. I can't. He pulls away.

"I accept all of you, Zoey, and I love you."

I open my eyes and see him. A wave of emotions hits me. Fear. Affection. Anxiety. Love. My entire body tingles with the realization that I don't ever want to be without him.

I nod my head. "Okay."

"Okay." He repeats, leans in, and presses his lips to mine; this time, I let him in. I part my lips and invite his tongue to me with mine. Our tongues dance and explore, and I fall into Jack.

CHAPTER 21

Jack

My hands release from her face, and I embrace her. I don't stop kissing Zoey as I lift her up. She wraps her legs around me and I carry her over to the bed. Then I lean down to take off her shoes, then her socks. Slowly, I grab her pants and panties and pull them down.

I softly start kissing her scars. The one on her shin, then her knee, over to her upper thigh. Gently, I grasp the hem of her shirt and lift it above her head. I kiss the scar on her forearm that I traced last night, then her upper arm. The spot above her eye is warm against my lips before I move down to kiss her tenderly on the mouth. My tongue swipes deep into her mouth as she raises my shirt over my head. I rip it off quickly so that our lips only separate for a moment.

She reaches for my belt, and I stand up, undo my pants, and lower them, watching her take off her bra, taking in how stunning she is. We lock eyes, and I'm filled with hope of a love that can grow between us. I make my way along her body, kissing right below her belly button, then her breast, cupping it and pulling it into my mouth. I clinch her other breast, teasing her nipple between my fingers. Her hands lower down my back as she arches into me.

"Jack?"

My eyes meet hers.

"I need you. I need you inside of me."

The moment is electric as I raise up and trace kisses along her neck and jaw, before our lips meet again and I enter her.

"*Zoey*. You feel so good."

Her breath catches as she wraps her legs around my hips and drags her nails down my back. I moan and thrust deep into her, desperate to get as close as possible to her.

"Jack," she gasps.

Hearing my name on her lips and her rapid breaths are undoing me. I slow my hips and almost pull out of her completely and then gently enter her again, savoring her warmth around me. I surround her with my love with each deliberate slide in and out.

She takes my bottom lip in her mouth, biting gently, and I lose all control and thrust deep into her. If I don't slow down, I'll finish before her. She pushes on my shoulder to roll on top of me. I'm desperate not to lose our connection for even a moment and continue kissing her. I resist as she pulls away. She sits up and grinds back and forth on top of me. I admire her. *Damn.* She's stunning, her head tilted up, back arched, breasts on display.

"Shit," she moans.

She falls forward, closing the distance between our bodies. I wrap my hand around her head and pull her back into an intoxicating kiss. My tongue is desperate, searching her mouth as her tongue matches my movements. I wrap my arms around her, embracing her completely. All the sensations are building within me. She bites and pulls on my bottom lip.

"Zoey," I moan, desperate for release.

She clenches around me and shudders. I thrust once, twice, and explode in release with her. We continue kissing, not wanting the closeness to end. She giggles into my mouth and then drops her head on my shoulder. I keep my arms around her, stroking her back.

"Wow." Her heavy breaths glide along my chest.

"Yeah, wow."

That's what making love with Zoey is like. She slides to the side, draping a leg over me. Not wanting to let her go, I hold her firmly, turn and kiss her forehead.

"I need to pee."

"No," I reply, squeezing her into me.

"Yes," she squeals.

"Fine. But come back." My lips meet her forehead again, and then she rises and kisses me quickly. "I will, promise."

I clasp my hands behind my head and stare at the ceiling. My heart is whole. My eyes close and I replay the last twenty minutes.

A noise wakes me. My eyes open and see the oddly pink wallpaper on the hotel room wall. As my mind makes sense of the space, my heart quickens as I think about making love to Zoey. I roll over and reach my arm out. Panic breaks me when I notice the bed is empty. Did she freak out again and run?

"Zoey?" I scramble out of bed, trying to find my boxers. "Zoey?"

"Hey, sleepyhead." She's in my T-shirt, walking over to sit next to me on the bed. She leans down and gives me a kiss, and my heart explodes. I pull her into the bed and give her a deep kiss, full of my relief and love for her.

She giggles into my mouth. "We still have no food."

"So?"

"I'm starving," she whines. Reluctantly, my arms release her and drop to the bed. Our eyes meet and my chest tightens. There's a spark growing in her eyes.

"Fine." I get up out of bed to get dressed and clear my throat. "You're wearing my shirt."

"Oh, yeah." I watch as she rips it over her head and tosses it at me. "Here you go." She's standing naked in front of me. All perky breasts and hard nipples.

"If you don't get dressed as quickly as possible, I won't be able to leave," I grit out. My hands ball into fists as she mocks horror and puts her hands on her hips. I dart toward her to wrap myself around her and pull her back into the bed. She dashes to the side, dropping her head back and laughing as she gets dressed.

"Ready yet?" she asks with an evil grin.

"Are you mocking me?"

"Maybe?"

"Yeah, let's go." I say and grab her hand, pulling her out of the hotel room.

As we drive to the store, my shoulders relax and I tap my fingers on the steering wheel to the music. Tension releases from me. I've finally told Zoey how much she means to me. And she accepted it, unlike when I confessed my love to her in college.

I glance at her, and I'm full of satisfaction. The drastic difference between Zoey over the last four months and right now makes me feel invincible. Her fun, playful side is resurfacing and I'm bringing it out of her. I'm determined to protect our relationship fiercely and eliminate any threats.

My palms are clammy as I grip the steering wheel. We made love; it was incredible. But he's still out there. *We're not safe.*

"Hey, did you hear me, Jack? Should we make a game out of shopping?"

Shit. I should pay attention to driving. "What do you mean?"

"We have fifteen minutes, and we must shop for the other. Get all our favorite foods and drinks, see what we remember about each other from the good old days."

My grip loosens on the steering wheel at the lightheartedness of her tone. With a deep breath, I push away my thoughts of him.

I smirk, challenging her. "You're on."

"Okay, time starts when we walk through the door."

We enter the store laughing as we both hit the timer on our phones. Zoey runs. *Shit.* Focus. My eyes scan the store, and I spot the candy aisle. She always had a pack of Starburst on her during high school. As I snatch up a bag of Starburst, I also grab a bag of Twizzlers—her second favorite candy.

When I leave the candy aisle, I spot the alcohol and dash to grab some wine. It's not a favorite from high school, but she likes to unwind with a glass now. Zoey's hair catches my eye as she darts out of the freezer aisle and I jump behind an end cap before she can see me. What else do I need? Cookie dough, Ritz crackers, bubble gum ice cream.

As I run past the deli section, I stop and grab a meat and cheese platter. We'll be sick if we only eat junk. The crackers and cookie dough are easy to find. Last on my list is bubble gum ice cream. I pace back and forth in front of the ice cream section, straining to read all the labels. *Dammit.* Bubble gum ice cream was her ultimate favorite. I always teased her about how gross it was.

"Finally!"

I buzz with disbelief. With my basket full, I stand in the aisle, wondering if there is anything else I should grab. Before I make my next move, I glance at my phone. *Shit*, out of time. As I reach the checkout line, I spot Zoey one lane over.

"Hey, no peeking," she pouts.

My head tilts to the ceiling as I laugh. Despite all that's going on, I cherish her amusement. We both finish at the same time and walk out of the store. When we get to my truck, I try to take her bags to load them, but she pulls them out of my reach.

"I said no peeking," she warns.

My hands raise in innocence as we climb into the truck, laughing. I can't take my eyes off of her as she buckles up. "What?"

"It's nice to see you smiling, having a little fun. It's been awhile." I swallow down the thoughts that are trying to surface of why she hasn't been herself. She reaches over and grabs my hand. As we ride back in silence, hands intertwined, my heart might explode.

When we pull into the hotel parking lot, I discreetly do a scan of our surroundings. I release her hand and step out of the truck. My senses are on high alert as I pull out my groceries. Quickly, I walk over to Zoey and follow closely as she walks into the hotel.

My body relaxes, knowing we've made it back to safety with no signs that anything is amiss. We step into our room, and she's still coy. "Alright, missy, let's see how you did."

Her eyes light up and her nose crinkles as she pulls out the beer I always have stocked at my house. "Easy," I respond, putting my hands on my hips.

She rolls her eyes, hands me one, and then puts the rest of the six-pack in the fridge. I'm astonished as she pulls out peanut M&Ms, Doritos, beef jerky, Fanta, and a frozen pizza. She remembered all my favorites from high school. The realization that our friendship was meaningful to her during high school hits me like a wave.

"What? You didn't think I paid attention, did you?" I step forward and draw her into a hug, words escaping me. She pulls away. "Now your turn."

I start with the Ritz crackers because that's all she ate for lunch in high school, which I never understood. She laughs as I toss her the bag of Starburst.

"Yes! My favorite." She beams at me.

Next comes the cookie dough and Twizzlers. Then I make a big show of dragging the bubble gum ice cream out of my bag.

"No way! Okay, you win. I can't believe you remembered and could find it," she says, slapping me on the shoulder.

"I know, I'm just that good." I say with a wink. "Let me get the pizza started. Why don't you go find something for us to watch? I'll bring over our spread."

She bounces over to the couch and raises her feet onto the coffee table, smiling. I'm not sure my heart will survive this night of witnessing Zoey return to herself.

"I picked up some wine, too. Want a glass, or a beer?"

"Wine, please."

I bring over our drinks, then take the two steps back to load up on the crackers and meat and cheese platter.

"An appetizer before our feast." Setting the food on the coffee table, I take a sip of my beer. "Find anything?"

"Well, there's the news, *Sports Center*, or I found *The Notebook*. It's just starting." She side glances at me, waiting for my reaction.

"It's your favorite. How could we not? Let's watch it."

"Really?" I see shock and excitement on her face.

"Why the hell not?"

Zoey sinks into the couch, taking a bite out of a makeshift cracker, meat, and cheese sandwich. We sit close together, watching the movie and munching on our junk food feast. Once we're full, she lies her head on my lap. I'm content and don't even care that I'm watching some cheesy romantic movie. Her breaths slow under my arm. She's asleep. My heart is full, and I can't remember a time when I was this hopeful. Once the movie is over, I wake her gently.

"Hey, let's go to bed."

"I fell asleep?" Her eyes hardly open.

"Yeah, you did. You left me high and dry watching *The Notebook*."

She gives me a sleepy smile. "Did you like it?"

I rub my chin. "I like it because it's your favorite movie."

A sleepy laugh escapes her as she rises and heads to the bathroom. We brush our teeth next to each other; it's natural, and I want to spend the rest of my life with evenings like this. I kiss her on top of her head and make my way to the bed, sliding out of my clothes and lying down in my boxers.

As Zoey undresses, I make a fist into the bed to contain my arousal. She slides an oversized T-shirt with the Chicago flag across her chest and climbs into bed next to me. My hand relaxes as she slides close to me, laying her head on my shoulder and her leg over my waist.

"Thank you, Jack. For today. It's been ..." I gently stroke her back as she tries to find words. "It's nice to forget all that's happened for a night. And you've shown me how it's supposed to be. To feel." She lets out a deep breath. "To feel loved. Thank you."

I kiss her, and the words fall around us as I take in the significance. Never again. My jaw tightens as anger brews, and then my shoulders tense as the wave of guilt crashes over me. I'm not losing Zoey again. Her breaths slow and mine follow. I fall asleep.

CHAPTER 22

Zoey

Jack's alarm wakes me, and I savor the warmth of his arm around my waist. I lean into his chest, allowing myself to be at home and safe in his arms. Then I roll over and snuggle up face-to-face with him. He's sleeping hard, and it's adorable. As his alarm rings, I kiss his cheek, lips, and other cheek, trying to get him to wake.

He responds by pulling me in tight and pressing his hips into me. I'm pleasantly surprised at his hardness against me. He leans in and kisses me deeply. As I let him pour his love into me, my chest tightens, and I'm overwhelmed by his strength. My body stiffens, as panic rises at how vulnerable I've let myself become with him.

"Hey, hey." He opens his eyes to me. "You okay?"

He could shatter my heart. As a vice grip forms around my chest, I count. In one, out two, in three, out four. My body slowly relaxes in his embrace.

"Are you counting?" he asks softly.

Stunned, my eyes meet his. "Yeah. It's something I do when I'm anxious or overwhelmed. It helps me clear my head."

He pulls away from me. "Are you okay?" he asks, concerned. The urge to run hits me and I sit up to get out of bed. Before I can stand, he reaches and covers my hand. "Zoey?"

My body goes rigid as I force myself to stay in bed. The last twenty-four hours were incredible. The way Jack loves and supports me, despite everything I've done. I've never felt that. But he could also hurt me deeply, so much that I don't think I could come back from it.

"Please don't push me away. Everything I said last night, I truly meant. I love you. I've accepted your past. Our future is all that matters to me."

My body resists as I turn to him. Fear laces his eyes, and my heart breaks. My head knows that he wouldn't hurt me. He's kind and generous, and he loves me. It's my heart that needs to catch up.

"I want that too. I do. It's just ..."

His hand pushes a strand of hair behind my ear. "That's all I need to know." He kisses my temple and gets out of bed. When I open my eyes, I watch his bare back as he goes to the bathroom. Damn, he's sexy. Today will be a long, lonely day while he's on shift.

I get up to make us some coffee. The room is a mess with our leftover junk food feast. As I clean up, the panic fades, and I think of him watching *The Notebook* alone.

"What's got you smiling?"

My eyes scan Jack as he tucks in his uniform shirt. *Dammit.* Why does he have to be so irresistible? I bite my lip.

"Don't do that. It'll really piss off Sarge if I'm late." He says with heat in his eyes.

"Sorry." I bite my lip again, and he drags me into a hug.

"I don't want to leave you today, and you're making it impossible right now."

I reach around and grab his ass. "Does it help if I tell you I really want you to stay?"

He drops his chin on the top of my head. "No," he growls.

I maneuver my way out of his embrace. "Okay, I won't then. Get out of here," I say with a forced scowl on my face.

"Not convincing enough."

I shrug and turn, trying to figure out what I'll put together for breakfast. There's nothing. "Do you have time to eat breakfast quickly in the lobby?"

He glances at his watch. "Yeah, a quick one."

"Good." I reach up, kiss him, and pull on some sweats.

As we leave the room, I grab his hand, and we walk down to the lobby. We're living in a bubble, and I don't want it to end. After eating watery eggs and soggy bacon, he walks me back to our room.

"Listen, I don't want you leaving today." He follows me into the room. "I'm serious. Keep the door locked, the chain on."

I study the determination on his face and the bubble pops. This isn't a time for teasing.

"I will. Promise. Don't you worry about me while you're working."

"I'll call and check in throughout the day," he says with his stern cop voice.

My arms wrap around his waist as I step into him. "Okay."

"I know today will suck for you, being alone here all day. I'll come home as soon as my shift is over." His tone softens.

"I'll be fine. I'll finish watching *The Walking Dead*. There's five episodes left. Then, maybe I'll start *Breaking Bad*."

Jack leans down and kisses me; I part my mouth to let him in. I fall into his consuming embrace, imprinting my memories with how safe I feel with him. Reluctantly, I pull away. "Go, so you're not late."

"Okay. I'll talk to you soon."

"Bye." I stand and stare at the closed door for a minute before turning the deadbolt and putting the chain in place. As I turn around, the depressing sight of the room deflates me. Shower. Then *The Walking Dead*.

In the middle of my third episode, there's a knock at the door. I look at my phone. I just spoke to Jack thirty minutes ago, and he didn't mention he'd be stopping by. Probably housekeeping. The Do Not Disturb sign is on the door, so I don't move, knowing they'll move on in a minute.

The knock happens again, harder this time. "Zoey?" I hear a muffled voice. Fear shoots down my spine. I pick up my phone and stare at it, hesitating to call Jack. Conflict stirs in my stomach. I don't want to worry him. Let me check who's at the door first. The knocking continues as I look through the peephole.

On the other side of the door is an older, round man holding a vase full of flowers. Did Jack send me flowers? That's over the top, even for him. I chew on my lip and then look again. "Zoey?" the man says and knocks again.

Jack doesn't need to woo me. My hands sweat as I unlock the door and remove the chain. It's just a flower delivery. I let out a deep breath and open the door.

"Zoey?"

"Yeah, that's me," I say as I reach for the flowers.

"You're not wearing what you said you'd be wearing," he says as his brows furrow on his oily face.

"What?" The room grows icy as fear travels down my spine. I move to push the door shut, but he blocks my way by placing his foot in the doorway.

"You sent me a picture of what you had on." He reaches into his pocket, and I push the door harder. He pulls out his phone, almost tipping the water out of the vase.

"What?" My voice is barely a whisper.

"Don't play games with me. You told me to come over, that you were waiting for me. You sent me a picture of yourself."

My heart races as he holds up a screenshot of the video of me, and I'm unable to move. *Shit.* The cold air around me sends a chill through me, and I take a step back.

"You've been chatting with me all night, teasing me with all that you would do to me. You told me you couldn't wait to meet me in person. This is you."

He's shoving the phone in my face. "I brought the flowers, like you asked." His voice is rising in frustration.

"There's been a mistake," I stutter out.

"What do you mean? I can pull up all our messages on Facebook."

Ned. Anger rises. "Listen, I didn't send you any messages, and if you don't leave, I'm calling the cops right now."

"Woah, woah. There's no reason to call the cops." I glance down and see a wedding band on his hand. Disgusting pig.

"I mean it. Leave now and don't ever contact me again, or I'm calling the cops and your wife will find out what you've been up to."

The man's face reddens, and I push the door hard, shoving his foot out of the way. I lock it quickly and try to get the chain back on with my trembling hands.

My stomach churns as I pace the small room. I'm infuriated, embarrassed. And then my body gives way to the weight of shame as I collapse onto the couch. I'm never going to get away from that video. It's going to haunt me for the rest of my life. What am I doing? Pretending I can have a future and build a life with Jack? That's never going to happen.

No matter what he says, my past will always be a part of my future. *Fuck.* I drop my head into my hands and my body shakes as I sob. Get. It. Together. This is not the time for a breakdown.

After a moment of collecting myself, I reach for my phone on the coffee table and wipe the tears from my face. It's heavy in my hand as I stare at it. I need to call Jack. He'd want to know about this. But he'd come over in the middle of his shift. He can't piss off Sergeant Graves right now.

The knot in my throat grows. I need to call the police. My grip tightens on the phone as I realize I'll be detailing the encounter to Sergeant Graves. I run to the bathroom as my stomach lurches.

My body collapses on the disgusting floor, and I heave my breakfast into the toilet. When I stop convulsing, I lean back against the wall. I'm completely drained. My head pulses with exhaustion as I stare at my phone on the ground next to me.

When I bring the phone to my hand and open it to dial the station, my stomach clenches again. My phone clatters against the floor as I dry heave into the toilet. I can't do it. Tears stream down my face as I grab my phone and stand.

My legs are heavy as I walk to the bed. I won't answer the door again. My head lies on the pillow, and I smell Jack all around me. My eyes squeeze shut. The old man did not fit Ned's description. I can tell him when he gets off his shift. My stomach cramps, and my head pounds as the flurry of emotions torments my body. I curl up in a ball and fall asleep.

The buzzing of my phone wakes me; it's Jack. Checking in again. I take a deep breath and answer.

"Hey," I answer with a mumbled voice.

"Zoey? Are you okay?" Concern laces Jack's words.

"Yeah, I'm fine. You just woke me up," I respond softly.

"Oh. Sorry. Oh shit. I've gotta go. Some kid just sped by. I'll call you when I get back to the hotel so you can let me in."

"Sounds good," I mutter.

The phone slides out of my hands, and I roll onto my back and stare at the ceiling. Devastation sits heavy on my chest. I can't do this with him. I don't know how long I've been staring at the ceiling when I finally grow tired of my self-loathing and rise to go back to the couch.

I turn on *The Walking Dead*. My mind numbs as I stare at the screen. I don't even notice time has passed as my phone buzzes again. *Jack.*

"Hey."

"I'm outside our room; let me in. I can't wait to get my arms around you."

"Coming." When I open it, we're still on the phone together, and he's picking me up in a hug.

"This is what I've been dying to do all day." He pulls back and kisses me desperately, completely.

My stomach churns as my dread resurfaces. He senses my unease and holds me back. "Hey, are you okay?"

My heart breaks as I turn away from him. Nausea takes hold. I can't bring the words to the surface to tell him what happened. The humiliation is choking me. Will this ever end? I step into the small kitchen.

"Yeah, I'm just tired. Everything is just catching up to me. Hungry? We still have leftovers from last night."

"I am, but I want to shower first." He raises his eyebrows at me. "Have you showered yet?"

I give him a small smile. "Yeah. You go. I'll get the food set up. A buffet of junk food."

As he enters the bathroom, I can't pull my eyes from his ass in his tight uniform pants. I cover my face with my hands and hold in a sob. Swallowing hard to steady my determination, I step into the kitchen. After the leftover pizza is re-heated, I take a plate to the couch, trying to appear like I'm eating.

As I stare off into space, my tension releases. He makes all my fear about Ned, my past, tolerable. His presence, his love, gives me hope. The conflict in me explodes to the surface as I catch Jack walking in his gray sweats, no shirt, out of the corner of my eye. Warmth floods my core, my toes wiggle as tears well up in me.

"What's wrong?" Jack rushes over to me.

He's alarmed, and by my side before I can even react. "Did something happen today? Why didn't you call me?"

I shake my head. "I can't. I can't do this with you. My, my past. It's too much." Words and tears are pouring out of me. "The things I've done, they're awful. They'll follow me always. They won't stay in my past."

"Zoey, shh. Take a breath. Breathe." His chest is against my face as I struggle to catch my breath. "Breathe. One, two, three, four." He's trying to help me calm down. I can't help but slow my breath and relax into him. His comfort and tenderness are exactly what I crave, and I'm safe. He pulls back.

"You've been through a lot of shit. Done a lot of things that you're ashamed of. I don't expect you to be okay overnight. I expect you to have good days and bad days." He tucks a hair behind my ear. "And I'm going to be by your side, *always.*"

His strength wraps around me. My breaths even as I realize I'm falling in love with him. I'd do anything for him, even share what I'm most ashamed of.

"Someone came by today," I whisper.

"What? Why didn't you call me?" He stands up quickly in the small space and looks down at me. I shiver at the shock of his sudden absence around me. My eyes meet his pleading eyes. I can do this.

"It was awful. I opened the door. I know I said I wouldn't, but I thought you sent me flowers. I thought the guy was a flower delivery guy."

He looks around to see if he missed a vase full of flowers. "What did they look like? Did you open the door? Tell me every detail."

"It wasn't a flower delivery." I steady myself, building the courage to share what happened. "The guy, the guy came here to have sex with me."

Jack goes entirely still. The muscles in his jaw twitch as tension radiates off of him. "What do you mean?" he grits out.

"He, he had a—," I choke back the tears. "He had a screenshot from that video. And he said I'd been chatting with him all night and promised to wear that outfit when he came over if he brought me flowers. He said I promised to have sex with him."

He's suddenly an explosion of pacing movement. "When? When did this happen?"

"Just before noon. This wouldn't be happening if I didn't make that video. I'm such a fool." I drop my head in my hands.

"This isn't your fault. Don't blame yourself. Why didn't you call me right away?"

The words are stuck in my throat. "We talked in the afternoon. Why didn't you tell me?"

He's angry with me. I'm struggling to keep my fear under control, my body trembling with the effort. "I didn't want you to worry while you were at work. Be distracted. I knew you'd come here. I didn't want you to get in trouble for visiting me on shift."

"Jesus fucking Christ, Zoey! I don't care about my fucking job. I care about you!"

Jack's staring at me, his face red and eyes hard. I flinch, fear wins out and I shake. My hands are sweating. The room is closing in on me.

"Oh, shit." His voice is full of remorse.

As fast as he was up, he's back down next to me. "Hey." He hesitates to touch me. "I'm sorry. I'm not angry with you. It's this *fucker*, Ned." Jack lowers his hands over mine. I'm struggling to breathe again. His hand moves in slow circles on my back.

"I really screwed up. I shouldn't have lashed out like that."

I stare at the floor. My emotions are all over the place. When will my body stop reacting to anger in such a way? The hold that Sam still has on my life leaves me defeated. Shame chokes me. I'm so stupid. I'm mortified that I made that video, knowing it will follow me forever. My entire being longs for Jack.

When our eyes meet, I collapse into his arms, wishing his love had the power to make this all go away. My throat goes dry with defeat, knowing that his love won't be enough. He doesn't really understand what a future with me will be like.

Hot tears fall down my cheeks. Why am I always crying in front of him? Isn't he sick of me yet? Despite my tumultuous state, I let him draw me nearer to him.

CHAPTER 23

Jack

My arms hold Zoey firmly as regret consumes me. How could I lose control? The minute I turned to her, I realized she was terrified of what I would do next. That *bastard* Sam. What I wouldn't give to beat the shit out of him. How could a man treat a woman like that? It's beyond comprehension. Words tumble out of me.

"I'm terrified of something happening to you. I mean it. You're the most important thing to me in the world. My life, before you came back, was empty. I'd lost purpose. I was going through the motions, miserable. When you came back into my life, you brought me back. There's a reason for me to dream again and pursue something greater. I hate it here. I always have. Half of a life—that's what I've settled for. Who I am when I'm with you is who I want to be. I want us to get out of West Plains and build a life together. Get back to those dreams we had when we were teenagers."

She twists in my arms and slides onto my lap. My chest is heavy. Is she trying to escape the moment? She raises her hands to my face.

"Even if I'm a rollercoaster of emotions? I don't know how long it'll take me."

"I love rollercoasters," I interrupt her. "Especially yours."

"I don't deserve you. I don't." She's leaning down and kissing me gently, then desperately. My arms wrap around her in a tight embrace. We need to talk about the incident earlier and what I learned about her tire, but I don't move.

A defeated sigh escapes me as she pulls away. "So, my day was shit. How was yours?"

"Shit, too. Sergeant is really pushing my limits of tolerance."

"Then you need a beer, and we can talk more about the creepy old married man looking for sex online." My admiration for her resilience causes a lump to form in my throat.

"Sounds good, because I also need to tell you about your tire."

Zoey pauses as she nears the fridge. "I'll get wine too."

Pain between my eyes pulses as I process the situation. My fingers massage my temples as I try to calm myself. She's in real danger. He's escalating. Impersonating her, sending men after her? What did he want by doing that? I'd feel a lot better if I could just get her out of town, but Sergeant is an asshole and still considers her a possible accomplice.

I meet Zoey in the small kitchen and grab some food off the plate she laid out. This is going to be a tricky conversation.

"I really hope I was right about the nail?" she says as she hands me a beer.

My eyes hold hers as to convey the seriousness of what I'm about to say. "Your tire was slashed."

"Shit." Her face loses color.

"He's escalating quickly."

She takes a shaky drink of her wine.

"And now, he knows you're here, and knows your room number. He knew you'd be alone, impersonating you online, sending someone to taunt you with that video and sex."

My grip tightens on the beer bottle as she processes all that I've just said. My hand reaches out to hers and I lead her to the couch. "This is serious. You're in real danger."

Zoey silently sits down on the couch, her back stiff. Her breaths quicken. Instinctively, I reach my arm around her. "I'm not leaving your side again until Ned's locked up. I'm calling in, quitting if I have to."

The muscles in my neck throb as I try to mask the desperation in my voice. I'm running out of time. There isn't anything I can do to speed the investigation along, or to increase her protection. It's just me and zero resources. Her head snaps at me.

"Jack, no. You can't put your life on hold for me. You can't lose your job."

I squeeze her in tight to my side. "I meant what I said. You're my life, my future. I don't want this fucking job. I'm happy to walk away and take you with me."

She reaches up and puts her hand on my cheek. I melt into her touch, turn to kiss her palm and tell her, "I love you."

"I can't hide again." She drops her hand and stares helplessly at a spot on the floor. With a gentle tug, I pull her back into me, not wanting to let go.

"I know." The promise that this will be over soon is stuck in my throat. I'm unsure right now. My confidence is fading. My hand strokes the side of her arm as we sit in silence.

We need to concentrate on the information that I already have. *Shit.* I left my notes at my place. *Dammit.* And I just got back to Zoey. A knot forms in my stomach.

"Are you ready to talk more about what happened earlier? I want to get a full picture and take notes to file a police report," I say, ignoring that I'll need to go back to my place to get my notes.

She nods and pulls away from my embrace. "I can."

As I reach for my bag and pull out my notebook and pen, I ready myself for a description. "Tell me about this guy." I say, my jaw tight with disgust. "Can you describe him?"

"Yeah. He was old, maybe late fifties or early sixties. He wasn't tall, and he was overweight. Gross, oily. He had a comb-over." She grimaces as she describes the man.

"And you've never seen him before?"

"No. I'd remember his appearance." She rubs her hands on her thighs.

"Okay, what about the flowers? What kind were they?"

"They were those cheap ones like you'd get at a gas station, but they were in a vase, so they'd look fancy. Wait, wait. Not a vase, a glass jar. I should've noticed when I saw them. They weren't something you would send me." Zoey shakes and drops her head into her hands. "I'm such an idiot."

He's clever. He had the old man use flowers to motivate her to open the door. I place my hand on her back. "No, you're not. You're being tormented and stalked. That's a lot to endure." I pause and rub circles on her back.

"What about what he said? He said you'd promised him sex?" I growl, not able to hide my primal urge to protect her.

She looks at me, pain in her eyes. She doesn't want to talk to me about this. "It's okay. You're the victim here. Take your time." I continue rubbing her back while I wait for her to speak and push away my fury at this bastard for what he's putting us through.

"He told me I wasn't wearing what I said I would be. He was expecting me to wear what I was wearing in that video." She swallows hard, as I continue slow circles on her back. I steady the pen I'm gripping tightly so I don't put a rip in the paper.

"I was confused, and that's when he showed me a screenshot of the video." Her voice trails off as she squeezes her eyes shut. I reach my hand up and massage some of the tension out of her neck.

"Then he said I'd been chatting with him all night on Facebook and promised him sex if he came to my room and brought flowers."

Her eyes open, and she lets out a breath. "That's it. Then I told him I was going to call the cops, and he freaked and left."

"This is good."

Her words hit me like a ton of bricks, and I need a moment to collect my thoughts. I knew he had to be impersonating her online. That he had to know that we were at this hotel and our room number, but hearing how he's using that video to continue to humiliate her ... my stomach cramps. This isn't good. I don't like these facts.

"I want to go on your Facebook and see if it's been hacked or if the messages were from a fake profile with your info."

Zoey's hands shake as she hides her face. "Okay."

She stands to get her laptop and anger ignites in me. Last night seems like a world away.

She sits back down and opens her laptop and pulls up Facebook. We stare at her page as she slowly scrolls, and nothing looks alarming. "Let's check your messages."

She stiffens next to me. "What is it?"

"I've got another message from this, Max Payne."

"Who's Max Payne?" I ask. My neck rolls as I learn about another detail Zoey has ignored.

"I don't know. I totally forgot to tell you about him. His first message came right before everything with the property manager happened. It was creepy, and he had a picture of my building in Chicago in his feed."

I watch as she clicks open the new message. We both freeze entirely.

We'll be together soon.

"What was the other message he sent?" I ask, and she clicks on it.

Sorry about what happened in Chicago. Things will be better for us in West Plains.

"I don't like how he uses *us*." I clip my words.

"Yeah, it gave me the shivers the first time I read it. I'm so sorry that I forgot to tell you. Everything's just been so crazy this week. It's all jumbling together."

I tuck a lock of hair behind her ear as I try to mask my regret. It's me that's distracted. Anxiety churns in my stomach. What if my incompetence causes me to lose Zoey?

"It's okay. You're doing great. I'm amazed you can talk about everything with such clarity."

I kiss her forehead. "So brave." My focus is back on the screen. "What about his feed? You said he had a picture of your building."

She clicks on her profile. "Shit," she whispers.

The laptop is shaking in her lap. "That's the antique shop below your *place*, Jack."

"Yeah, it is. This Max Payne has to be Ned."

I close the laptop and set it on the coffee table, taking her hands in mine to soothe her. Her face transforms with terror as she accepts the reality that she is being stalked.

"I know this is scary, but it's good. It means he's coming out of the shadows. He wants us to know he's near, and if he's near, then I can get to him."

I pull her onto my lap. "I mean it. We're sticking together." My words linger in the silence, and I hold her tight.

"This is enough for tonight." She nods against my chest. We sit in silence for a moment, and I soak in her warmth. I need a distraction before I spiral with anger.

"Need more wine? I could use another beer."

She nods again as she slides off my lap. Her weight shifts and the warmth of her body leaves mine. As I stand, I grab her glass to get us refills. The tension is thick with my anger and her fear. I'm desperate to change the energy and return to last night's playfulness.

"Let's find something to watch," I tell her as I sit on the couch. "But I'm picking tonight."

"Only if it's a romantic comedy," she teases.

"That was a one-and-done. Don't get used to it." I smirk at her.

She relaxes and leans up against the arm of the couch as I'm clicking through the channels. "Oh yeah, *Top Gun*."

I pull her feet into my lap and begin rubbing them to work out the emotions from tonight, for her and myself. Every few minutes, I steal a glance at her to see if her defenses are going up again. Each time I confirm she's relaxed against the couch, I let out a breath. When she finally starts nodding off, I turn off the TV.

"Let's go to bed," I say and she responds with a sleepy smile.

We repeat the routine from last night and my body relaxes at the normalcy. We climb into bed together, and I bring her body against mine. She leans up and kisses me gently and then parts her mouth. In return, I open myself to her, welcoming her tongue to explore me. My dick hardens as our tongues continue their familiar dance.

As much as I want to make love to her, the day's events have left me exhausted. After I give her a squeeze, I draw back and place my hand on her cheek. "I love you." I kiss her forehead before she tucks herself into my chest. We fall asleep to the rhythm of our breaths.

CHAPTER 24

Zoey

I wake up to sunshine and Jack's arm over me, holding me close. His warmth envelops me with a sense of peace. Despite all that's going on, I finally have hope for a different future. He pulls me closer and my ass rubs up against his hardness. Surprised by the sudden tightening in my stomach, I roll my ass a little into him and pull his hand over my breast.

"Mmm, good morning," he mumbles.

I roll over and snuggle into him, throwing my leg over him and pressing my hips into him, creating friction on his hardness. "Good morning."

I tilt up and kiss him gently. Jack moans into the kiss and presses his hips into me. My need to hold him is overwhelming, and I slip my hand down between us and into his boxers to grasp his hard smoothness in my hand. I palm the length of him, lowering down to cup his balls. I slide my hand up, tickle his tip, and slide down to grasp his balls again.

"*Fuck*, Zoey," he gasps into our kisses, and I giggle.

His kisses intensify, and he reaches for my T-shirt to pull it over my head. I gasp as my breasts press against his warm chest. He reaches down and grabs my ass before sliding his hand firmly up my side and palming my breast. Kneading and teasing my nipple while rocking into my hand that's still stroking him. I tug on his lower lip with my teeth.

"You're going to be the end of me."

"That's the plan."

I kiss his chin, then along his jaw and down his neck. I continue down the center of his chest, and he moves his hands to the back of my neck, fisting my hair. His hips lift into my chest as I reach his belly button. I slide my tongue down along his trail of hair as I pull his boxers down.

He releases my hair and grasps the sheets next to him. I smile as I bring him into my hand and lick the tip. He moans as I drag my tongue down to the base. I continue lower and pull one of his balls into my mouth and tease it with my tongue. Jack growls.

"*Fuck.*"

I move to the other and do the same as I continue stroking his length. He moans in response and then I take him fully in my mouth, bobbing a few times before I lift to make my way back to his mouth. I stop on the way, lowering my breasts around his hardness and squeeze him between them and slide up and down.

"*Zoey.*"

His hands are back in my hair as he looks down to see himself covered between my breasts. I lick his tip and climb up, and before I can get to him, he flips me onto my back, lowering down to return the teasing. I gasp as his tongue teases my bundle of nerves.

"*Jack.*"

He lowers his tongue through me, and the intensity throws my hips up while I rock up and down on his face. The need to have him inside me explodes. I pull him up, forcing him to look up at me. "In me, now."

The hunger in his eyes almost does me in, and I drop my head back as he thrusts into me. How can this all be real? I lift my legs around his waist and wrap my arms around his neck. Small moans escape my lips with each deep thrust.

I'm completely lost in the moment, in Jack. Our eyes meet, and the intensity threatens to overpower me. There's a vulnerability to looking into his eyes that leaves me completely exposed. And then his head drops back in release. The passion of his last thrust puts me over the edge, and I shake with him.

He lowers and gently kisses me, filling me with love. "Can we wake up like that every day?" he asks breathlessly.

"I'm not opposed." I smile into the kiss. Jack drops beside me, draping his arm over me. My chest tightens and then releases. It's scary as hell, but it also feels like this is where I am always meant to be—with Jack.

"Coffee?" He interrupts my thoughts.

"Do we have to get up?" I'm not ready to return to the reality of stalkers and dingy hotel rooms. My eyes close and I snuggle up to him. He leans down and kisses the top of my head.

"Yes, but you stay. I'll make your coffee and bring it to you." He rolls away from me. "And don't you dare get dressed."

I watch his naked ass walk out to make us coffee. My head drops back, and my cheeks hurt from smiling. I slide off the bed to pee and then climb back in and anxiously wait for Jack to return, with a strange sense of anticipation that I can't quite explain.

The anxiety isn't desperate and pain-filled. My heart is full of hope. I bring the sheet over my head and take a deep breath. The crushing loneliness I've been carrying is fading. These past few days have been hell. The weight of all my secrets has lifted and I have a new sense of clarity.

My legs kick a little as a small squeal escapes me. My shame isn't all-consuming anymore. I'm still aware of it, yet I'm determined to move on and leave it behind. Trust again. Be happy again. As he walks back in, a wave of joy washes over me.

"I can't help but be a little nervous that you listened to me." He hands me a coffee with a skeptical face. I sit up, still bare from this morning.

"Don't get used to it," I say and narrow my eyes at him.

"Trust me, I know better." He leans in and kisses me on the forehead.

We lean against the headboard and drink our coffee in silence. I'm holding onto this moment for as long as I can. With each sip of coffee, a knot in my stomach grows at the uncertainty of the day ahead. If it's anything like the last few days, it will be a nightmare. My head drops to his shoulder.

"Are you sure we can't stay like this all day? In this shitty bed, with scratchy sheets?"

"There is nothing more that I want to do, but we need to keep working through the details of everything. I'm ready to put this all behind us, and to do that, we need to identify who Ned is." There is an edge of irritation to his voice.

"Uhh. You're right." I turn to kiss his shoulder. "I'm going to take a shower. Then let's go eat some shitty breakfast."

I leave him sitting on the bed, staring at the wall while drinking his coffee. He's troubled. His usual confident disposition is faltering.

As I get dressed after the shower, I try not to let fear creep in, taking a moment to count my breaths. The last thing I want is for Jack to grow even more anxious about everything. When I step into the small living space, he is in those damn gray sweats and a T-shirt. "Ready?" he asks flatly.

"Yeah, let's go eat some shitty eggs." I try to keep my eyes bright as I take in the grimness of his demeanor.

As we leave the room, I entwine my fingers with his, wrap my other arm around his, and drop my head to him as we walk. I'm holding onto the safety he brings me. I flinch inwardly, dreading the moment something will bring my guard up again.

Jack steps up to the buffet and fills his plate. He's been quieter than usual this morning. I follow him to a small table with my plate of runny eggs.

"Is everything okay? You're pretty quiet this morning."

"I've got a lot on my mind," he responds without meeting my eyes.

"Oh."

I sit back and stiffen, insecure that he's changing his mind about everything. He reaches to place his hand on top of mine. "Not about us. The way I feel about you, that's not changing."

My grip tightens around my mug as I take a sip of coffee.

"I'm on edge because we're running out of time," he says.

My throat tightens, and I force myself to swallow. Deep down, I know he's right. "Do you want to go somewhere else?"

I feel like I'm drowning and need to regain control of my life. He shakes his head.

"Leaving here won't help. Ned's tracking you. Knowing he knows where you are gives us an edge."

I let out a breath, relieved to not be running and trying to find a new hiding spot. Done with my breakfast, I rise. "What's the plan for today, then?" I ask as Jack follows, grabbing my hand as we return to our room.

"Can I ask you more specific questions about what you remember about David Slim? I hope it will uncover some clues we didn't see before." His voice is distant, troubled.

I turn into his arms as he closes our room door. "Okay, detective. I'll do my best."

He reaches down and kisses me while palming my ass. I soak in the moment of peace, knowing that things are about to get complicated. A whimper escapes me as he steps away and sits on the couch.

"This is going to be over soon. I promise." Determination and anger darken his face.

My heart takes his assurance and warms as I sit next to him, propping my legs on the coffee table. I chew on my bottom lip and rub my hands on my legs. "I hope so. What do you want to know?"

He squeezes my hand before picking up the notepad he was writing notes on last night. "What was David like?"

I take a moment to recall those fuzzy nights of talking to him.

"Well, he was kind. Easy to talk to. It was like we were in our own little bubble around the noise of a party."

"Anything stand out to you about who he was? Any specific life events?"

I side glance at Jack. He's all serious and professional. I suppress the urge to lean in and kiss him.

"I remember we were both from small towns. He was in Iowa, and I was in Missouri, obviously. We discussed how small towns didn't allow space for bigger dreams."

He nods beside me. He understands. We spent hours as teens talking about different big cities we'd love to live in.

"What about his family? Did he ever talk about them?"

"Yeah, I remember we bonded over both being an only child."

His brow furrows. He's concentrating, and it takes every ounce of control not to slide onto his lap and kiss him. I'm desperate for a distraction, to forget why we're having this conversation.

"Can you think back to your interactions with David? Did you ever sense that it changed?" He's not breaking from his role as an investigator.

I chew on my bottom lip and remember the nights we were talking and making out before Sam, and then the few times I remember after Sam and I got together. A memory of that one time we were in a booth at that dive bar slams into me.

"This one time, he brought up the possibility of us dating. I remember he said something like he and I would be like oil and water; never would've worked out."

I try to remember the details of how he acted that night. It was different. He seemed agitated. Jack is listening to me patiently, not wanting to rush me.

"He was a bit off. We were in a booth, and he was against the wall. He pushed me out of the booth, and I almost fell when I stood."

Jack's presence is calming, allowing me to focus on the details.

"This is good info. Did he ever send you texts, or emails, or contact you outside of late-night talks?"

"No." I sigh. "Wait!" I sit forward. "One time, he fixed my phone for me. I'd left it on a bar and a beer spilled all over it. He worked some sort of magic on it to get it working again."

Jack nods as a flash of concern crosses his face, and then it's gone. He looks toward the door.

"Have you ever felt like anyone was following you? College? St. Louis? Chicago?" His voice is becoming increasingly tense.

"No, I can't say if I've ever had that feeling. Did you figure out if he lived in Chicago?"

"No, I haven't found anything on him in the last three years. But he's the best lead we have. That's why I'm focused on everything you can remember about your relationship with him. See if any memories give some insights into him." A muscle twitches in his jaw as his knuckles grow white from gripping the pen in his hand.

"Okay," I respond softly.

"You're sure you've never felt like someone was watching you? In Chicago, did you go to a gym or bars regularly?"

I've always been on edge since I left St. Louis. I close my eyes and take a deep breath, frowning.

"No, nothing stands out," I say, defeated.

"You're doing great. Really." Jack squeezes my leg. As I look at him, he leans over to kiss my forehead. My heart flutters.

"I'd like to move on, to more recently. Outside of this Max Payne profile, any additional strange online messages or contact?"

My hands rub back and forth on my thighs as I think through the creepy profile and messages.

"No. I've been off social media for months," I respond sheepishly. "And before, I was always more focused on the image I was curating than interacting with anyone. If someone tried, I didn't notice."

A pain pierces my chest. I was so stupid. All the desperate things I did in Chicago to build a life that would be the opposite of my life with Sam. I sink into myself.

Jack senses my growing unease and draws me into him. "I think this is enough for now. You've given me some additional details about David. I want to compare them to my notes from my research on him."

I close my eyes, breathe deeply, and push out my thoughts of running away from him. My body relaxes into him as he kisses the top of my head. I'm not sure how long Jack holds me.

"Zoey?"

He meets my eyes with apprehension. My stomach twists.

"I need to go back over to my place. Something's nagging at me and I left all my notes on David there."

I slide onto his lap, not wanting him to leave. My head bends to kiss him, and he opens his mouth to my tongue. I explore his mouth and grind into his lap. He hardens beneath me as he grabs my ass. His hands glide up my back under my shirt. I sigh into him, welcoming the distraction. My hips rock into him harder, slow and deliberate.

"Zoey." He pulls away from me, and I pout down at him. "I really don't want to go. I mean, really." He pumps up into me.

"I can't help this nagging feeling that there's something I'm missing. I need to grab the notes, and I'll be back here. Thirty minutes tops."

I rock my hips again. "Thirty minutes? Promise?"

"I promise," he responds hoarsely and leans in to kiss me thoroughly, sealing his promise.

"Okay." I step off him, dropping my eyes to the bulge in his pants. I can't help the grin forming.

"You think it's funny? Huh?" Reaching to grab me, he pulls me into a hug. "I'm going to make you pay for this later. I'll have you begging, pleading for me." He kisses me on the forehead. I grab his ass in response.

"Is that a threat?"

"It is." Jack returns my ass grab by palming mine and squeezing roughly.

"Now, I know I do not need to say it, but do not open this door. No matter what. If anything freaks you out, just call Nine-One-One. Then call me. Got it?"

"I'm not opening the door for anyone but you, promise."

"I'll be back before you know it."

Jack turns and gives me another kiss and then heads out the door. I lock it and put the chain in place.

CHAPTER 25

Jack

As I turn down the hall, my hands clench and unclench on the way to the parking lot. *Fuck.* I hate leaving Zoey right now, but I can't shake the feeling there's a critical clue in my notes. I slam my truck door. Why didn't I grab them when packing for the hotel?

I concentrate on the road ahead, pushing the speed limit as I race to my place. The last thing I need is any delay. My stomach has been uneasy since I woke up this morning.

He's growing desperate. My knuckles turn white as I squeeze the steering wheel tight, thinking about that creep coming to the hotel room for sex.

"*Fuck!*"

My palm slams onto the steering wheel. I have to get to David and put an end to this. We need a lead that will help me track him down. This has gone on long enough. A rush of emotions hits me. I knew that when she finally opened up to me, our connection would be unbreakable.

Zoey watched me all morning. As distracted as I was thinking about finding David, I couldn't help but hope that she was falling in love with me. Her trust in me is growing stronger. I refuse to let anything stand in the way of making that happen.

Nothing else matters right now but our relationship. Throwing my truck in park, my body is humming with energy. My phone vibrates in my pocket. *Shit.* Zoey. I pull it out, annoyed to see it's my mom.

"Hey, Mom."

I take the stairs to my place two at a time.

"Hi. Are you okay? You never called me again to plan dinner." Her voice raises.

My teeth clench. *Shit.* "I'm really sorry. Sarge has me working school duty, so I've been slammed."

I get to my door, unlock it, and take in the leak's aftermath. This is going to take a while to get cleaned up.

"You're not still hanging out with Zoey, are you? She's only trouble."

I'm pacing now, anxious to get off the phone with her.

"I really wish you'd stay out of the town gossip. You don't have the full story."

"Well, I wouldn't have to rely on the town's gossip if my *son* would keep me informed." I cringe in response to her chastising tone.

"Point taken. I hate to let you go, but there was a water leak at my place. I'm trying to get it cleaned up."

"A water leak, really? How bad is it? Do you need to come stay with me for a few days?" she asks.

"It's not great. But, no, I got a room at the extended stay." I bite back my annoyance.

"What? Why would you do that? You're always welcome at home." Pain radiates from her voice.

My grip tightens on the phone. I turn to stare at my notes on the table. "I know, Mom. My hours are crazy, and I didn't want to trouble you."

"You're no trouble. Why don't you check out of the hotel and come stay with me? I'll make us dinner tonight," she pleads.

"By tonight, I should be back. I'm just finishing up cleaning now. I really need to go so I can get it all done. Can I call you next week?"

"Okay." She lets out a sigh. "I miss you. Promise we'll do dinner soon."

I shake off the guilt she's trying to burden me with. "Promise. Love you."

My hand runs through my hair, trying to soothe the exhaustion from the conversation. I look down at the notes. What is it that's pulling at me? I shift the notes into a pile, and that's when I see it. David had a little brother. Patrick Slim. It was what Zoey said about him being an only child—he isn't.

David's younger brother died when he was six in a drowning accident at a lake. David pulled him out of the lake and tried to save him. He was nine. That's what is troubling me. David could use Patrick's identity. He'd have access to his social security number to create an identification and get a job, rent a place, buy a car. I can't believe I didn't check out Patrick's history when I learned David had a brother.

I need to run a background check. See if any vehicles, apartments, or jobs are in his name. Anything that could link David point to where he is hiding out. I see my phone.

"Shit!"

I've been gone for twenty minutes. Mom really slowed me down. I call Zoey.

"Hey. How are you?" I ask breathlessly.

"Hi. I'm good. *You?*" I hear unease in her voice.

"I'm good, but listen. David had a brother, Patrick. He died when they were kids. I want to run a background check on him and see if anything comes up."

"He never mentioned a brother. Could this be the lead we need?"

Zoey's hope radiates through the phone. My shoulders ache as I force myself to keep my focus.

"I think so. Are you good if I run to the station? It means I'll probably be at least another half hour before I'm back."

"Yeah, go. It's fine. No one is getting in this room, and if anyone comes, I'll dial Nine-One-One."

"Okay. I'll call you when I get back to the hotel. We're close. It's almost over. I love you."

I hang up and rush out to my truck. As I speed over to the station, my stomach twists. I'll have to manage Sergeant. It doesn't matter. I'm right about this. I'll prove it to him.

As soon as I hop out of my truck, I'm running. I burst through the station doors and head over to my desk.

"Woah, woah. Moore. What's the rush? Isn't this your day off?" Sergeant barks at me.

"Hey, Sarge. Yeah, it is, but I have a lead on Ned. I want to check it out."

"You're not on the case."

"On the kidnapping case. But I've been looking into who is stalking Zoey. I think it's that guy from college, David Slim."

"Don't play semantics with me. Don't go messing up this investigation for us."

My jaw tightens with a force that may just crack my teeth. I ignore him and turn to my computer and type Patrick Slim into the records search. I wait as it's processed, pressing my fists into the desk. Fucking hurry.

"Yes! I found him!"

"What, Moore?"

"Look, I found him. This Patrick Slim here; he's dead. But he has an ID, a vehicle registered to him. He even got a parking ticket for staying overnight in the Walmart parking lot. Three days ago."

"Let me look at that," Sergeant commands.

"It's him, has to be. David Slim's brother Patrick died when they were kids. He's been using his identity for the last three years. Fuck, yeah!"

"It's possible," Sarge responds skeptically.

Bastard.

"Can you put out an APB on his vehicle? Let's find this asshole and arrest him."

"Don't get ahead of yourself, Moore. We'll put out an APB, but he still needs to be questioned, linked to all of this."

"You got it, Sarge." I slap him on the shoulder.

I wait to see that he announces the APB over the radio. And then I'm out the door when I hear him call after me.

"Where are you going?!"

I don't answer as I climb into my truck and make my way back to Zoey. Despite the urge to call her, I hold back. I don't want to be distracted speeding through town. My palm slams on my steering wheel.

"Fuck, yeah! It's almost over!"

Adrenaline is rushing through me as I imagine our future. Waking up each day and making love to her like I did this morning. Showers with her torturing me by playfully teasing and washing herself. Cuddles on the couch, watching more romantic comedies because I won't be able to say no to her. I'm full of emotion at the possibility of what's next for us.

As I pull into the hotel parking lot, my entire body warms at the future I've envisioned. I jump out of the truck and start running toward the entrance.

Bang.

I look around. "What the fuck?" I put my hand to my shoulder and pull it away. Is that blood? What the hell? I've been shot. I fall to my knees. The world goes black.

CHAPTER 26

Zoey

I recheck my phone. It's been forty-five minutes since Jack called. He said he would be back in about thirty minutes. Panic pierces my chest. I'm freaking out and restless. I get up and pace the small room. Fifteen minutes isn't that much time. Chewing on my lip, I don't have a good feeling. *Fuck it.* I'm calling him.

No answer. Dread lands in my stomach like a rock. That's not like him. I call again. Nothing. My heart is racing, and my palms are sweating. Having a meltdown isn't going to help things. My steps are frantic as I pace the small space.

I pick up my phone and call him again. Just before I turn around at the door, I hear a buzzing and a rattle at the door handle. *Jack.* The pain in my chest eases as my trembling hands fumble to undo the chain. I'm ready to jump into his arms as I throw the door open.

My phone slips out of my hand, and the thud on the floor unlocks a memory.

I'm pressed against the rough brick wall as David's fingers dig into my arms, his face twisted in rage. We're in a dark alley as I try to explain to him that Sam and I are exclusive. A sharp pain in my wrist brings me back to the present. I'm staring at that same twisted face.

The world slows. My eyes drift to David's hand clamped around my wrist as he drags me back into the hotel room. My feet trip underneath me and my heart is racing. The only sound I can hear is my pulse thundering in my ears.

My body crashes onto the couch, and I am instantly aware of my surroundings. David is standing over me, a gun in his hand at his side. My throat constricts. *Jack.* Where's Jack? No, no, no. That loud bang I heard moments ago was a gunshot. *Fuck.*

I'm trembling uncontrollably with adrenaline as fear threatens to consume me. *Get. Your. Shit. Together.* I rub my hands against my thighs and look up at David. His eyes are dark with rage.

"David?" I whisper.

"Hi Zoey," he responds.

He takes a step toward me, and his eyes soften. It takes every ounce of my control not to flinch at the movement.

"You don't need to be afraid of me." His voice is eerily calm. "I'm here to save you."

The sensation of my throat closing in on itself causes me to swallow hard. My eyes close as I focus on my breaths. In one, out two, in three.

"ZOEY!" David's voice echoes through the room.

My eyes spring open. He wants me helpless, needing him. I give up trying to hide my fear and let my body tremble.

"I'm not the threat to you," he says, taking a step back. "You're safe with me." His head tilts as his lips curl into a cruel smile.

In one, out two. *Play along.* In three, out four. *Let him believe you want him too.* In five, out six. *I can do this.*

"Okay." My eyes meet his and I force my body to relax. "But I don't really like guns and ..." I glance down at the gun at his side. "You're holding one. That's making me a little scared."

David raises the gun up and looks at it in his hand. He lets out a deep breath and then his head drops. "Jack pushed me to do this. If you'd just stopped trying so hard to make me jealous by being with him, then we wouldn't be here right now."

David takes the gun and tucks it in his pants behind him. "Better?" he asks, putting up his empty hands in front of him. I nod in response silently. "Good." He looks around the room.

"Well, we don't have to worry about Jack anymore," he says with finality, and my hands tremble as I place them under my legs.

My chest constricts, and the pain is so great I might pass out. *No.* I refuse to believe it. My body threatens to collapse with relief as the sound of sirens fills the room, signaling help is on the way.

And then I see pure hatred on David's face. "We should go," I blurt out and stand up, taking a step toward the door. David's hand grabs my hair and pulls me back.

"Where do you think you're going?" he seethes into my ear.

"We need to leave before they come to my room. If we hurry, we can make it out the back door." Pain from his grasp shoots through my body, down to my toes.

I have to get him out of this room. Jack said there was an APB out for his car. If we just leave this room, someone will stop us. The sudden release of my hair forces my body forward, and I land on my hands and knees.

"Get the fuck up. We're going." David's voice coils around my chest, constricting my breaths.

I scramble up, and my vision blurs. David's hand on my arm yanks me forward as the door opens. And then I'm collapsing to the ground as a deafening shot blasts around me.

The ringing in my ears is disorienting. I try to focus on what's happening. Suddenly, a body hits the ground next to me. David's empty eyes are staring at me as blood pools in his mouth. My stomach lurches.

"Jack?" My voice is soft. "Jack?" I force out. A sob escapes me as my eyes search the room and land on Jack laying on the ground in the hall.

"Oh my God! Jack!" I cry out and crawl toward him. Before I reach him, a paramedic appears and turns him onto his back. Blood covering his shoulder. A gasp escapes me.

"Zoey, are you hurt? Zoey?" Sergeant Graves asks, and I flinch when his hand grasps my arm.

"No. No. I'm fine. Help Jack." I force my voice to be strong. I can't breathe. Counting isn't working. In one, out. In one. I can't get to two. There are voices around me, but I can't understand what they're saying. Arms surround me, lifting me. "Jack?"

I open my eyes, but no. It's not Jack. It's Sergeant Graves guiding me down the hall. "I want to go to the hospital."

My voice is trembling, and my hands are shaking. I'm in shock. Jack's been shot. Oh my God. Oh my God. "We will. In just a minute. Let me get you some water and then we'll go, I promise."

I take a shaky drink of water and set the glass on the front desk counter. "Can we go now?"

"Yeah, let's go. I'll drive you myself."

Sergeant Graves guides me out the doors, unsure if my legs will hold me. I don't know if they will either. He has an arm around my shoulder and guides me to his car. Everything is a blur.

I'm in his police cruiser. Red and blue lights flash in my vision, overwhelming my senses. And then we stop. We've made it to the hospital.

"Okay. Let's get you in there and checked out. Jack's in surgery right now."

I nod my head. Surgery. Oh my God. My breathing is intensifying.

"Hey, hey. That means he's alive."

He's alive. Okay, he's alive. I can't make out any details of the hospital as Sergeant Graves guides me through the entrance, into an elevator, and onto a floor. He pushes down on my shoulder and I realize there's a chair behind me to sit in.

I'm in shock. My mind is blank. I can't move. I vaguely sense officers coming to sit next to me. People are talking to me, but I don't hear anything. Jack. Not Jack.

Tears fall down my cheeks. I never told Jack that I love him. I never said to him I loved him back. That I want a future with him too, to chase new dreams with him. How could I not tell him? What if I never get the chance to tell him? I drop my head into my hands and shudder with sobs.

I'm not sure how much time passes. It must be hours. I hear that he's out of surgery but not awake yet.

"Is he going to be okay?" I ask into the room. I can't comprehend who is with me. Someone grabs my hand. I turn, and it's Andy. Loud Andy.

"Is he going to be okay?"

He puts his arm around me. "The surgery went well. Now we just need to wait for him to wake up. He lost a lot of blood."

Andy's tone puzzles me. I've never heard him speak so softly.

"Can I go see him?"

"His mom is with him now." Andy squeezes my shoulder.

"Oh." I stare at a spot on the floor.

"When do they think he'll wake up?"

"They're not sure. He just needs time for his body to heal."

My hands rub over my thighs. I wish I could crawl out of my skin. The waiting is killing me. I stand up to pace. The room comes into focus. The wood and teal vinyl chairs. I'm in a waiting room. Willy and some other officers are chatting. I can hear Sergeant Graves, but not see him. He must be in the hall. A strange wallpaper in shades of blue, purple, and pink covers the walls.

"He can't die. He's going to be okay. Jack's strong."

I'm talking to myself now, still trying to figure out what to do. All my resolve, my strength to get through any crisis, is gone. This past week has been the worst of my life, and Jack has been by my side through all of it. He's been my strength. Oh, God. He's got to be okay. I see Sergeant Graves walk in.

"Zoey, can we talk for a minute? It's about the case. Feel up to it?"

No. I don't. But I'm helpless right now, and it's killing me. I need to do something. "Sure."

"Let's step out to the hall." I follow Sergeant Graves out of the waiting room. Clearly, the week's been hell for him, too. He looks like shit. He turns around to face me.

"Jack was right about David Slim. We found evidence in his car linking him to Madison's kidnapping and stalking you."

Sergeant Graves looks to the floor. All bravado has left him.

"So, it's over? You arrested David?"

"No, I mean, yes. It's over because David is dead. Jack shot him just before we got there," he says.

Silence stretches between us. I wait for the relief to come that this nightmare is truly over. It doesn't come. I just want to see Jack.

"I'm trying to get Jack's mom allow you to go see him. He'd want you in there. She's just protective, and with everything, you know."

He shrugs and looks away again.

"All that everyone knows about me. Yeah, I get it. I appreciate you trying."

I save him from having to spell out all the terrible things I've done. The mess I've made of myself. I turn and head back into the waiting room and sit next to Andy.

"Jack's mom doesn't want me in his room."

"Well, that's bullshit." Andy's voice rises, and eyes around the room look at him.

I warm, appreciating his high volume. Yeah, it is bullshit. I just want to see him. Hold his hand. Tell him I love him, even if he can't hear me. I sit with Andy. We take turns getting coffee for each other. Fatigue is taking over, and I should eat something, but I can't bring myself to leave.

The smell of pizza catches my attention. Sally's brought us all pizza, her way of getting involved in the situation, no doubt. Reluctantly, I grab a slice and force myself to swallow a few bites. I watch in astonishment as Andy houses three slices in the time it's taking me to make it halfway through one slice.

"Zoey?" Sergeant Graves says and steps in front of me. I stand immediately and hand Andy my half-eaten slice.

"He's waking up and asking for you. Come with me. I'll take you to his room."

I'm floating as I walk down the hall, following Sergeant Graves. He's awake, and he's asking for me. Of course he is. A rush of emotions floods me; I wiggle my toes as I walk. I'm not going to go in there crying. Jack needs me to be strong.

As I turn into his room, I choke on a sob. He looks terrible. There are so many tubes coming out of him. His mom is in a chair next to him, glaring up at me, clearly not thrilled that he's asking to see me. I don't care. He is awake. I walk over, pick up his hand, bring it up, and kiss it.

"Hi."

Jack's face scrunches as I realize he's trying to smile at me, but it comes out like a painful grimace.

"Don't talk."

I pull his hand to my chest and cover it with mine. Dammit. A tear falls down my face. Jack has a matching one. I realize he's just as relieved to see me as I am to see him. He must've thought that David had gotten to me.

"I'm okay. You saved me. David didn't get to me."

I bring his hand to my cheek and kiss his palm.

"Jack needs his rest. Maybe you should come back tomorrow."

I watch Jack slowly turn his head toward his mom and croak out.

"No. She stays."

The effort it takes for him to speak to his mom causes me to cringe. I steal a glance at her, not meeting her eyes that are piercing me like daggers. My focus returns to him. Strong, generous, tender Jack. I lean forward, put my hand on his face, and whisper in his ear.

"I love you."

I press a kiss to his cheek and wipe away another of his tears.

"You saved me. Not just from David. You saved *me.*"

I kiss him again on his cheek before pulling away. And then I stand at his side, not letting go of his hand. I'll stand here all night. I don't care what his mom thinks. She can stay in the only chair in the room. She does not know how hard I will fight for him. I watch him turn back to his mom.

"Go home, get rest," Jack says, his voice barely a raspy whisper.

My heart cracks at the effort it takes to speak to her. I watch her shake her head.

"I can't leave you." Tears roll down her cheeks. I get it. Jack is all she has. The thought of losing him would leave her all alone. I know exactly how she feels.

"Can we take shifts, Mrs. Moore?"

She looks up at me and makes eye contact.

"He's going to need a lot of support. It won't do him any good if we're both exhausted."

Jack nods slightly at his mom.

"You've been here all day. I can take tonight's shift, and I'll leave and get some rest when you come back in the morning."

I hold my breath, waiting for her to answer. She watches Jack trying to talk, pain covering his face.

"He really needs us at our best, Mrs. Moore. Please? Let's work as a team."

"Okay. I'll be here first thing in the morning," she warns.

I release a deep breath. "I'm counting on it."

She leans forward and kisses Jack on the forehead. The tension in the room leaves with her. I go to sit in the chair and grab his hand, holding it tight. A painful grimace of a smile appears on his face.

"You love me?"

"Shh. You shouldn't be talking right now." I give him my best you're in trouble face. I can't hold it. My mouth meets his dry lips. "Yes, Jack Moore. I love you."

As I sit back, his eyes close, and his grimacing smile is still on his face. His face softens, and he falls asleep. Watching the rise and fall of his chest, I realize I've loved him for quite some time.

Memories of that first night come back to me. When I slid on his lap to avoid answering questions. The rush of arousal for him entirely shocked me. His kiss was so different from high school. That night, it was like I was coming home. Jack was the missing piece of me.

I fall asleep in the night and wake up to Mrs. Moore shaking my shoulder. As promised, I kiss Jack good-bye and let her take her shift. When I return at night, Jack's awake. His grimace looks more smile than pain now. The color is returning to him.

"He's had a good day. They're happy with his progress. Tomorrow, they want him out of bed, walking, sitting up."

"I like the sound of that." I smile down at him. "I'll see you in the morning," I say to his mom, dismissing her.

Once his mom leaves, I lean over and kiss him. He parts his lips slightly. I smile at him.

"I didn't hear your mom talk about you being cleared for sex."

His chest rises with a chuckle and then coughs with pain. I raise to his forehead and kiss him. "Too much, too soon."

"Never."

I sit down, smiling at him. Full of love. It's over. It's all over, and we get to move forward.

"Did you say something to me yesterday? It's all kinda fuzzy."

I glare at him skeptically, and he gives me a grimace of innocence. He's not fooling me.

"I love you."

"Oh yeah, that's what it was. I love you too."

I hold his hand tight and tell him to get some rest. As he closes his eyes, I lean back and take in the peaceful expression on his face.

The days continue in a steady rhythm. Mrs. Moore helps him walk the halls during the day. And I try to keep myself busy, helping to put his place back together as I wait for my shift. At night, I move him from his bed to the chair and then back to the bed. Mrs. Moore is warming to me, but we haven't moved past updates on Jack's progress.

On the third day, I can't stand being away any longer and I arrive early. Sergeant Graves is in his room.

"Do you remember anything from when you pulled into the parking lot?" he's asking Jack as I walk in. Jack's sitting up in his bed, chin high, not wanting his boss to see him as weak.

"No, I was in a rush to get back to Zoey." He glances around Sergeant Graves and meets my eyes.

Sergeant Graves turns around and nods at me.

"Did the front desk clerk see anything?" Jack asks.

"No, they called Nine-One-One when they heard the gunshot, but then hid behind the desk."

"Is Jack in trouble?" My voice rises in disbelief.

"No, there's plenty of evidence that proves David is guilty, and no evidence that Jack's actions weren't justified. This is just a formality," Sergeant Graves reassures me. "And I think I have enough. Jack, get some rest."

He pauses and studies me for a minute and then turns and walks out of the room. Jack pats the side of his bed. "Come here. I need you close." His face is stricken.

"Are you okay? In pain?" I ask as I take the few steps and sit sideways on his bed.

"No, I just miss you while you're gone." He pulls my hand up to his mouth and kisses it. I lean down and kiss him in return.

Jack's mom clears her throat from the doorway. "You're here early," she grumbles.

"Mom, give it a rest."

She stops in the doorway for a moment. "Alright then, I'll just get my things and be on my way. I know when I'm not needed."

I watch in silence as she gathers her things. Any affection she may have toward me, instantly gone.

The next morning, Jack's mom and I are back to quick exchanges. And with each passing day, I arrive earlier and earlier. A week to the day of his shooting, I walk in, and they're talking about going home.

"What's this? You get to go home?"

"They say tomorrow."

Jack's beaming. Mrs. Moore doesn't seem as pleased. I look between the two for a minute.

"We're just discussing where he should go." Her words expose her feelings of betrayal.

Oh. I see. I've ensured his place got put together this week. It's ready for him to come home, but I'm guessing Mrs. Moore wants him to go to her house.

"It would make sense for you to go to your mom's so that you have support twenty-four/seven."

He side-glances at his mom and then back at me. "I was hoping you'd stay at my place to help me recover."

My heart races as I try to process what he just asked, leaving me stunned for a minute. Of course, I'd stay with him while he recovers.

"Are you sure? I mean, yes, of course, but are you sure?" I ask, as my face flushes under his mom's disapproval.

"I'm sure. Mom, as much as I appreciate you offering, I need to recover at my place. You'll be welcome over anytime to help."

Mrs. Moore's face reddens. She isn't happy about this, but she also can't fight what her son wants.

"Okay. But I'll be checking on you every day. Bringing you meals."

"I'd expect nothing less."

I smile sheepishly at her. My hand squeezes Jack's as I try to contain my excitement that he's going home tomorrow, and I'll sleep next to him. After his mom leaves for the evening, I snuggle into the small hospital bed with him.

"Did you just ask me to move in with you in front of your mom?"

He squeezes my hand and kisses my forehead.

"I absolutely did. I love you. We're not waiting any longer to start our future together."

"I love you too."

CHAPTER 27

Jack

Z oey bounces out of the room to head back to *our* place to grab me some clothes. Everything has fallen into place. I inhale deeply, and as I exhale, the weight of fear, anxiety, and panic lifts from my chest. A trace of frustration remains. I didn't foresee David going off plan and keeping Madison overnight.

He was more unhinged than I'd assessed. Memories of how it all started come back. The heart monitor's beeping speeds up. I came so close to losing Zoey for good.

I'm not sure how long I've been laying in my bed staring at the ceiling when there's a loud knock at the door. *Shit.* The pizza. I jumped out of bed and pulled on the first pair of shorts I saw. Disappointment settled deeper in my gut with each step I took toward the door. When I opened the door and saw two pizza boxes in the delivery guy's arms, my jaw clenched.

Why wouldn't Zoey just stay with me? My neck stiffened as the familiar feeling of rejection took hold. I reached for the pizzas and let the door slam in the guy's face as I walked over to my kitchen table. I refused to be *friend-zoned* again.

Zoey was the first, but she wasn't the only woman that pushed me aside. Only wanting to be my *best friend*. Sarah's words resurfaced. The distance making her realize she was in love with me as a friend, not a boyfriend.

My fist slammed into the table as I forced those memories away. This time was different. Zoey and I had chemistry. Our attraction to each other was undeniable. She just needs to see me as the man she will spend the rest of her life with. What was holding her back?

I needed a drink. A strong one. As I poured myself a full glass of my expensive bourbon, an idea emerged. Understanding Zoey's reasons for resisting our relationship would help me break through the wall she had up.

A hiss escaped me as I gulped down a large drink of bourbon. The burn down my throat a welcomed distraction from the ache of her dismissal. Getting close to her wouldn't be easy. I'd need to watch her, understand how she spent her time when not with me. Was there someone else?

My grip on the glass tightened at the thought. No, I knew when she arrived back in town she'd been single. I'd also known that there was no one in Chicago, either. My old buddy from the Nashville force was now in Chicago and I'd asked him to ask around about her when she moved back.

I downed the rest of my drink and grabbed the bottle for a refill as I remembered the tone of his voice. Disapproval laced his words when he told me about her giving a co-worker's husband a blow job at the holiday party. *Fuck him.*

I rose from my table, grabbed my laptop, and sat on the couch. First, I'd memorize her schedule so I could plan my shifts. It'd be easier to follow her when I was working because I'd have many excuses if she noticed me.

After reviewing her schedule for the next few weeks, there were only a few shifts I needed to switch for myself. I wrote them down and then refilled my glass again and sipped on it as I drafted my plan to learn everything about Zoey.

My eyes drifted open and then shut as the room came into focus. I'd passed out on the couch. A pounding in my head reminded me I'd turned to the good stuff last night. I caught sight of my laptop on the coffee table and a notepad with a few pages of scribbles on it. I picked it up.

Zoey's schedule. *Shit.* What was I thinking last night? Was I really willing to do this? To stalk her? I dropped back against the couch and covered my face with my hands. *FUCK!* Desperation radiated through me. I slammed my hands down next to me, and rose to get my ass in the shower and put that delusional idea behind me.

When I entered the bathroom, memories of Zoey and me yesterday crashed into me. All my muscles stiffened with anger at her refusal to stay with me. I let the burn of the hot water pelt me as I tried to think of anything else besides her in this shower. My dick wouldn't let it go.

I pounded my hands against the shower wall and looked down at my throbbing cock. *Fuck it.* I gripped myself hard and pumped my hand along my shaft as I let my fury unleash. With my release, I only felt emptiness.

My body ached with fatigue as I toweled off and entered my bedroom. I pulled out my uniform, dressed, and made my way to the kitchen to make some coffee. As I waited for the coffee to brew, I grabbed a slice of pizza I left out overnight and sat on the couch.

My notes on Zoey's schedule pulled my attention. She was off today and I was on. What was the harm to check up on her? She'd never know. The beep of the coffee maker pulled me from my thoughts.

After I filled my mug, I leaned against my counter. What would she be up to today? I could swing by her place and see if her car was there. There's nothing wrong with me keeping an eye out for her car and noticing her activities. My mind wondered through different scenarios of tracking her, what to do if she saw me, and how to stay out of her sight. I placed my coffee mug in the sink and grabbed my belt as I walked out the door.

As I drove to the station, the panic that had taken root when Zoey walked out on me lifted. Hope and confidence replaced it. There was a lift to my shoulders as I entered the station and nodded at Sarge.

"I want you out on patrol today, Moore," Sarge said.

"Sounds good. Anything I need to keep an eye out for?" I asked.

"Nope, just the usual. Broken fences, hazards on the roads," Sarge said, and then walked into his office.

My anticipation grew. I was in a perfect scenario to focus on Zoey today. As I pulled out of the station lot and headed to her apartment complex, I told myself only for today would I watch her. Just as I was about to pull into her complex, I saw her walking down her stairs. So I continued past her place.

I turned around at the next road and parked on the side and waited for her to pull out of the parking lot to see what direction she went. She turned in the opposite direction of me, so I pulled back onto the road to follow her at a distance. Just as I was about to reach her place, another car pulled out right in front of me.

I should've pulled him over for cutting me off, but I didn't want to lose Zoey. It looked as if she was heading to the grocery store, but I couldn't be sure. *Fuck it.* I followed behind the jack ass and learned quickly I was right. She pulled into the grocery store lot. And so did the jerk.

I drove past and pulled into the gas station that gave me a full view of the grocery store doors. As Zoey walked toward the entrance, movement caught my eye. The guy had parked at the back of the grocery store parking lot and was walking in.

Something immediately struck me as off about him. With his eyes fixed on Zoey, he took a step forward. *Shit.* Who is this *asshole?* I waited at the gas station for her to leave the grocery store.

After about twenty minutes, sure enough, she leaves and a few minutes later, so does the creep. Now this is a completely unexpected development. Is he following her? Determined to understand who this guy was, I pulled out behind him as he drove back toward her place. He didn't pull in, so I abandoned my surveillance on her and followed him.

At some point, he realized I was following him and he pulled over into a deserted field. I parked right behind him, blocking him in. He stepped out of his car and I stayed in mine and locked eyes with him.

He had balls, I'd give him that. His eyes never shifted. Finally, I got out of the car.

"Why were you following that woman?" I asked.

"Why were you following her?" He asked, boldly.

"That's none of your business. It's a police matter. I'd like to see your identification," I responded and took a step toward him, my hand resting on my gun.

He huffed and reached his hand in his pocket. As he handed me his identification, I asked him again.

"David Slim, what are you doing following Zoey Miller?"

I noticed he had a St. Louis address. Interesting. I knew Zoey lived in St. Louis after college, but I struggled to track her down. She'd deleted all of her social media.

"How do you know I was following her?"

My jaw clenched in anger. I didn't have time for his games.

"Let's cut the bullshit. What are you doing so far from home, following Zoey around West Plains?" I asked, my voice firm and commanding.

"I'm an old friend from college. Just here checking up on her," he said with concern.

"Sure." I said flatly. "I'm going to run your information. If anything suspicious comes up, I'm bringing you in."

As I made my way back to my car, I realized this guy could be stalking Zoey. Is this the reason she's so closed off? Why wouldn't she tell me? I entered his information, and he came back clean. *Shit.* My hands fisted over my keyboard.

I stared at the screen, trying to think of my options. Proving stalking is extremely difficult, and the chances of actually convicting someone and them doing time is even less. My eyes glanced out to where David stood.

He doesn't seem like he could be an actual physical threat. He can't be over five foot and five inches, maybe one hundred and twenty-five pounds. I'll just need to monitor Zoey and him.

I opened my car door and walked back over to him. "It's your lucky day, *David*. I'm going to let you go with a warning," I said and stepped right up to him. There was less than an inch between us as I looked down at him.

"You stay away from Zoey. I don't want to see you near her again, or I'll make your life a living hell."

A smug smirk spread across his face. "You don't know her at all, *Jack Moore.*"

What happened next was a blur. I slammed David up against his car. My fists grasping his shirt as I looked down at him. "You don't want to fuck with me," I said, rage radiating from me. "Or her."

"You're an idiot if you think she'll ever be with you. Zoey's plagued with the shame of her past. She'll never be with you," he said, arrogance dripped from each word.

I did not like this guy at all. He didn't even flinch when I warned him. I dropped my hands and took a step back. He laughed in response. My eyes met his, and I knew I needed to get this guy locked up and away from Zoey for good.

It took every once of my control to turn and walk back to my car. I needed time to come up with a plan. It had to be something that would put David in prison for good. A cool wave of excitement swept over me as I shifted the car into reverse. What if I could use him to break down Zoey's walls? I would finally get the future I deserved with the woman I've loved for most of my life.

The room comes back to focus as a nurse cheerfully enters, asking me if I'm ready to go home.

"Yes, ma'am," I respond.

She steps up to the side and begins chatting with me as she unhooks the monitors. I mindlessly nod to her as she finally pulls out my IV needle.

"Alright, that's it. The doctor will be in shortly to go over your discharge instructions."

I rise from the bed and enjoy the freedom of movement. When I reach the window, I see Zoey walking in from the parking lot. In the end, I won.

David thought he could outsmart me. My plan minimized the harm inflicted on Madison and Zoey while ensuring his arrest for kidnapping. When he went beyond just getting Zoey to confess to the blow job, I almost intervened. But as he continued, Zoey needed me more. So, I switched my focus to getting

Madison home and finding him. I knew if I'd played my cards right, I could end David's life and ensure a future with Zoey.

Made in the USA
Coppell, TX
30 November 2023

25064263R00134